The Days of the Deer

Liliana Bodoc was born in Santa Fe in 1958. She took a Modern
Literature degree at the National University of Cuyo. Her narrative
works, including the fantasy trilogy *Los Saga de los Confines*, were
published by Grupo Editorial Norma and became bestsellers in
Latin America. The first volume of her most recent saga, *Memorias
Impuras*, was published in 2007 by Planeta/Argentina.

THE
DAYS
OF THE
DEER

LILIANA BODOC

Translated from the Spanish by
Nick Caistor with Lucia Caistor Arendar

CORVUS

Published in trade paperback in Great Britain in 2013 by Corvus,
an imprint of Atlantic Books Ltd.

Originally published in Spanish by Grupo Editorial Norma as
Los Días del Venado.

10 9 8 7 6 5 4 3 2 1

A CIP catalogue record for this book is available
from the British Library.

Trade paperback ISBN: 978 1 84887 027 7
E-book ISBN: 978 1 78239 016 9

Printed in Great Britain by the MPG Printgroup

Corvus
An imprint of Atlantic Books Ltd
Ormond House
26–27 Boswell Street
London
WC1N 3JZ

www.corvus-books.co.uk

Contents

Introduction

It all took place so many Ages ago that not even the echo of a memory of the echo of a memory remains. No trace of these events has survived. Even if archaeologists dug deep down inside caves buried beneath new civilizations, they would find nothing.

It took place in the most remote of times, when the continents had a different shape and the rivers ran a different course. In those days, the hours passed slowly for the Creatures; the Earth Wizards roamed the Maduinas Mountains in search of medicinal plants, and on the long nights in the southern islands it was still common to see the lukus dancing round their tails.

I have come to bear witness to a great and terrible battle. Possibly one of the greatest and most dreadful ever fought against the forces of Eternal Hatred. All this happened as one Age was drawing to a close, and another fearful one was spreading to the most distant places.

Eternal Hatred was prowling around the edges of the Real World in search of a shape, a tangible form to allow it to gain entrance to the Creatures' world. It lay in wait for a wound it could crawl inside, but none of the Creatures' faults was large enough for it to gain a footing.

Yet since everything can happen in Eternity, an act of disobedience became a wound, a scar that created enough space for hatred to come into being.

Everything began when Death, disobeying the law not to create any other beings, made a creature out of her own substance. This was her son, whom she loved. It was thanks to this ferocious offspring, born in

1

violation of the Great Laws, that Eternal Hatred found its voice and a presence in this world.

Stealthily, on the summit of a forgotten mountain in the Ancient Lands, Death brought forth a son she called Misáianes. At first he was no more than a puff of air his mother incubated between her teeth. Soon he became a viscous heartbeat. Then he cawed and howled. When he laughed, even Death trembled with fear. Afterwards, he sprouted feathers, and flew against the light.

Misáianes' vassals were numerous beyond counting. Beings of all kinds bowed before him, obeyed his every word. Yet every kind of being also fought against him. In this way, war spread to every forest, river, and village.

When Misáianes' forces crossed the sea that lay between them and the Fertile Lands, Magic and the Creatures united to confront them. These are the events I will now recount in human tongue.

Part One

1

THE RETURN OF THE RAINS

'It will be tomorrow,' Old Mother Kush said softly when she heard the first peals of thunder. She laid down the yarn she was spinning and went to the window to look out into the forest. She was not worried, because in her house everything had been properly prepared.

A few days earlier, her son and grandsons had finished sealing the roof with pine resin. The house was stocked with sweet and savoury flour, and with huge mountains of squashes. The baskets were filled with dried fruits and seeds. There were enough logs in the woodshed to burn through a whole winter. She and the girls had also woven thick woollen blankets that were now heaped, a colourful labour of love, in a corner of the hut.

As had happened every winter in living memory, another long season of rains was returning to the land of the Husihuilkes. The storms came from the southern seas, brought by a wind that spread heavy clouds over the Ends of the Earth and left them there until they had exhausted themselves.

The season began with showers that the birds watched from the mouths of their nests, the hares from their burrow entrances, and the Husihuilkes from their low houses. By the time the downpours began in earnest, no being was outside its refuge. The lairs of puma and vixen, nests in the trees or on the mountain tops, underground caves, dens hidden in the bushes, even worm holes were protected. So too were the Husihuilkes' houses, thanks to a store of knowledge that taught them how to make the best use of all the forest and the sea could offer. Here at the Ends of the Earth, the Creatures faced the wind and rain with strategies almost as old as the elements themselves.

'The rains will start tomorrow,' Kush repeated. She began to hum a farewell song. Kuy-Kuyen and Wilkilén crept closer to the old woman's warmth.

'Start again so that we can join in,' the eldest of her granddaughters begged her.

Kush hugged the girls, pulling them towards her. Together they began to sing again the song the Husihuilkes chanted whenever the rainy season returned. This was the warm, broken voice of the southern people; a voice unaware that soon the ones who were to bring these bountiful years to an end would be putting to sea.

The women sang as they waited for the men to appear along the path from the forest, loaded with the last provisions. Old Mother Kush and Kuy-Kuyen sang as one, never making a mistake. Wilkilén, who had only lived through five rainy seasons, had trouble keeping up with the words. She looked gravely at her grandmother, as though promising to do better the next time. The Husihuilke women sang:

> Until we meet again, deer of the forest.
> Until then, run and hide!
> Fly far away, bumblebee, rain is on its way.
>
> Father Hawk, make sure
> That you protect your young.

Friends, beloved forest,
We will meet again when the sun
Shines on our house once more.

The three faces peering out of the hut had dark hair, dark skin, dark eyes.

The Husihuilke people had been forged in battle. That was why their men were so tough; and the long periods of waiting had made their women caring and patient. The only decoration they wore was sea coral threaded into their plaits and headbands, or fashioned into arm-bands and necklaces. Their garments were light-coloured tunics reaching below the knee, sandals, and cotton or warm woollen shawls depending on the season. This was how the grandmother and her two granddaughters looked now, generous with the beauty of their people.

'The lukus! There are the lukus!' shouted Wilkilén. 'Old Mother Kush, look at the lukus!'

'Where can you see them, Wilkilén?' her grandmother asked.

'There, over there!' she said, pointing straight at a huge walnut tree growing halfway between their house and the forest.

Kush followed her gaze. It was true: two bright tails were curling and uncurling round the tree trunk, as if seeking attention. One was red, the other a faint yellow. Their colour was a sign of their age: the older they became, the whiter their tails shone.

Kush was not surprised. The lukus were coming for honey and squash cakes, just as they had done every evening during the dry season since the day of Shampalwe's death. Kush put two fresh cakes in a basket, left the hut and headed for the walnut tree to leave them their cakes and then return. The lukus never spoke to her; they had never done so in all the five years they had been visiting.

They never made friends with mankind, and whenever possible avoided them. They would sink down onto their four legs and run away as fast as they could. But if they were caught by surprise deep inside the forest, they would remain completely still, heads tucked down and claws gripping the earth, until the human being passed by. Yet despite this reluctance, it was the lukus who had brought Shampalwe back to the house, already close to death from the snake bite, and it was they who had laid her gently under the walnut tree. That was the first time Kush had seen a luku's eyes from close to. 'There was nothing we could do for her,' the eyes had told her. Now Old Mother Kush was about to see a similar expression on their faces.

The old woman had put the basket down on the ground and was about to go back to the girls when a whisper from one of the lukus kept her there. Recovering from her astonishment, she whirled round, thinking she was being ambushed. Instead, she found herself staring into the eyes of the yellow-tailed luku, who was gazing at her in exactly the same way as the other one had the day Shampalwe died. Realizing that sorrow was on its way to them once more, she faced it with the calmness learnt from her people.

'What is going to happen now?' she asked.

The luku remained silent, its huge eyes filled with foreboding.

'Talk to me, brother luku,' Kush implored it. 'Tell me what you know. Perhaps there is still time to remedy things.'

In reply, the luku turned back towards the forest, and leapt away on all fours. Oblivious to the preoccupations of its elders, the younger one was not going to let the feast go to waste. It was only after he had scooped up both the cakes in the basket that he sped off to join his companion.

Kush walked very slowly back along the path to the hut. As she walked, that day long ago when Shampalwe died and Wilkilén was born flashed through her saddened mind.

Shampalwe had married Dulkancellin shortly after the Festival of the Sun. She was from Wilú-Wilú, a village close to the Maduinas Mountains. Her heart was the sweetest of all those that beat at the Ends of the Earth.

'When she sings you can see the pumpkins grow,' people who knew her would say.

After the wedding came the good years. Dulkancellin went hunting with the village men. He took part in all the border patrols and came back safely from two battles against other clans. Kush and Shampalwe shared the household tasks. Children were born. Shampalwe and Dulkancellin had five of them; all were a delight to Old Mother Kush. First came two boys: Thungür and Kume. Soon afterwards, Kuy-Kuyen was born. Then Piukemán, the third boy. Then at the height of summer, Wilkilén was born. Kush liked to look at each of them in turn, because in one way or another they all reminded her of Shampalwe's beauty and grace.

On the day Wilkilén was born, Shampalwe left the children in their grandmother's care and set out for Butterfly Lake. She wanted to bathe in its waters, renowned for helping new mothers recover strength in their bodies and serenity of mind. It was from there that the lukus brought her, with still just enough life left in her to kiss her children and beg Kush to look after them on her behalf. Shampalwe did not breathe her last until Dulkancellin returned from hunting fresh meat to celebrate the new birth. In the mouth of a lakeside cave, a grey serpent of a kind not seen for years in those parts had bitten Shampalwe on the ankle. She had been picking flowers, and still had them in her hands when the lukus found her.

'Flowers that did not grow from any seed,' muttered Kupuka the Wizard.

The Earth Wizard tried to bring her back to life with remedies he had found in forest and mountain. But neither Kupuka's medicines, Shampalwe's youth, nor the pleas of a man who had never pleaded before were able to save her. She died that same day, as the sun was setting over the Ends of the Earth.

That was why Kush had asked the lukus to come and receive a gift at sunset whenever it was possible to venture out.

'That is how we can show them our gratitude, and it will help you remember your mother,' she told her grandchildren.

The lukus had left. Kupuka left as well. Dulkancellin fired his arrows at the stars. And, under Kush's protection, the children grew.

The old woman heard distant laughter. Kuy-Kuyen and Wilkilén were laughing at her because she was so absorbed by her memories that she had come to a halt a few feet from the house door, her arm stretched out in front of her.

'That's enough... there's more work to do,' Kush said as she walked into the house. She was pretending to be angry, but the children were not fooled.

'What happened with the lukus?' asked Kuy-Kuyen, who had inherited her grandmother's ability to see beneath the surface of things.

'What could have happened?' she answered, trying to convince herself. 'Nothing... nothing.'

Wilkilén spoke in her own way:

'I think they sang you their song, grandmother Kush. The song of the lukus... I can sing it too.' She tried to whistle like them, hopping from one foot to the other. Little Wilkilén had inherited the gift of happiness from her mother.

Before their grandmother could tell them to get back to their weaving, they heard familiar voices approaching the hut. Dulkancellin and his sons were returning from the forest. With them they brought more firewood, aromatic herbs to burn in the long nights of story-telling, and the last hare of the season, which they would eat as soon as Kush could prepare it.

The men did not head straight for the house. First they stacked the new logs on the pile, sorting them according to size. Then they went over to a low circular stone building. This was where they washed and rubbed a light oil over the scratches they had got in the forest.

The first to enter the hut was Dulkancellin, followed by his three sons.

Outside, night closed in. The tall trees drove their roots into the ground. The wind started to blow, bringing with it a flock of crows, and everything turned dark.

Cooked in broth, the hare lay steaming on a stretched animal hide. Hare with herbs, corn bread and cabbage was that day's meal for the warrior and his family.

In the firelight their seven faces looked dream-like. The Husihuilkes ate in silence. It was only once they had all finished that Dulkancellin spoke:

'Today in the forest we heard Kupuka's drum calling to his brothers. We also heard the reply they sent. I could not understand what their message was, but the Wizards' drums sounded very strange.'

The name of Kupuka always intrigued the elder children and silenced the younger ones.

'Which direction did the sound come from?' Kush asked her son.

'Kupuka's drum came from the volcano. The other one sounded fainter. Perhaps it came from...'

'The island of the lukus,' said Kush.

'Did you all hear it too?' Dulkancellin's question remained unanswered because Old Mother Kush was once more recalling the look on the face of the yellow-tailed luku.

'Kush!' her son called to her. 'I'm asking you if you heard the drum here too.'

The old woman came out of her sombre reflections and apologized, but she did not want to tell Dulkancellin what had happened earlier that evening.

'We didn't hear anything,' she said, quickly adding: 'I like to guess what the future may hold.'

'Tomorrow I will go and visit Kupuka in the Valley of the Ancestors. I'll talk to him,' said Dulkancellin, signalling that the conversation was at an end.

Each year, just before the rains started, the Husihuilkes assembled in the Valley of the Ancestors to say farewell to the living and the dead. It was an occasion to eat, sing, and dance. Above all, it was an opportunity to barter their surplus goods for anything they did not have enough of, so that they would get through the rainy season. A day for exchanging abundance and scarcity so that everyone would have all they needed.

Within a short space of time they would be separated by the sodden earth, the winds, and the cold. There would be no chance to hunt, sow crops, or to fight. All communication between them would be reduced to the bare essentials.

2

THE WARRIOR'S NIGHT

Even though the night was calm and a multitude of stars persisted in the last clear gaps in the sky, Dulkancellin could not sleep. Life at the Ends of the Earth lay curled up on itself; even the distant rumble of the storm was another kind of silence.

The warrior closed his eyes, waiting for sleep. He turned towards the wall facing the forest, the wall where his axe was leaning. He did not want to think about that day's events, and yet much later he found he was still puzzling over the meaning of the drums. Dulkancellin remembered what Kush always said: that sleep never came when it was pursued, but always when it was ignored. Trying to disregard it, he concentrated on the breathing of each of the other six people sleeping in the hut. Before he could discover whether Old Mother Kush was right or not, he heard noises that seemed to come from near the walnut tree. He leapt silently to his feet, and was outside the hut in an instant, axe in one hand and shield in the other. He stood stock still outside the door until he could be sure no one was close enough to slip inside while he went to discover what was going on. Then he stole noiselessly towards one end of the building. When he had almost reached it, he jumped round the corner. For once, though, the Husihuilke warrior was taken completely by surprise.

Between the house and the forest, dozens of lukus were spinning round apparently aimlessly, their luminous tails flailing through the air. From the expression on their faces, it seemed as if they were all whistling, but Dulkancellin could hear no sound. He took a few steps forward so that they could see him. As soon as the lukus caught sight of him, they all rushed to the bottom of the nearest trees, and soon were no more than a host of yellow, unblinking eyes. One very old luku ventured towards him. Considering the distance and the darkness between them, the warrior could see him far too clearly. The creature from the island stretched a thin arm towards the west. Dulkancellin followed his direction. From their house, the Lalafke Sea was only visible on clear, summer days; even then it was no more than a line that appeared on the horizon and then disappeared in an instant. But now when the Husihuilke warrior looked, he saw the sea blocking out the sky, crashing down on his house, his forest, his life. Dulkancellin gave a mighty cry, and instinctively raised his shield. All at once, the giant wave paused, then flowed round the house like a furrow in Kush's vegetable garden. Crushing everything beneath their feet, along the furrow came pale-faced men mounted on huge animals with manes. They were both near and far, and their garments did not flap as they ran. For the first and last time in his life, the warrior drew back. By now the lukus' whistling was almost unbearably shrill. Beyond the pale-faced men Dulkancellin could see a landscape of death: a few flayed deer were wandering among the ashes. The poisoned fruit of the orange trees fell to the ground. Kupuka was walking towards him, his hands amputated. Somewhere Wilkilén was crying, making the sound of a bird. And Kuy-Kuyen, her skin covered in red blotches, was peering from behind a dust-storm.

The warrior woke with a start. Once again Kush's words had proved true. The axe was still leaning against the wall. Everything was still silent.

Dulkancellin remembered it was a day of celebration. It would soon be dawn, and even sooner his mother would be up to light the fire and begin her daytime tasks.

Wrapped in a fur cloak, Dulkancellin left the hut, feeling as if this were the second time he had done so that night. The world outside was the same as ever: the warrior took a deep breath. A dull grey light spread through the darkness. To the south, another grey that was as solid as the mountains began to cover the landscape.

Dulkancellin's hair was tied back by a band across his forehead: the way the Husihuilkes always wore it before going off to war or when they were training their bodies.

The forest was far enough away for him to sing the song that only the warriors knew. Each time they sang they promised that every day they would honour the blood that had lain down at night, and begged to be allowed to die fighting.

When Dulkancellin reached the tall trees, he took off his cloak and left it on the roots of a tree. Flexing his body like a young cane, he ran through the undergrowth, leapt like a jaguar, climbed to impossible heights, and finally hung suspended from a branch until the pain made him drop. On his way back to the hut, he recovered his cloak and picked some seeds to chew on.

Ever since Shampalwe had died he had become harsh and silent. Before, they said he fought with no fear of death. Now they complained they saw him fight with no regard for his life.

3

WHERE IS KUPUKA?

The Husihuilkes lived at the Ends of the Earth, in the furthest south of a continent its inhabitants called the Fertile Lands. The warriors' territory was a forest between the Maduinas Mountains and the Lalafke Sea. A forest crisscrossed by mighty rivers, with cypress trees growing right to the mountain tops, and laurels and orange trees reaching down to the sea. The land of the Husihuilkes was a forest in the south of the Earth.

A long way north from the Ends of the Earth, several days' hard climb up a steep slope, lived the Desert Pastors, a tribe of llamel breeders that died out with the last oases. Still further north, on the continent's distant shores, was where the Zitzahay people lived. And beyond the Border Hills, the Lords of the Sun created a civilization of gold. Perhaps other peoples lived and died in the mists of the ancient jungle, without ever emerging. And finally there were those who lived where the seas turned to ice and the sky was always dark because the sun forgot to shine there.

At the Ends of the Earth on the morning of the day the rains would start, Dulkancellin and his family drew near to the Valley of the Ancestors.

When they were halfway there, Thungür asked his father if he could go on ahead a little. Kush and the girls were walking too slowly for him, and he did not want to waste the morning. His wish granted, he wasted no time and was soon out of sight.

The spot where the Husihuilkes were to meet was a rough circle, completely covered in spreading grass and surrounded by patches of big white mushrooms. Trees and bushes crowded in around it as if they wanted to see the celebrations without trespassing.

The family had almost arrived when they saw Thungür coming back along the path towards them. He was carrying something. From the way he was holding it with his arm outstretched it must be very precious.

'What has he brought? What can he have found?' Kume wondered out loud. Intrigued by his elder brother's excitement, he ran to meet him.

Piukemán and Kuy-Kuyen ran after him. As they ran, they tried to guess, their words fragmented by their leaps: an animal's fangs... a blue stone... a shell... a luku's claws. Behind them, Wilkilén shouted as loud as she could in her weak little voice:

'An orange! Thungür has brought me an orange!'

Thungür had come to a halt, the treasure hidden behind his back until they reached him.

'Let me see!' begged Kume.

But Thungür shook his head. Kume and Piukemán understood that this time it was not a game, and that they should not surround and jostle their brother until they forced him to show them what he was hiding. At that moment, Kush and Dulkancellin caught up with them. Dulkancellin had no need to say anything: he stared at his eldest son and waited to find out what had made him so agitated. Thungür slowly brought his hand from behind his back. The others could finally see what he had been concealing from them.

'Is that all?' Piukemán protested. 'A black feather, and not a very big one, at that.'

For Piukemán and his two sisters, the mystery had been solved, and so they lost all further interest in the matter. The rest of the family, though, saw at once that this was a feather from a golden oriole. Old Mother Kush, Dulkancellin, Kume and Thungür were all aware that, depending on the manner in which it had been found, a golden oriole feather could mean many things. It was a message from the forest that could not be ignored.

'How did you find it?' asked Dulkancellin, taking the feather from Thungür's trembling hand.

'I had already skirted the marsh and was about to run down into the Valley. Then, just at the spot where the old holm oaks are, I heard someone calling my name. I covered my ears, but still could hear it. It was coming from somewhere high up, from the top of an oak on my left. When I raised my head, I saw the feather fall. At that moment I heard the oriole sing.'

'And what did you do, Thungür?' This time it was Kush asking the question. She moved closer to her grandson, who was already much taller than her. Thungür knew what was expected of him.

'I was very quiet, and I didn't move an inch from where I had come to a halt. I raised my hands with the palms cupped upwards.'

'And you closed your eyes…' Kush whispered.

'I closed my eyes so as not to try to catch the feather or avoid it. I waited. Time went by, and I thought it must have landed on the ground by now. But just as I was about to open my eyes, I felt it drop into my hands.'

Kush spoke again, as if remembering:

'The oriole sang once more…'

'That's right,' Thungür said. 'Then it circled round my head, and flew off.'

The forest was placing an oriole feather in the hands of a Husihuilke male. It was telling him that soon he would have to take on the responsibility for feeding and protecting his family. From among its many voices, this was the one the forest had chosen to warn them that somebody was about to leave his home and his duties there. And that someone else had to take them on himself. This time, the message was for Thungür. What was going to happen to Dulkancellin? Why would he no longer be at home, as he had been ever since Thungür could remember? How could he possibly take the place of his father? Thungür tried hard to disguise his dismay, but his arms felt very heavy, and his legs were far too weak. What was going to happen? Who was going to show him what he had to do?

Thungür had no need to say any of this, because before he could speak he already had his answer.

'Keep on walking towards the Valley. That is what you have to do now,' Dulkancellin told him.

Thungür hesitated, but Dulkancellin insisted, barely raising his voice: 'Come on, Thungür, let's go on.'

So the family set off again towards the Valley of the Ancestors, walking as close as possible to each other. The youngest could see from their elders' faces that something unusual was going on, but preferred not to find out what it might be.

Yet the same forest that had caused their anxiety now came to relieve it. The smell of the approaching rain and the clear outline of the trees as the wind swept over them convinced the family that any suffering was still remote. In no time at all, their hearts were filled with optimism once more.

Kume picked up a stone and skimmed it along the ground as far as he could. Thungür and Piukemán accepted the challenge. The three of them ran to where their stones had landed, decided who had won, and threw them on again.

Kuy-Kuyen and Wilkilén were walking hand in hand singing a lullaby. Kush smiled tenderly, and rummaged in her belongings until she found her wooden flute. To play it more easily, she put her bundle on her back and rolled up the sleeves of her cloak. The simple, repetitive tune added to their renewed sense of tranquillity. Old Mother Kush was so concerned about sounding the right notes that she walked more and more slowly.

Her son and her granddaughters slowed down too, because they did not want to leave her behind.

So it was to the rhythm of the flute that they finally reached the summit. At the Ends of the Earth, the land rose from the seashore through villages and trees until it became part of the Maduinas mountain range. Often, the rising terrain was interrupted by a marsh or lake. It fell sharply for a waterfall, or sloped downwards for a while, and yet all the time it rose towards the mountain peaks. The point where Dulkancellin and his family paused for a moment before they started out on the last stretch was where the descent into the valley began. The trees descended too, until they were held back by the ring of white mushrooms.

People from every village were gathering. Most were coming in large groups down the three main tracks. Some families were arriving on their own because they had been late setting off, or because their homes made it easy for them to take a short cut. This was the case for Dulkancellin's family: they had taken a path that allowed them to reach the Valley of the Ancestors quite quickly.

When they arrived, the Husihuilkes unloaded their bundles and started to greet their relatives. They saw some of them quite often, but others they only met up with on rare occasions. In the same way that they had different skills and tasks, here the men and women met in separate groups.

As soon as they saw Dulkancellin appear, several warriors came forward to greet him. The women gathered round Old Mother Kush. She greeted the married ones with a kiss on each cheek, and the single women by laying her hand on their foreheads.

The people of the Ends of the Earth loved their elders, and no one more so than Kush. All those who had grown up with her were long since dead, yet she still roamed through the forest.

'I've been left forgotten here,' Kush would explain whenever the matter was brought up. 'It must be because I never make a sound.'

21

Old Mother Kush had given birth to her son at a very mature age, when nobody thought it was still possible. The other Husihuilkes saw it as a miracle.

'It's a reward life has given Kush for having such a soft heart and rough hands,' was what they whispered for a long time afterwards.

The gathering was becoming more lively. The Husihuilkes were coming down from Whirlwind Pass and Partridge Hill, from The Corals and the villages to the north of the Cloudy River, even from distant Wilú-Wilú.

Most of them made the entire journey on foot. Those who lived on the far side of the river left their canoes tied up on the bank, and walked to the Valley of the Ancestors from there. Only a few, especially those from the high villages, came riding on llamels.

Blessed with amazingly fertile lands, the Husihuilkes were as self-sufficient as the animals of the forest. They knew the apple trees would bear fruit each year, that the animals they hunted would have their young each season, that a single gourd contained the seeds of many more. It never occurred to any of them that there should be more than this.

The only exception was shortly before the rainy season was due to start. Then the Husihuilkes stored more than usual so that they could survive the long days of isolation, when sea and land turned in on themselves, and the forest withheld its riches. Both men and women redoubled their efforts. They hunted or wove, made pottery, tanned hides, or made baskets. Some of them fished and preserved their catch in salt; others dried fruits. Yet no one ever kept more than was necessary for themselves. The rest was traded in the Valley of the Ancestors. In that way, abundance in one village helped make up for a shortage in another. And everyone benefited from each other's skills.

The inhabitants of Wilú-Wilú gathered valuable stones from the mountainsides: small flints for lighting fires, larger ones to make axes and arrowheads with. But in exchange they needed the salt and dried fish that the people of The Corals brought in reed baskets. These baskets were made in the villages on the banks of the Cloudy River, where the reeds grew in great profusion. The same villages made clay pots: pitchers, bowls, and small jars that were greatly appreciated in the Sweet Herbs villages, where the beekeepers could use them to store the golden honey from their honeycombs. The women from Whirlwind Pass, who were excellent weavers, brought the cloaks and woollen cloths that during the winter were so precious to the fishermen who lived on the coast at The Corals.

All these goods were laid out in rows that the Husihuilkes inspected at their leisure. Since every village was aware of what the others needed, and as each one took into account any unusual events that had changed the lives of their neighbours for good or ill, most of the exchanges were predictable and were repeated in almost the same fashion year after year.

This time Kush had brought three woollen cloaks. They were dyed green, with red and yellow borders. In exchange, she chose a bowl to grind corn in, leather to repair her menfolk's shoes, medicinal herbs and some dried fish.

Once the time for giving and receiving was over, Old Mother Kush joined the rest of the women in preparing the food.

Located in different parts of the valley, the musicians were visited by small groups of people who crossed each other as they made their way between the different instruments. Those who had just come from hearing the heavy beat of the drum looked preoccupied. Others were still dancing to the rattle of the dried gourds. The sounds of the bound-together reeds died slowly away, while the listeners remembered events from the past. Only the man with the flute did not stay in one spot, but walked round and round the valley playing his tune. The crowd following him changed each time he appeared.

When the flute went past Kush, the old woman paused in her task to greet it.

'Come and sing with me,' said the flute.

'You have plenty of people with you,' Kush replied. 'I need to get on with my chores.'

She raised her hand in greeting, then concentrated once more on arranging palm hearts on a piece of bark. When she was done, she called out to her elder granddaughter:

'Kuy-Kuyen, come here!' The girl appeared at once. Kush went on: 'Take this tray and offer it around. When it is empty, come back here for more. But first, have one for yourself.'

. Kuy-Kuyen took one of the palm hearts and bit into it with great delight. Wilkilén stood close by, watching all this.

'Grannie Kush! Give me something to offer around!' the girl begged her.

'Come here so I can straighten your clothes a bit,' said her grandmother. She tied the straps on her little leather boots, straightened the cap with earflaps that framed her face with strips of colour, and made sure above all that her cloak was properly done up. While she was doing this, Wilkilén stared up at the wind above the valley, imitating it by blowing out her cheeks and stretching her arms out as though they were the branches of a tree.

'I would be done more quickly if you kept still,' said Kush.

Wilkilén lowered her gaze from the sky, still lost in thought.

'I wanted to know if people grow tired of being the wind,' she said, lowering her arms. She added: 'Yes, they do.'

Kush looked at her granddaughter, remembering the golden oriole feather. She hugged the little girl to her, and kissed her freezing cheeks to try to calm the fears that had suddenly come rushing back. Then she immediately set about granting her granddaughter's wish.

'Let's see what I have to give you,' she murmured, partly for her own sake, partly for Wilkilén. She hesitated, then chose a medium-sized pot in which she had made a thick paste of nuts and herbs. Perfect for spreading on bread.

'Take it like this so that they can serve themselves,' she said, pushing several wooden sticks into the paste. 'It will be well received.'

Wilkilén went off with the pot, carefully watching where she put her feet. Old Mother Kush stared after her. Just when she was almost out of sight, Kush saw Dulkancellin striding towards her.

Her son was looking for her. They had to go together to talk to Shampalwe's family, who had come all the way from Wilú-Wilú.

'Are you ready, Kush?' he asked her.

'Yes. Take the presents I have brought for them out of my pack and let's go.'

They walked away without another word. It was not easy for either of them to see Shampalwe's eyes again in the faces of her brothers and sisters. But the gathering in the valley was one of the few occasions when they could see the children and hear the latest news. Wilú-Wilú stood at the foot of the Maduinas Mountains, a long way from Whirlwind Pass, so that they could meet up only a few times each year.

The sky was rapidly turning dark; the air was growing colder. Sheltered in the valley, the Husihuilkes stared up at the wind above their heads just as Wilkilén had done, and predicted it would be a hard journey home. The celebration would soon be over, and one single question was on everyone's lips: where is Kupuka?

Kupuka was not in the Valley of the Ancestors. The Earth Wizard, who saw further than anyone and knew the language of the drums, had not arrived as he usually did, his pack filled with mysteries, to await the arrival of the rain with everyone else. The Husihuilkes felt strangely abandoned, and wondered what the reason for his absence could be.

Someone who was not thinking about Kupuka heard the question repeated time and again, but paid no attention. Walking as if he wanted to remain invisible, he went through the mushroom ring and carried straight on. He took the track to the west until the route forked into a narrow path. Branching off from the main route, this path did not head uphill, but immediately went down a steep slope. After reaching here stealthily, the small figure immediately started down at a surprising speed, compensating for the incline by leaning backwards. Almost at once, though, he heard a familiar voice calling to him:

'Piukemán! Piukemán, wait for me!'

Somewhat surprised, but even more annoyed, Piukemán stopped and looked back. Wilkilén had followed him, and was coming down the path almost sitting down to avoid falling. Piukemán climbed back up towards her.

'What are you doing here, Wilkilén?' he shouted furiously. 'You always spoil everything!'

'I don't...' the girl stammered. Piukemán cut her short:

'Don't say a word!'

Wilkilén's black eyes brimmed with tears. As she always did when she was sad, she started playing with her plaits.

'And don't cry either!'

This only brought on more tears: Piukemán was her beloved brother, and he had never treated her like this before.

But Piukemán was no longer even looking at her. He was trying to decide whether to return to the Valley of the Ancestors, or to take his sister with him in his adventure. He could not let her go back on her own. Then again, if he missed this opportunity he would have to wait until the Festival of the Sun, and that seemed too far away. Taking Wilkilén by the hand, he started down the slope again.

The path the two of them had taken was the only one that reached the Owl Gateway, beyond which it was forbidden to go.

Of all the males in the family, Piukemán was the one who most resembled his mother. He had inherited from her a restless curiosity about everything. Shampalwe had paid with her life for her interest in the strange flowers from the cave. Piukemán too would one day pay a high price. Ever since he was of an age to understand, he had been asking what lay beyond the Owl Gateway and who had forbidden the Husihuilkes to go there. He had never received any answers, and so now he was determined to find out for himself. In previous years he had twice left the celebrations and ventured as far as the boundary of what was permitted. Twice he had been overcome by fear, and had returned without daring to disobey the ban that came from time immemorial. Now, though, Piukemán had lived through eleven rainy seasons, and refused to let another one go by without crossing the Owl Gateway. He would not be defeated a third time. Wilkilén's sudden appearance made him hesitate, and yet he could not accept having to back down again. He decided to go on, even if he had to drag his sister by the hand.

The steep, narrow slope they climbed down with difficulty ended in a dark, gloomy hollow. The air was so cold and damp that it hurt when they drew breath. A deep carpet of leaves buoyed them up, so that they could continue without getting muddy. Plants of the shade proliferated at the foot of all the trees. Creepers, toadstools, and tiny worms that appeared whenever their feet dislodged a stone were the most obvious signs of life. Piukemán had been here before, so he strode on to join the path again, even though it seemed to be deliberately concealed. They zigzagged from side to side through thick vegetation as they advanced across the dark hollow. By now they were shivering, and their teeth were chattering. Not even the cloaks they wore wrapped tightly around them offered much protection because the damp cold rose from their feet. Then all at once the path straightened out and the undergrowth thinned. They had reached the Owl Gateway.

In front of them stood two enormous trees. The gap between them was about the width of a man with his arms outstretched. From a distance it was plain to see that the outline they made had the shape of an owl. Wilkilén and Piukemán stood motionless, staring at the silhouette of the bird of many names, close kin to the Earth Wizards.

Piukemán was the first to recover. With what he hoped resembled a gesture of defiance, he signalled to his sister that they should keep going. Clasping each other tightly by the hand, they stepped towards the Owl Gateway. As they drew closer, the outline of the owl became less clear, making it easier for them to pass through the forbidden gate.

Piukemán wanted to whistle to show he was not afraid, but the sound would not come. Not even Wilkilén, normally so talkative, could utter a word. Although everything around them seemed normal, never before had the forest made them feel so sad.

As it was, they did not manage to get much further. As they rounded a bend, in a clearing by the side of the path they caught sight of Kupuka. The Wizard did not seem to hear them. He was squatting down, his back towards them. In one hand he held a branch in the shape of a snake; with the other he was drawing something on the ground that the children could not make out. His silvery locks cascaded down his back, and below the deerskin cloak they could see his bare feet, toughened from walking through forests and over mountains.

Quickly, the two of them hid behind a bush, fearful of Kupuka's reaction if he discovered them on this forbidden territory. The Earth Wizard was chanting a sacred chant. When he finished, he turned his head towards his heart, revealing his profile. As soon as they saw it, the children realized there was something different about it. This was not the face of the Kupuka they knew. The change was hard to define, but was no less terrifying for that. His flaring nostrils quivered strangely. His chin was jutting forward, and his breathing had threads of colour in it. If the brother and sister had been able to move their legs, they would have run away as fast as they could, all the way back to Old Mother Kush's welcoming arms. But their legs refused to move. All at once, Kupuka gave a howl and leapt to his feet. He sang words in a language they did not recognize. As the two petrified children looked on in horror, he began to spin round on one foot, the other one stamping the ground as he did so.

Kupuka's face seemed to change each time he spun round. His voice, though, stayed the same, and he went on singing, although the sound seemed to come from a long way off. At the first turn, his face appeared to have grown feathers. The next time, he had a hare's muzzle. A lizard's tongue darted out from between the fangs of a wild cat as he came to a halt, sniffing the air.

Piukemán could not think. Wilkilén could not cry. They remained stock still, until a stab of pain roused them from their state of fascination. Red ants had climbed their boots and begun furiously to bite their legs. Stifling the urge to cry out, they tried desperately to brush them off, forgetting Kupuka for a brief instant.

Before they succeeded in getting rid of all the tiny creatures by now crawling all over them, they heard a sound that quickly made them straighten up. A growing cloud of white butterflies had appeared from nowhere and was fluttering between the sky and their heads. It was as if they had come into existence through a hole in the air. As though responding to an order to attack, the mass of butterflies flew at them. Hundreds and hundreds of wings beating against their faces. So many that they completely covered the clearing where Kupuka was performing his ceremony.

Piukemán and Wilkilén staggered back, waving their arms to try to get the swarm off them. They had little success, and before long they were two human shapes covered in butterflies. Their hands were smothered in them as well, and so were of no use to try to brush the rest from their faces. Blinded by the beating wings, Piukemán groped for Wilkilén, who in her efforts to fight off the attack had become separated from him. As soon as he reached her, he clutched her tightly against him. Then he ran as fast as he could... poor Piukemán ran and ran, still pursued by a howling wind of white wings, until he was back across the other side of the Owl Gateway.

Not a single butterfly crossed the threshold of the gate. They hung in the air on the other side, and then flew off again. As soon as Piukemán was certain they would not come back, he set Wilkilén down slowly, and sank to the ground himself to get a moment's rest. After two or three deep breaths they were able to continue on their way. A few steps further on towards the Valley, Piukemán turned to look behind him. Between the two trees, the Owl Gateway was completely covered in an intricate spider's web that must have taken several days to spin. Although he could not understand what had happened, Piukemán felt relieved. Perhaps they had never been on the other side.

The remainder of the walk was easy. Comforted by the fact that they were on their way back, they were not even afraid of Dulkancellin's anger at their absence, which he must have discovered by now.

The same path took them down into the Valley. The celebration was still going on. They mingled with the crowd, heads down, ashamed to imagine that everyone already knew they had broken the rule. Before long, they bumped into their grandmother and their father. Piukemán and Wilkilén slowly raised their eyes, fearful of Dulkancellin's flashing, angry eyes, and Kush's sad look. But they were in for another surprise: both adults smiled at them.

'We were looking for you. We all need to go together to greet your mother's family,' said Kush.

'There's Kuy-Kuyen,' said Dulkancellin, pointing to her. 'Go on ahead with her. I'll look for Kume and Thungür.'

Piukemán and Wilkilén simply nodded their heads and did as they were told.

The celebration was coming to an end. All the families were packing up their things and saying goodbye. Under a heavy sky, the Husihuilkes set off into the icy wind rising from the sea and whistling round the forest up to the mountain peaks.

The Valley of the Ancestors was deserted until the next fine day. With only the souls of the dead to inhabit it.

4

A TRAVELLER

A man was leaving Beleram at dawn. At that time of day, the city was already busy. Some servants from the House of the Stars were raking the games court. Tardy street-sellers were carrying their goods as quickly as they could down the narrow lanes to the market. Savoury odours from the food stalls filled the air. The man stopped at one of them to buy a tortilla wrapped in leaves. It smelt particularly delicious, and only cost him a few cacao seeds. This early halt had not been part of the strict itinerary the Supreme Astronomers had set out for him, and yet how often on his journey did the memory of that taste give him the strength to go on!

He was known to many people in Beleram, and several of them greeted him as he passed by. His pack made it obvious he was setting off on a journey. In fact, he had left the House of the Stars with less than half of the treasures he had entered with: a bag full of unusual objects, as well as others he usually carried with him. The Supreme Astronomers had insisted he reduce his load, and despite showing them why each and every one would be useful to him, he had finally to resign himself to leaving behind a wealth of wonderful things. 'Remind me to ask for them back when I return,' he protested as he left. Although they could see he was carrying enough for a long journey, none of the people who saw him pass by bothered to ask him where he was going or why. He was always someone who came and went.

The first part of his journey was back along the way he had come a few days earlier. He crossed the market and the games court. He walked along the street leading to the market, then out past the orange groves and the outlying dwellings. 'Farewell, Beleram!' he said, without looking back. 'I'll make use of my long journey to compose a song to you!'

He crossed the bridge over the river, and went on to Centipede Yellow. From there he climbed towards the Ceremonial Mountains, which he crossed by a steep short cut. At the top, he praised the countryside around him out loud. 'I've reached the most beautiful valley in the world!' The valley was called Thirteen Times Seven Thousand Birds. 'Perfumed like few others, and more musical than any of all the many I have heard.' The traveller would have liked to spend several days in the valley, but knew this was impossible. Instead, he continued on his way towards the sea. One fine day he slid down the sand-dunes of the beach.

The Astronomers had ordered him to wait on the shore for the arrival of the fish-women. They came at first light, bringing with them a small boat that they left close to the shore. The traveller had no difficulty reaching it. A wind from behind blew their hair over their faces. When they left at dusk, it streamed out over their shoulders.

The craft was no different from one any Zitzahay could make out of bundles of reeds and a few secrets. Inside it was a pair of oars and a generous amount of food. The sun shone once more, and although the wind had died down, the Zitzahay prepared to set off. 'Farewell, my Remote Realm. I shall be further away from your stars than I have ever been.'

He sailed across the Mansa Lalafke because the sea there was calm, sheltered between two shores. Crossing the sea saved him many days, because the path along the land here was very long, and grew steep where it met the foothills of the Maduinas Mountains.

From the morning when he disembarked, things changed for him. From that moment on, his journey had to become stealthy and silent so that he did not give away his secret. No one was to see a Zitzahay in this part of the continent. That was why the traveller was so thankful for the boat that had brought him, even though he destroyed every last trace of it.

Anybody wanting to reach the Ends of the Earth from the north had to cross the country of the Pastors of the Desert. The Astronomers had instructed him to stay close by the shore of the Lalafke. If he did that, no one would see him, because the Pastors never went near the sea. 'Of course I did as I was told. I went where the Astronomers said I should, and, as far as I know, not a single human being laid eyes on me.'

This was what he said long afterwards, each of the many times he told his story.

He said 'human being' because from the moment he arrived in the Land Without Shadow an eagle circled above him. Occasionally it disappeared – once for a whole day – and yet it always returned. The man was pleased to see it back, flying high in the sky above his head. 'It made me happy the way one feels when you see your home again in the middle of a lightning storm.' And of course he had reason to be pleased with the bird. Travelling on one's own through foreign lands it is easy to lose one's way, mistake a landmark, become disoriented on the plains or to go wrong at a crossroads. Whenever that happened, the bird swooped down with a loud screech. Then it flew back and forth between the bewildered traveller and the right path, showing him the right way to go. In addition, the eagle often carried fleshy leaves in its beak that were filled with a comforting juice. These helped augment the traveller's scarce supply of water, which he could only replenish in the rare oases he came across near the coast.

So they travelled together for countless days. 'She in the sky, me in the sands; never the other way round.'

The desert seemed endless. Days of scorching heat; icy nights. Days and nights, nights and days, the landscape always the same. Every so often, the figure on his own in the desert threw a pebble in front of him just to convince himself he was advancing. 'You've caught up with the pebble you threw. Calm down, you are moving. And with any luck, you're moving in the right direction,' he told himself in consolation.

The Supreme Astronomers had instructed him how to plan his time: when to make an effort, and when to rest, so that he would survive the desert. While he was in the Land Without Shadow, he had to start walking at sunset. 'To wrap myself in my cloak and walk. To make progress at night and in the early hours of the morning, because as soon as the sun rose in the sky I had to set up my tent in the meagre shade of the thorn bushes, drink my water, and get some sleep. Sleep and then wake at the red sunset, bathe in the sea, and then go on with my journey.'

Often at night a sandstorm arose, stinging his body. Then there was no chance of going on. His eyes tight shut, his mouth set in a taut line while he sheltered under his cloak waiting for the wind to drop, his mind went back to the smell of that tortilla he had eaten when he left Beleram. The wind took a long time to drop, but gradually the grains hurt less; the sand returned to the sand. It was only then that he could set off again.

'The Land Without Shadow is a strange place! The sea and the desert meet at the coast, but there is no telling which of them is dying and which is doing the killing!'

Then one dawn, a day before his belt had a hundred and forty knots on it, he reached the Marshy River. The traveller knew that once he had crossed it he would be entering the Ends of the Earth, the lands where the Husihuilkes lived. The air here was different, and the first few clumps of vegetation started to appear.

In order to cross the Marshy River he had to leave the coastline, because the river estuary was one huge swamp. If he did not do so, he would be bound to sink in the mud. His map showed he should head inland. And even though this held its risks as well, they were not as deadly or as unavoidable as the ones he faced in the swamp. Leaving the coast meant he might be spotted by the Pastors of the Desert, who often came down to the estuary for their flocks to drink and graze. They also crossed the river to trade. Their llamels were greatly sought after in Husihuilke villages, and the Pastors exchanged them for flour, medicinal herbs, and other things they could not obtain in their oases. This meant there was a greater chance the traveller would be discovered, as he had to use the same bridge as they did.

He had just set out across the river when the eagle started to circle round his head, screeching loudly. What was it trying to tell him? He could not be going the wrong way this time. The river was the river. The bridge was the bridge, and only offered two possibilities: to the south lay his final destination, to the north was the way back. 'My friend, you can't want me to return to the desert, can you?' He peered in the direction of the eagle's flapping wings, and soon understood why the bird was making such a fuss. A big flock of llamels was heading for the river. He could only make out the nearest animals; the rest of the flock was an indistinct blur. But where there are llamels, there are Pastors. And since there were no bushes near by, let alone trees he could hide behind, the man decided he had to get as far away from them as he could. He walked on as fast as his stumpy legs would allow.

So as not to think about how tired he was, he started to think about the llamels. He soon found himself wondering what those enormous red-haired beasts would do in the jungles of the Remote Realm. How could they possibly get through the undergrowth with their splayed feet and heavy bodies? They could not climb or fly; nor could they make themselves thin the way jaguars did, or crawl like snakes. He imagined them hopelessly stuck, longing to be roaming again through their vast deserts. At that point he suddenly realized that he too was stuck, longing for his home. 'What about you, Zitzahay? Isn't the jungle your home, and despite that, haven't you just crossed the desert?'

Yes, he had crossed that vast expanse safely! As he took his first step beyond the bridge, he looked up to find the eagle. He wanted to ask her to laugh with him, but she was nowhere to be seen. Eventually he felt so happy he laughed on his own.

Behind him lay the empty wastes, the Marshy River, and the flocks of llamels. The forest was close at hand, and with it came the promise of an easier journey.

He walked on. He soon realized that the eagle had not followed him, but was not concerned: he had learnt by now that it was the bird's habit to disappear. When he reached the first well-defined shadows he looked for her again. He stared so hard into the sky that he confused her with other birds. And because he was looking up so much, he stumbled over everything he met in his way. He called out 'Eagle' softly, because he could not shout. 'My friend,' he said. He looked and looked, until finally he realized the eagle had stayed in the desert. 'And there I was, thinking only of the llamels!' Despite the welcoming forest, he could not forget her. 'And as you can see, I still haven't,' he told his listeners.

Nothing was sent to replace the bird to help him on his way. At least, he was not aware of anything. Although he would have liked to have someone to talk to, the fact was that once he had crossed the river, the journey became so easy that he had no need of help. The path he had been told to follow kept him well away from the villages of the southern warriors. Added to that, his hearing, his sense of smell and his ability to walk silently kept him safe. 'I have no idea if the stars were on my side too!'

In order to avoid the Husihuilke villages he had to take a winding path full of detours. He often had to double back, and yet he never got lost. The landmarks he had to follow were unmistakable: quite the opposite to the Land Without Shadow. There all he could see were the Maduinas Mountains in the east, the Lalafke to the west, and sand all around him. In these forests at the Ends of the Earth, a waterfall or pool never failed to point him in the right direction. Impossible to get lost somewhere where everything seemed to be a signpost for the way he should take. Rivers flowing west, a huge cypress wood charred by fire from a lightning strike, twin lakes, springs, lava flows, caves... 'The landscape was such a good guide that I walked along singing to myself, as I did in my own land,' he told people in later days.

5

TWO VISITORS

'Why are you scratching your legs like that?' Kume asked his brother and sister.

Thinking they had successfully disguised the persistent itch and pain the ant bites had caused them, the pair looked at each other, not knowing what to reply. They did not dare tell the truth, but neither of them had the courage to invent an excuse either. So they carried on walking, without acknowledging they had even heard their brother's question. Kume shrugged his shoulders and forgot about it.

If it had been Thungür or Kuy-Kuyen who had seen them scratching in this way, either would have pestered them until they gave an answer. Kume, though, was naturally taciturn. He spent many hours on his own, observing the world from his solitary lair with a mixture of melancholy and hostility. It was not surprising therefore that he left them alone without repeating his question. Now he soon fell into one of those self-absorbed moods they all knew so well, but did nothing to try to change. He walked in silence a little way back from the others until they reached home.

'Here we are at last!' exclaimed Old Mother Kush. 'Take off your cloaks and sit by the fire. I'll make some mint tea with honey to ward off the cold.'

Dulkancellin was hanging up his cloak when he saw the carved wooden chest that appeared together with the rain and disappeared as soon as the sun shone again. He smiled to himself, and shouted to Kush, who was busy with the fire:

'What will you choose from your chest this time?'

'Who knows?' his mother replied.

'I hope it's Shampalwe's comb,' said Kuy-Kuyen. 'Then you can tell us again what her wedding was like.'

'No,' Thungür objected, warming his hands at the fire. 'I'd like it better if you took out the red rock from the volcano and told us about the day the earth opened and the lakes were bubbling with heat.'

'All I can promise is that I will tell you a story.'

Every Husihuilke family kept a chest that was passed down through the generations. Even though it was less than two hands high, and could be carried by a young child, in it were keepsakes of everything important that had happened to the family throughout time. When the nights for story-telling arrived, the chest was turned over four times: first forwards, then backwards, and finally to each of its two sides. Afterwards, the oldest member of the family would plunge a hand into the chest and pull out the first thing it touched, without hesitating or choosing. That object was a token of the story that would be told that year. Sometimes this referred to events none of them had witnessed, because they had happened many years before. Yet the story-teller talked of them as surely as if they had indeed been there. In this way too the tales became rooted in the minds of those who would have to tell them again years later.

The Husihuilkes said it was the Great Wisdom that guided the hand of the oldest member of the family so that their voice would recover from memory all that had to be remembered. Some of the stories were repeated tirelessly. Some were told only once in the course of a generation; others perhaps would never be recounted.

'I wonder about the old stories that have always remained in the chest,' said Thungür. 'If no one has told them, no one has heard them. And if no one has heard them…'

'… No one remembers them,' said Kush, coming over with her bowl of herb tea. 'You always say the same thing, and I always give you the same answer. When something really important happens, many pairs of eyes are witness to it. And many tongues will say what they have seen. Just remember, old stories which are not told around one fire will be told at another one. And the memories one family forgets will still live on in other homes.'

Kush dragged over a hide rug to sit by the fire.

For a moment, none of them spoke. Then Dulkancellin said:

'Thungür is concerned about the stories in the chest. I'm worried about Kupuka…'

Wilkilén and Piukemán jumped when they heard the Wizard's name.

'I wonder why he didn't come to join us,' Dulkancellin went on. 'What could be more important than our meeting in the Valley?'

'A lot of things have been happening,' said Kush, finally deciding to share her disquiet. 'Too many not to notice. The lukus' strange behaviour, the drums in the forest, the oriole's feather, and Kupuka's absence are all threads from the same weave.'

Dulkancellin looked round at his five children. The memory of the previous night's dream flashed through his mind. *Old Mother Kush, I know of another thread for your loom*, he thought.

A longer silence left each of them to their own thoughts. Kuy-Kuyen was thinking of her mother; Thungür of the message from the golden oriole. Kume was thinking about Kume. Dulkancellin's mind was on the Husihuilkes, while Kush was remembering her family's earliest ancestors. Piukemán could not forget Kupuka, and Wilkilén was asleep… until there was a loud, sharp knock at the door.

43

'That's Kupuka,' said Kush in astonishment.

'It's Kupuka,' the others whispered. His way of knocking was unmistakable.

Dulkancellin strode across the room. Lifting the bar from the door, he let the Earth Wizard in. All the family had risen to their feet to welcome him. All except Wilkilén. She was so sure Kupuka had come to scold them for crossing the Owl Gateway that she hid behind a pile of cloaks. None of the others saw her, so she lay there, curled up in her fear.

Kupuka set aside his bag and his staff. He was obviously very tired, with an age-old weariness that made his slanted eyes seem even narrower than usual.

'Greetings to you, brother Dulkancellin,' said Kupuka, following the Husihuilkes' traditional words of welcome. 'And I ask your leave to stay here, in your lands.'

'Greetings to you, brother Kupuka. I give you my permission. We are happy to see you well. We thank the path that brought you here.'

'Wisdom and strength be with you all.'

'May the same be with you, and more.'

The best rug had been brought out for the Wizard to sit on. Kush got up to bring him some corn bread, but when he saw what she was doing, Kupuka stopped her.

'Come back, Old Mother Kush! I will gladly have a slice of your bread, but in a little while.' He turned to Dulkancellin. 'Before anything else, I have to tell you that your life is about to change as the colour of the air changes from day to night. I trust that the signs which went before me have succeeded in preparing you and your family for this.'

'Yes, there have been signs,' replied Dulkancellin. 'But they were as unclear as your words are now.'

The tone of her son's reply made Kush think that it was time for her and her grandchildren to leave and go to the room where they all slept.

She stood up cautiously; but once again, Kupuka halted her.

'I bring news that concerns you all. It's important for you to stay and hear it. If Dulkancellin agrees, of course.'

The warrior nodded, so Old Mother Kush sat down again without a word.

'Good,' said Dulkancellin, 'let's hear the news you bring.'

Taking a dark root out of a small bag hanging from his waist, the Earth Wizard chewed on it for a while. Tied back with a thong, his long white locks left his thin face uncovered. His face was a mass of contradictions. Deep wrinkles were a sign of the many years he had lived, and yet in his eyes shone the same proud gleam as that of the young warriors when they entered the field of battle.

'A man is walking through the forest towards this house. He is already very close. He is a Zitzahay, and has been sent by his people as both messenger and guide.'

Dulkancellin raised his hand a little, asking to speak.

'Wait a moment, Dulkancellin,' said the Earth Wizard, trying to calm the warrior's anxiety. 'Everything I know is hazy and vague. I have many doubts and little clarity about what I am going to say. It will save time if you let me speak without interrupting. Afterwards you can ask me whatever you like, although, believe me, I will not have many answers. Possibly the messenger who is about to arrive will be able to respond more adequately than I can.'

Dulkancellin seemed to acquiesce. He sat elbows on knees to listen to what the Earth Wizard had to say. Everyone else gazed at Kupuka expectantly. Behind her pile of cloaks, Wilkilén was trying to work out whether what she had heard was related to the Owl Gateway.

'The Brotherhood of the Open Air is experiencing days of great turmoil. They are trying to complete a difficult task in time and without making any mistakes. A very hard task, and one that is to some extent impenetrable even to those of us who are helping to carry it out. Everything began when the Brotherhood decided it was imperative to send out some news. It seems that at the same time, they decided this news was not to be spread to the four winds. The Supreme Astronomers advised that it should not be announced publicly, but be treated as a secret. That it should be passed on surreptitiously so that it would only reach the recommended ears.' At this, the Earth Wizard peered round at each of them in turn before he went on. 'I mean that a piece of enormously important news had to reach all parts of the Fertile Lands without any attention being drawn to it. And in addition, with hardly any time to do so. Did I already say that? Well, I am telling you now: we have no time to spare. An important message, but it must remain concealed. Unusual activity on all the roads: but no one must notice! That is a hard thing to achieve, even for Magic. I know that a complex network was created in Beleram, the city of the Supreme Astronomers, and that it spread from there like the points of a star. I also know that fortunately all the messengers have reached their destination. All of them apart from the one coming here. Our messenger left Beleram before the others, but he had a long road to travel. Something must have held him up... Who knows? We will soon learn the reason for his delay, because he is almost here with us.'

Like the vast majority of Husihuilkes, neither Dulkancellin nor anyone else in his family had ever seen a Zitzahay. What they knew about them and the Remote Realm came from stories or songs. The idea that soon one of them would be there, stretching his hands out to the fire, made their hearts beat faster and left them speechless. A Zitzahay was arriving on the very same day that the rains from the north of the Fertile Lands were about to start. Why had he made such a long journey? And on whose behalf? Kupuka had spoken of 'recommended ears'. Were they the ones who were supposed to hear the message? Kupuka talked of the Supreme Astronomers. The Astronomers were so far away! They were nothing more than an ordinary Husihuilke family with their corn bread and fire. Even Dulkancellin preferred not to say anything, but to listen to what the Earth Wizard could explain to them.

'The Astronomers gave a command, and immediately all the resources of Magic were set in motion to carry it out.' Silence and consternation greeted Kupuka's words. 'This task brings with it many risks. A piece of news had to secretly speed along the difficult roads of the Fertile Lands until it reached those chosen to hear it. Only them, and no one else. The news could easily have become distorted on its journey, intentionally or otherwise. The secret could come out either through carelessness or by design. The messengers could lose their way or be intercepted. As soon as great events appear on the horizon, errors and betrayal can spring up anywhere.' At this, the Earth Wizard started to chew once again on the root he was holding. The sweet juice he sucked from it gave him obvious pleasure.

'Well then?' said Dulkancellin, who was starting to grow impatient.

'Well,' Kupuka continued, 'in order to protect the mission, precaution after precaution was taken. The news was sent in two different ways. Human messengers set out on land, while other emissaries took routes unknown to man. The hawks sought me out. They took me to meet them on the other side of the Owl Gateway. On the day of the celebration in the Valley, I came down from the mountain and walked there. Beyond the gate it is possible to clearly understand the language of the animals. Woe betide anyone entering the forbidden place to see and hear what is not meant to be revealed!'

Saying this, the Wizard rapidly turned his head towards Piukemán, his two eyes flashing like lightning. No one apart from the boy saw the snake's tongue dart out from Kupuka's slight smile, flicker in the air for a second, then vanish. Kupuka saw how the boy turned white and caught his breath. Satisfied with the lesson he had taught him, he went on with his story.

47

'The Wizards who live on the islands of the lukus learnt of these new happenings through the fish-women. The oldest Wizard dreamt of them in a dream he usually has before he wakes at the foot of a tree.'

As Kupuka spoke, many things began to make sense to the Husihuilkes. The call from the hawks, which the Earth Wizard had to answer as soon as he received it, explained his absence from the Valley of the Ancestors. And the drums which had sounded so oddly in the forest must have been conveying a similar message. Dulkancellin could contain himself no longer.

'Many things are still dark for me,' he said.

'If you can see them, they can't be that dark,' replied Kupuka jokingly. Then his voice took on a more forlorn tone. 'The really dark things are those you stumble over before you even know they exist. But go on, ask away!'

The warrior bit his lip. On this occasion, Kukupa's puzzles were annoying.

'Answer me this,' he said. 'Why were human messengers chosen? You spoke of other kinds of messenger. Aren't they more to be trusted? Aren't their tongues more truthful than those of men?'

'They may be more truthful, but they are less subtle,' Kupuka replied. 'Only human languages can describe the shape of a feather or the roughness of a patch on a bird's beak. Human messengers will tell the news in much greater detail than any other creature could.' The Earth Wizard suddenly became agitated. 'And men will be far more than the heralds of these events. They will be the makers. Men will take decisions, choose which direction to take. Afterwards there will be consequences.'

'Let me see if I have understood,' said Dulkancellin. 'The Supreme Astronomers have chosen a few persons from all round the Fertile Lands whom they are going to inform of great events that are happening or are about to happen. Now tell me this: what does this mean for us? Why should my life change more than that of the other Husihuilkes?'

'Oh, my goodness!' Kupuka protested. 'Nothing seems to be clear enough for you! You, Dulkancellin, are one of the few whom Magic has chosen. The Zitzahay messenger will knock at your door, and make you see these things.'

The Husihuilke family retreated into silence once more. They all knew they still had to hear the most important part.

'Brother, your life will change. You would do well to accept that without protesting. And so will all their lives.' Kupuka, who no longer spoke in a joking manner, included the others with a wave of his gnarled hand. 'The Zitzahay messenger will take you with him. And it will be for a long, long time. Perhaps—'

'Take me with him? Where to?' Dulkancellin interrupted him.

'Far away from here. To the Remote Realm.'

Dulkancellin stood up and went over to the Wizard. Kneeling down, he looked him in the eye.

'I am nothing more than a Husihuilke warrior. Here, I live among my living and my dead. Everything I need is in this forest. Tell me the reasons why I have to leave for the lands of the Zitzahay and become caught up in the labyrinths of Magic.'

'I'll tell you why,' replied the Earth Wizard. 'You have to do so precisely because you are a Husihuilke warrior, because here is where you have your living and your dead, and because you can find all you need in your forest. And possibly because all that is in danger.'

Dulkancellin was about to ask him more questions, but Kupuka quickly stopped him.

'That's enough! The messenger is about to arrive. There will be time for words afterwards.' He turned to Kush: 'You need to warm up that mint tea! The visitor will be cold when he gets here.'

Old Mother Kush rose to her feet at once. Partly to carry out Kupuka's instructions, and partly to hide her sadness. The warrior stood up too, and shifted away from the fire. The Earth Wizard also moved off his rug and, with all the children staring at him, went to one side of the room. When Wilkilén saw him coming close to her hiding place, she began to tremble like the leaves outside their hut. Yet Kupuka did not seem to notice her presence. He slowly began to untie his pack. To judge by the difficulty he had in finding what he was looking for, he must keep many things inside it. Finally, he pulled out a clay pot the size of a walnut. Holding it between two fingers, he showed it to the whole family. Kush gave him an enquiring look.

'This is for the children,' Kupuka said in answer to her silent question. 'Should they need it, this will help soothe certain stings they may have received.'

The Earth Wizard raised his head towards the ceiling and chuckled in a way that nobody but two youngsters in the hut could understand.

'Here he is! At last he's arrived!' said Kupuka, still laughing.

The visitor rapped on the door with his knuckles. When Dulkancellin opened it, he had to look down to see who was there. From below, a man no taller than a child greeted him, a smile like a crescent moon spreading from ear to ear. Dulkancellin was so amazed at this extravagant creature that it took him some moments to react, giving the newcomer the chance to quickly slip past him into the hut. With two bounds, he was in the centre of the room. Dulkancellin whirled round, ready to take him to task for such an impolite entrance, but the little man was already introducing himself:

'My name is Cucub. I come from the Remote Realm, where I first saw the light of day. I travel all around performing tricks and recounting great deeds. I am a travelling minstrel by trade: that is what I know best. Unwittingly, I have been chosen as a messenger, and I must say, have not done badly at that either. I may have been a little late. Only a very little. But I am here now. I reached the end of my difficult journey, and that is the main thing. Brothers, Cucub greets you all!'

This torrent of words was uttered quickly in a squeaky voice that sounded far too loud for the small hut. The Zitzahay embellished his speech with all kinds of gestures, exclamations and bows, like a ham actor playing to his audience. When at last he finished, they all seemed pleased that Cucub was among them. Almost all of them.

6

AN IMPORTANT CONVERSATION

'What's this?' said Dulkancellin, unable to hide his irritation.

'He has already presented himself,' Kupuka replied. 'I don't think I have anything to add.'

'All I heard from this man's mouth was idle boasting.' Dulkancellin advanced towards the Zitzahay, pointing an accusing finger. 'Who in our present situation needs to hear you praising your own talents as an artist?'

Cucub looked round to see if everyone else was on his side.

'The others do not seem to think that way,' he said. He was beginning to behave more in keeping with his surroundings, yet still his attitude seemed extraordinary to the Husihuilkes. 'You must be... Dulkancellin! Brother Husihuilke, you have a fine name! Fine and sonorous. But do you agree with me that it's too long? If you are willing, I'll call you Dulk.'

'I have no idea how you know my name. I ought to have been the one to tell you, but you spoiled our welcoming ceremony. Yet you are right about one thing: my name is Dulkancellin. And you are never, ever to call me anything different.'

'Now I come to think of it, Dul-kan-ce-llin is the right length,' Cucub readily agreed. 'Dulk isn't right, it sounds like a bird cawing. Dulk! Dulk!'

As he said this, the Zitzahay strutted up and down, imitating a bird. There was stifled laughter in the room, until the warrior silenced it with a scowl. Kupuka thought it best to step in.

'Let's help our guest recover from his long journey. You, Kuy-Kuyen, serve him a cup of mint tea. And make sure it's piping hot.'

Kush and her elder granddaughter saw to it that Cucub was made comfortable. The old woman asked his permission and took his bag, placing it alongside Kupuka's. Kuy-Kuyen took his cape and staff. The little girl had never seen anything like them. The jaguar skin of the cape and the jade stones set in the staff fascinated her. Old Mother Kush thought her granddaughter's curiosity might upset their visitor, and so hurriedly caught her attention.

'Come on, Kuy-Kuyen! Hurry up and serve that mint tea as you were asked.'

Sitting close to the warmth of the fire, Cucub sipped the tea with pleasure while he devoured the bread the little girl brought him.

'A feast! A delight for the hungry traveller!'

Everything about Cucub – his tone of voice, his attire, the way he was always gesturing – seemed outlandish and extravagant compared with the Husihuilkes' naturally austere manner. Faced with this performance, Dulkancellin lost his last reserves of patience. Cucub was so far removed from his idea of someone he could trust that the warrior could not and would not hide his suspicions any longer. How was he meant to trust such a loud-mouthed, impertinent man, someone who was so small and skinny? Dulkancellin stroked his chin, ready to explode. The Zitzahay must have realized this, because he put down his bowl and surprised them yet again:

'You, dear mother, must be Kush. Or rather Old Mother Kush, as you are known at the Ends of the Earth. And you must be Kuy-Kuyen. I'm not wrong, am I?' The girl gave an enchanted smile. 'You are the eldest, your name is Thungür. And you are the youngest boy, and are called Piukemán. And you? Of course! You are Kume.'

Kume glared back at him, but the messenger simply smiled. There was no doubt that, like his father, the boy disapproved of him.

'But there's someone missing,' said Cucub, as if he had not noticed anything. 'That is… that is…'

'That's me!' said Wilkilén, popping up from behind the pile of blankets. 'Do you know my name?'

The rest of the family were startled when they saw her appear. Kush was ashamed she had not realized her granddaughter had vanished. Wilkilén came out from her hiding place and stood in front of Cucub, waiting for him to answer her question.

'Let's see.' Cucub pretended not to remember. 'Your name is Wil… Wilti… Wilmi… Wilkilén!'

Wilkilén's eyes shone with joy.

'You may be tiny, but you know a lot,' she said, stretching out her hand to touch the visitor's.

A pang of nostalgia caused a fleeting shadow to cross Cucub's smiling face.

'I'm far from home,' he said. 'So far that by the time I return the rain will have ended in your land, the trees will be in blossom, and the first fruits will have ripened. Believe me, when the distance separating you from your own hammock can be measured in harvests, a friendly hand is a great comfort.'

'I think it's time we heard what has brought you here,' insisted Dulkancellin.

'This time, sister Kush,' Kupuka interrupted. 'This time I must ask you to leave us on our own.'

Kush and her five grandchildren started to leave the room. But before she did so, Kush stepped back a few paces. A guttural sound, accompanied by a rapid darting of the tongue, came from the old woman's mouth. The others greeted this strange behaviour enthusiastically. The children skipped round her. Dulkancellin and Kupuka laughed out loud.

'You have won again, Mother,' the warrior said. 'You are the lucky one.'

Cucub had not the faintest idea what was going on.

'Just look at you, Zitzahay! For once you seem lost for words!' Kupuka said gleefully. 'What happened is that Old Mother Kush here has just told us with her Water Cry that she was the first to hear the rain start to fall. That gives her a right she can call on whenever she considers it essential.'

'A right? Explain that to me.'

'From this moment on, until the start of the next season of rains, she has the right to impose her authority on one occasion. That is our Husihuilke custom! The first person to hear the rain has the right to settle matters should there be a disagreement, if she thinks it is necessary. As you have seen, it does not matter that she is not the head of the family.'

'You said "if she thinks it is necessary". Does that mean she can decide not to exercise her right?' asked Cucub.

'That is often the case,' said Kupuka. He turned to Kush: 'Isn't it true, Old Mother Kush, that you have never used what our visitor calls "your right"?'

'Never, ever,' replied Kush, leaving the room with her grandchildren. 'Never. And that's a good thing.'

Cucub's face shone.

'Explain one final thing to me if you would,' he asked. 'How do you know for certain that the person who says they have heard the rain really did so?'

'How little you know the Husihuilkes!' said Kupuka indignantly.

Cucub squirmed on his rug and muttered an apology. By now the rain had started lashing down on the Ends of the Earth.

The three men were left alone in the room. A Husihuilke, a Zitzahay, and an Earth Wizard sitting facing each other. The time for explanations had arrived, and Dulkancellin came straight to the point.

'What is the news you have travelled so far to bring us?'

'Since I can see I will have no opportunity to introduce any persuasive rhetoric or significant silence as befits a true artist, I will simply tell you what I have been sent to say, as if I had no skill in oratory.'

Neither Kupuka nor Dulkancellin quite believed he would keep his word, but they remained silent and waited for the Zitzahay to begin.

'I have to inform you of events which are happening as we speak. It was for this and something more that the Supreme Astronomers sent me on such a long journey,' said Cucub. 'You, Dulkancellin, know nothing about them. You, Kupuka, know something, but not enough. So listen closely! The Magic of the Open Air has learnt beyond a shadow of doubt that there will soon be a fleet from the Ancient Lands coming to our continent. It is known that the strangers will sail from some part of the Ancient Lands and will cross the Yentru Sea. All our predictions and sacred books clearly say the same thing. The rest is all shadows. Shadows in the stars and our books. Shadows that prevent us from seeing the faces of those who are coming. Who are they? Why are they travelling here? The answers to these questions will decide the fate of everyone living in the Fertile Lands. One thing is certain. Whoever they may be, they must have powerful reasons for wanting to face such an arduous crossing. If this were not the case, nobody would risk sailing across the fearful Yentru from shore to shore. All three of us know that it is an endless voyage, full of dangers and anguish. And yet they will undertake it. The question is: why?'

'With your permission,' Kupuka interrupted him. 'Perhaps the real question is: will it be for our good, or for our ill?'

'Well said!' Cucub congratulated him. 'You have reached the point I was aiming towards. For our good, or for our ill? Is this a good or evil shadow for the Fertile Lands? As yet this question has no answer, or at least no simple one. The Astronomers cannot interpret the signs from the skies with any certainty. They are confusing and do not fit together. Our Magic cannot discover the truth in all this fog and darkness.'

'Well then?' asked Dulkancellin.

'Then decisions have to be taken,' replied Cucub. 'It's no easy matter to decide when there is so much uncertainty and so little time. The strangers will soon set sail. Who knows? They may already be doing so. That is why we inhabitants of the Fertile Lands have to decide without delay what to do, and how to be prepared for their arrival. The Supreme Astronomers say we must form a Great Alliance. They say we must unite in our aims and in our movements, because nothing that has happened in the past bears any resemblance to what is about to happen now.'

'Well then?' Dulkancellin repeated.

Cucub slapped himself on the knees and shook his head in disbelief.

'I suppose that Husihuilke warriors are as sparing of their arrows in battle as they are of their words in conversation.'

'That's enough joking; just answer what you have been asked,' said Kupuka, trying to ward off Dulkancellin's anger.

'At once!' Cucub said again. 'The reply is easy to imagine. I think that you, Dulkancellin, have some idea what it is.'

'Possibly,' said the warrior, not taking his eyes from the Zitzahay's face. 'But unless I am mistaken, you came all this way to spread light on what little we know.'

'You are right. And I have not forgotten my duties,' said Cucub. 'I was simply giving an introduction before I came to the heart of the matter.'

'The heart of the matter is the only important thing,' said Dulkancellin. His voice sounded more bewildered than discourteous.

Yielding at least for the moment to the demands of his audience, Cucub tried to get to the point.

'What they are talking of is a Great Council. A council to be held in the city of Beleram, in the House of the Stars. Representatives from every village in the Fertile Lands have been invited. Together with the Supreme Astronomers they will seek to interpret who the strangers are, and what are their real reasons for coming. Even if they fail in this, the Council will have to decide what is to be done. In the House of the Stars a few men will decide on behalf of everyone how the Fertile Lands should prepare to receive the Ancient Lands.' Cucub sighed. He knew the hardest part was still to come. 'They have chosen you, Dulkancellin, to speak for your people in the House of the Stars. You are to go to the Council on behalf of the Husihuilkes. And I have to take you there.'

'There are so many brave warriors at the Ends of the Earth. And so many wise elders. And yet I was the one chosen,' said Dulkancellin. 'Truly, I do not understand why.'

Kupuka cut in before Cucub had a chance to speak.

'Brother, you talk of the tasks before you as if they were some kind of unjustly awarded privilege. You think that many others deserve this more than you, as if they would be happy to be chosen. But listen carefully to this old man, and believe what I say. This is not a reward we have given you. No, it is a heavy burden we are placing on your shoulders: so heavy few people could bear it. From now on you will think and act on behalf of your people. If you are right, all the Husihuilkes will be right too. If you get things wrong... oh, if you do that! Do you really think this is a privilege?'

Dulkancellin realized it was an order he must obey, and began to accept his fate.

'I will do as you ask, since it has been so decided.' The warrior thought this was the right moment to make a demand of his own: 'I will go to the Remote Realm, but without any companion. I will not need the Zitzahay on my journey.'

'"I will not need the Zitzahay on my journey,"' Cucub mocked him. 'What do you think of that, Kupuka? The warrior does not need me!'

'You will need him,' said the Earth Wizard. 'The journey to Beleram is long and complicated. Without his help you would find it hard to reach the House of the Stars in time. Above all, we must make sure you take part in the Great Council. If you went alone you would be exposed to too many dangers. With two of you, you can watch over each other's sleep, cure the other's wounds, and if necessary one of you can sacrifice himself so that the other can continue.'

Cucub yawned and concentrated on rubbing his arms and legs. His gesture showed both his weariness and his satisfaction at the reply Dulkancellin had received.

'Everything has been said,' Kupuka concluded. 'I am going to leave now. I also have difficult days ahead of me. You two have only a few days to prepare for your journey. Don't let the seventh sunrise still find you here!'

'The rain will be a wall against us,' said Dulkancellin.

'Of course, but you will have to overcome it. You know the forest better than anyone.' With this, Kupuka got to his feet and asked Dulkancellin to bring Kush and the children back in.

By the time Kush and her five grandchildren had entered the room, the Earth Wizard was already standing by the door loaded with all his belongings, his cloak wrapped round his shoulders. They went over to him. Kupuka placed his palm on the forehead of each in a sign of farewell and protection. Then he turned to the men.

'Two of you rather than one are setting out, in order to defend each other and protect the outcome of your mission. Two of you rather than an army, so that your movements will go unnoticed, and the secret be kept as has been ordained.'

'Are we to see you again?' asked Dulkancellin.

'Yes. I will appear at some point on your path, before you finally leave the Ends of the Earth. Oh, I was forgetting!' the Earth Wizard smote himself on the forehead. 'You must ask Cucub for the sign that shows he is the true messenger sent by the Astronomers. It is one of Kukul's feathers. He is sure to have it.'

'I've never seen a feather from that bird,' Dulkancellin objected.

'That is why you will instantly recognize it.'

'Shouldn't we have done this as soon as the Zitzahay arrived?' the warrior said in surprise.

'As I told you, I forgot. I must be older than any of you imagine.'

Dulkancellin was not convinced by Kupuka's excuse.

'Wait. We'll ask him for it right now,' he insisted.

'That's impossible. Cucub will take ages rummaging in his belongings, and I cannot wait.'

Kupuka said farewell and went out into the rainstorm. They closed the door behind him. Wind, rain and cold were left outside once more.

'Look! Look!' shouted Thungür, pointing to one of the walls.

Kupuka's shadow was still there, with his pack, his staff, and his cloak. It slowly faded away, with all of them watching until it had completely disappeared.

7

'I CAN STILL HEAR THE RAIN BEFORE YOU!'

'It's true Kupuka must be very old,' said Wilkilén. 'He forgot his shadow as well!'

'I think he left so quickly it could not keep up with him,' Kuy-Kuyen argued.

'That can't be right,' said Piukemán, who did not agree with her. 'Arrows fly more quickly, and yet they take their shadows with them.'

'Kupuka does not do things without a reason,' said Thungür.

'I know the reason,' said Kume with a nervous grin. 'It's because he enjoys scaring people now and again.'

This children's chatter helped the family recover from their unease at the sight of the shadow. Dulkancellin remembered his duties, and spoke to the messenger, who at that moment was gazing round the room, taking in every last detail.

'Show us the sign so we may know you are who you say you are,' he asked, then added: 'Show us the feather which for some reason or other you failed to produce of your own accord.'

'Of course I didn't show it!' Cucub protested. 'I had orders not to do so until I was asked. You must understand that we too need proof that you are who you say you are. What if I took an impostor with me right to the House of the Stars! But since Kupuka has already demonstrated that he knew of the sign, and that it is a feather from Kukul, I must now let you see it as evidence of my faithfulness to the Astronomers and their commands.'

Cucub dragged his bag close to the oil lamp, and knelt down to rummage in it. The Husihuilkes took advantage of this to get a good look at him. They found it hard to understand how he could move easily beneath all he was wearing. Kuy-Kuyen stared at the green stones set in his earrings, his arm-band and the seven loops of his necklace. *There are no stones like that in the forest. And the people who come down from Wilú-Wilú never bring them either*, she thought. Thungür's attention was drawn to a slender rod hanging from the Zitzahay's belt, which flexed without snapping as he knelt. For her part, Old Mother Kush preferred to look at the string of seeds that kept appearing and disappearing among the folds of his clothes. 'Those seeds he has strung on a thread must be from the cacao tree,' she said to herself. Wilkilén was amused by Cucub's short, wiry hair. Dulkancellin noticed the blowpipe he was carrying. However hard he tried, though, he could not make out where the darts and poison were concealed. The Zitzahay's astonishing appearance meant that all the Husihuilkes forgot their good manners as hosts, and stared at him openly.

Cucub meanwhile had removed almost everything from the bag. Things were not going well for him; they grew worse when Dulkancellin returned to the charge.

'What's wrong? You should have no doubt where you put the feather.'

Despite the abruptness of his question, Dulkancellin was sure Cucub was going to find the proof at any moment. But this certainty evaporated when the Zitzahay looked up, his face pale. Glancing across at the warrior, he began to speak hesitantly:

'It was here... I know it was... here somewhere. I put it away carefully, but... now I can't find it.'

'You say you can't find it?' Dulkancellin said. 'You're telling me you have lost the proof that you are the true messenger, that the feather was there, and now it isn't? And you expect me to believe that?'

'Yes. I mean, no,' stammered Cucub. 'I don't expect you to. You're right, quite right. I understand it must be hard to believe me. But let me look again. That Kukul feather has to be somewhere.'

The Zitzahay started going through his things all over again. He looked in every cranny, turned the bag over, shook it hard. No use. 'It has to be here... it has to be here,' he kept repeating. He wiped his brow, patted his clothes despairingly, then began the search again. Finally, after admitting to himself it was impossible, Cucub gave up: the Kukul feather had vanished, and he could give no valid reason for it. There was no excuse for losing the token the Astronomers had given him to prove he was the true messenger. Cucub knew that not being able to produce it put him in a dreadful position, and put his future in doubt. He peered round, hoping against hope he might spot the special green colour of a Kukul feather in some corner of the room. No luck there either. Straightening up and seeing the Husihuilkes looking gravely at him, he attempted to smile.

'Listen, Dulkancellin,' he said. 'I can't tell you how this has happened. I don't know if an ill wind blew it away, or if an enemy has turned it into grains of dust. Whatever it was, it must have been close to here, because just before I arrived I made sure I still had the feather. I saw it with my own eyes! Believe me, warrior, I am the messenger Kupuka and you were expecting.'

'I will not believe you,' said Dulkancellin. 'It's impossible for me to believe you. The Earth Wizard was clear. You were supposed to show us a Kukul feather to prove that your words and your intentions are one and the same. You have been unable to do that, and anything you say from now on will only confirm you as a traitor.'

65

'We ought to wait for Kupuka,' said Cucub, trying to postpone the decision Dulkancellin had already taken.

'You know Kupuka will not be coming back here. You and I both heard that he will meet us on our path,' the warrior sighed. He knew what he had to do, and also knew that putting it off would only make it more cruel for Cucub. 'I was ordered to take this mission, and I will. They want me to think and act in the name of the Husihuilke people. That means I must think and act as they would. Since my own judgement has to take the place of the council of elders and warriors, I will not declare anything they would not have said. I sentence you in the same way we have always sentenced traitors since the sun saw us awaken at the Ends of the Earth. Death is justice for you, Zitzahay. And it will take no more time than it takes us to walk into the forest.'

In Dulkancellin's voice, the death sentence sounded dispassionate. There was no trace of hatred, but nor was there any weakness. It was clear that nothing Cucub could do or say would change anything. Staring helplessly at Kush's warm presence, the Zitzahay slid slowly down, until he was slumped on the floor like another of the jumble of objects he had scattered around.

Dulkancellin walked away from him without another word. As Cucub saw the warrior leave the room, he suddenly began to think of how he could escape. His hands and feet were not tied... perhaps he could slip away and run towards the trees. Then he remembered the heavy bar across the door. That, and the fact that Thungür and Kume would be bound to try to stop him, made him change his mind. He would wait for Dulkancellin to return. He could do nothing by force, but he could by stealth. If he could load the blowpipe before the warrior reappeared... A well-aimed dart would paralyse him. The rest would be easy. Cucub remained very still. Nothing about him revealed how his mind was spinning as his thoughts collided with each other. The final decision, though, was surprisingly simple: he had nothing to lose. The Zitzahay bent over so that Kush and the children could not see what he was up to. He felt for the poisoned darts, and took one from the stiff plant sheath they were kept in. His hand moved imperceptibly towards the blowpipe. Yet before he could touch it, a long time before, before he had decided there was nothing to lose, even before he had left Beleram to travel to the Ends of the Earth, his time was up. Dulkancellin was standing beside him, gripping his arm.

Cucub felt despair take hold of him. It weighed so heavily on his chest, pressing all the air out of him, that the little man had to take in great gulps so as not to pass out.

'Stand up and walk by yourself,' Dulkancellin ordered him. Allowing Cucub to reach his place of execution without being bound was a mark of respect the Zitzahay could not appreciate.

'Take everything you brought with you,' added the warrior, 'it will keep you company.'

Trembling, Cucub stuffed all his things back in the bag and slowly stood up.

'Allow me to get the rest,' he said, pointing to the cape and staff Kush and Kuy-Kuyen had earlier put aside.

Cucub's state of mind must have changed as he walked over to pick up his other belongings, because when he turned back to the Husihuilke family he was no longer trembling. He held his head high, and his face had become almost noble-looking. They all understood that he had accepted he was going to die.

'We can go now,' was all he said as he stood next to Dulkancellin.

His spirit did not even seem to waver when he noticed the axe that the warrior was carrying beneath his cape.

'You will not suffer,' said Dulkancellin, whose eyes had followed Cucub's gaze. 'And then time will not be able to harm you. I will look for a tree with branches that can support your body, and I will cover it with my cape so that no scavengers can get at it.'

The two men made to leave. But just then, Kume stepped forward.

'Father, stop!' he said.

At this, Old Mother Kush stretched out the palm of her hand to tell the boy not to go on. Instead, she was the one who spoke:

'Dulkancellin, don't take the Zitzahay to the forest. Let him live, and go with him on your journey to the north. You will meet Kupuka before you have left the paths you know. Let Kupuka decide the fate of this person who says he is called Cucub!'

'You know I cannot do that,' replied Dulkancellin, failing to realize his mother was not begging a favour from him.

'I am exercising my right,' the old woman said gently. 'I still hear the rain coming before you do. And I say, regretfully, that the moment has come for me to go against your decision.'

'You are going against our laws,' murmured her son.

'But it is our laws which also give me the power I am calling upon. I was the first person in this house to hear the rain on the leaves.'

Every season since Dulkancellin could remember, Old Mother Kush had won this right. Yet never before had she used it. The warrior was confused. Why did his mother want to get mixed up in such serious matters?

'Old woman, you are also going against justice.'

'Has this old woman said you should not make sure justice is done?' Kush responded sharply. 'I did not say that, simply that you should wait until Kupuka learns what has happened and approves the sentence. Our justice is not in the hands of any one person. And the person who has decreed Cucub's death is not the Council, although he has acted as if he were.'

'I can think of no better way to act,' said Dulkancellin.

68

'Do as you say: observe the laws,' his mother replied. 'For once, I am imposing my will on yours. I have this right. Do you understand how rarely we Husihuilkes use it? Do you understand that I have never done so? Yet I am doing so now, because that is what the voice inside me is telling me.'

Dulkancellin still hesitated between his own sense of right and his mother's.

'Be careful, my son. It is not good that a man and his laws are at odds with each other.'

'I will respect your right,' said the warrior.

All this time the Zitzahay had been standing with his eyes closed, and seemed to have distanced himself from the discussion. So much so that Dulkancellin now shook him roughly.

'Listen to me! I don't know what charms you used to cloud this woman's understanding. But neither they nor any others will succeed in fooling Kupuka. You will leave here as my prisoner.'

Dulkancellin took some of the clothes Cucub was wearing from him, as well as most of his possessions.

'Sit over there!' he ordered. 'We will leave when the sun has risen three times. And remember, you may still be alive, but you are not free.'

The Zitzahay's expression at his reprieve was far from joyful. He walked slowly over to the corner where Dulkancellin had pointed, and slumped down.

'Come on, daughters!' said Old Mother Kush. 'We have a journey to prepare for.'

The old woman was beginning to feel the pangs of doubt. She realized her decision had changed the course of great events, and was afraid she might be wrong. For his part, Dulkancellin hardly dared ask himself whether the need he felt to take a deep breath of the damp night into his lungs was due to a sense of relief.

8

THE PRISONER'S SONG

The following day was spent in preparations for their imminent departure.
The whole family took part, so that by nightfall nearly everything was
complete. Dulkancellin and the three boys were polishing the last arrow-
heads. Old Mother Kush, Kuy-Kuyen and Wilkilén were smearing grease
onto all the leather gear. The quiver, cape and boots had all to be carefully
polished so that they would not let in water or split.

'Tomorrow the Zitzahay can gather together his things,' said Dulkancellin to no one in particular.

Still sitting there, hands tied, Cucub watched them hard at work. The
previous night he had been given a good meal and a bed close to where
Dulkancellin slept. The Husihuilke warrior trusted in the sharpness of
his hearing. The Zitzahay was no longer thinking of trying to escape. Yet
both of them spent the entire night awake, until at last dawn came. The
sky at the Ends of the Earth barely grew light, changing from black to
dark grey. The household was up very early: they had much to do, and
very little time. Dulkancellin realized he could not keep a proper watch
on the Zitzahay, and so had decided to tie him more securely. Taking a
leather thong, he had skilfully wrapped it round his hands several times

until he could not move them. He was about to do the same with his feet, but thought it over for a moment and decided not to. It was not necessary.

Cucub had spent most of the day tied up like this, thinking it would have been good to be able to play his pan-pipes. The rain came lashing down all the time. The morning went by. Midday arrived, but brought with it no more than a faint glow in the sky. Then the afternoon slowly dragged by: so slowly for the Zitzahay! No one had spoken to him the whole day: they had scarcely exchanged a few words with each other. If only the beautiful one with long tresses would speak to him!

By now evening was drawing in. Cucub was beginning to feel tired. He tried to rouse himself by watching what the Husihuilke family was doing, but achieved only the opposite: the repeated polishing of the arrow-heads and the leather acted on him like a sleeping potion. The more he watched, the heavier his head felt, the more his eyes smarted. Why not sleep? thought Cucub, close to dozing off. If he fell asleep, he might dream of Mother Neén and his distant jungle. Slumped over, in his dreams the prisoner saw himself back in his own hammock. It was so good to be there! Lying in it, rocked by the fragrant night breeze, Cucub was folding tobacco leaves as he watched the moon glide through the palm trees. He was out in the jungle once more, thinking that at first light he would go to the market to eat some spicy fish. But this happy sensation soon deserted him when his uncomfortable position woke him with a start. He slowly stretched his aching neck. He could not stay awake without wanting to cry. Everything he could see made him sad: the walls, the oil lamps, and these people he could have been friends with. Cucub decided it was better not to fall asleep again. *I'll sing instead*, he thought.

> I crossed over to the far bank
> And the river took care of me
> So I was not afraid.

72

> I asked the tree if I could
> Climb to its highest branch;
> I saw things far in the distance
> But I am a man
> And so I climbed down
> And walked on the ground again.

Just as he was finishing his song, Kuy-Kuyen and Wilkilén also completed their task. They both stared at the Zitzahay.

'Your hands!' their grandmother reminded them. They took a handful of ashes out of a pot by the fire and rubbed their forearms to remove all the grease. Then they went out to rinse their arms, and finally spread some oil on them.

'Hmm… that smells good even from here,' said Cucub, trying to engage them in conversation. His previous attempts that afternoon had proved fruitless. This time was different, however. Kuy-Kuyen and Wilkilén came over and sat on either side of him.

'Who taught you that song you were singing?' Kuy-Kuyen asked.

'No one,' replied Cucub. 'It's my song, I made it up. Up there in the Remote Realm everyone has their own song. We invent them the day we become adults, and then they go with us for the rest of our lives.'

'Sing it again,' Kuy-Kuyen begged him.

The Zitzahay did not hesitate. He cleared his throat and began:

> I crossed the other river
> And the tree took care of me
> So I was not afraid.
> I asked the man if I could
> And climbed to the top,
> I saw things in the distance.

But I am a river bank
So I began again to walk
On the ground.

'That's not the same song!' Kuy-Kuyen protested. 'It's not the same as the one you just sang!'

'Yes and no. That's how our songs are. The words don't change, but their order does. We like it that way, because it means they can accompany us when we are sad, but also when we are happy. On days without sun and moonlit nights, when we return and when we leave.'

Cucub had recovered his spirits. After all, all he had to do was wait: he had no doubt Kupuka would be more reasonable than Dulkancellin. And besides, the two girls were keeping him company, and he could smell a good meal being prepared on Kush's fire.

All of a sudden, the eight people in the hut raised their heads. The noise was followed by a movement... a dull, harsh sound. The roof beams shook, the oil lamps swayed, the earth seemed to change shape beneath their feet. The ground moved at the Ends of the Earth so that no one would forget it was a living creature. When the shaking finally finished, all their hearts had turned pale.

Dulkancellin wrapped himself in his cloak to leave the hut, just as all the other heads of family were doing. The Husihuilke men listened through the wind and rain to discover whether the voice of a drum could be heard from any village calling for help. They listened intently for a long while, but no request came.

'Nothing serious has happened,' said the warrior, coming back inside.

Kuy-Kuyen and Wilkilén were still clinging to Kush.

'It's not good to stay still like that,' the old woman told them. 'It's better to be doing something to recover your calm. Come on, girls, give me a hand! There are many things we need to put back where they belong.'

'Look!' shouted Thungür. The urgency of his voice was mirrored by the way he was jabbing his arm towards the ceiling.

Several baskets piled on some bundles of reeds, together with some rolled-up hides, had come crashing down, revealing the green tip of a bird's feather.

'How is it possible?' said Cucub, in a delayed reaction to what he could see. 'That's the sign! Warrior, there's the sign you were demanding! Please get it!'

Dulkancellin did as he was asked. He carefully removed the feather from in among the baskets and held it up for them all to see. It was shiny, and about two handspans long. Its green colour was completely unlike any of the greens that the Husihuilkes had ever seen.

Dulkancellin quickly forgot what the feather looked like to ask himself – as the Zitzahay was also doing – how it could have got where it did. Someone must have hidden it there on purpose. But... who? And why? The only possible answer was no consolation: it must have been one of the family. One of them, or Kupuka.

The warrior untied the Zitzahay's hands. Then he spoke for all of them:

'Gather round. We need to know what happened.'

Dulkancellin sat on the floor. One by one, the others did the same.

'We all saw the same thing, and at the same time,' said the warrior. 'The earth uncovered the Kukul feather. It also uncovered someone's evil intention. This feather is the sign of the messenger, the proof of his loyalty, the difference between his life and his death. Somebody wanted to hide it... Does anyone here know something they wish to tell us?'

Several of them shook their heads.

'Confusion added to confusion,' Dulkancellin growled. 'I am reluctant to ask myself, as I must, who among us is not telling the whole truth. I don't want to think it was Kupuka, because—'

'I have a question to ask,' Cucub butted in. 'Listen to me, Kume. When your father and I were about to go to the forest, you were going to say something... Kush interrupted you, so you kept silent. What were you going to say but didn't? Perhaps you would like to tell us now.'

Kume turned scarlet.

'Speak, my son!' Dulkancellin could sense the note of desperation in his own voice.

Visibly uncomfortable, Kume could not find any words.

'Reply to the Zitzahay's question!' his father managed to add, before the desperation reached his soul.

'I don't remember very well...' the boy began.

Dulkancellin stood up, and so did Kume. Father and son confronted each other in a ring of astonished faces.

'I did it.' Kume's voice was a faint whisper. 'I hid the feather.'

'Go on,' said Dulkancellin.

'I took advantage... I did it when you were all looking at Kupuka's shadow.'

'Continue.'

'I was not going to let you... to let him die. But Kush got in before me, and invoked the right of rain. So the Zitzahay's life was saved.'

'Only just in time.'

'I didn't want to...'

'Continue.'

'I was only waiting for the right moment to slip the feather back into his bag. I was going to make sure you found it before you set out.'

'Why did you do it?' his father insisted.

'I didn't... I don't trust the Zitzahay, even if he did bring the Kukul feather with him. That's why I thought of hiding it. If he could not find the sign... I was wrong. I thought you would ask him to leave, that's all. And that you would stay with us.'

'You have no further explanation?'

'No.'

The warrior waited for the blood to settle in his throat. He knew that his words would be hard to speak.

'I do not know you,' he said.

Kume was in disgrace. If he did not live long enough to wipe out the stain of his dishonour, he would die without a name. Old Mother Kush could not hold back a sob. The father was disowning the son. And although none of them realized it, that increased the power of their enemy even before he had set sail.

9

FROM MINSTREL TO MESSENGER

A long while later, the Husihuilke family and Cucub were sitting in a semicircle on rugs, eating red prickly pears. Kume was not with them: he could no longer share the warmth of the fire. How different this was from previous nights they had spent together! Evenings of friendship, perfumed with laurel, when Kush told stories or played her pan-pipes late into the night. Would they ever return?

Cucub would have gladly interceded on Kume's behalf, and yet he refrained from doing so. He had learnt enough about the Husihuilkes to know his defence would be in vain. The Zitzahay wondered how he could ease the sadness of these good people, and decided the best thing would be to talk about other things.

'It may be that you all would like to hear certain details,' he said. 'I would be happy to tell you about how I went from being a minstrel to becoming a messenger. And if there is time, I can tell you about the most exciting parts of my journey here.'

None of them was sleepy, and the Zitzahay deserved some reward for the unjust way he had been treated.

'Tell us about them, if you so wish,' Dulkancellin agreed.

So Cucub began his story, which no one interrupted.

'I was in a town we call Centipede Yellow when I received the order to go to the House of the Stars. Since that is in Beleram, two suns away from where I was, I set off at once. I was very sorry to leave the wedding at Centipede Yellow where my flute and I were the guests of honour. Oh well, I told myself, you have no choice! Someone else can provide the music for the celebrations. Walking day and night, I reached Beleram sooner than I expected. Would you believe me if I tell you I did not even stop at the river? I crossed two villages near the city, then the orange groves that surround it. I walked down the street to the market, then across the games court, and the main square. I paused for breath outside the House of the Stars. I was glad I did, because I still had to climb the flights of stairs leading to its entrance. You will soon see it, Dulkancellin! There are thirteen times twenty steps, built into the side of a hill. To climb them I had to rest more often than I had done in my whole journey there, but eventually I reached the top and called my name. You all should see that place! It is partly excavated from the rock, and partly a stone wall. The main entrance to the House of the Stars opens onto an enormous empty chamber, with no more decoration than the shafts of light that pour in through the narrow windows and glint off the stones. As I was waiting for the guard who had taken my name to reappear, several young apprentices went by. They were all in a great hurry: they went down one staircase and up another one on the other side, came out through one interior door and disappeared through another. And to tell the truth, none of them was the slightest bit interested in me. The guard finally returned. "Follow me, Zabralkán is expecting you," I remember he told me.

'We went up one of the lateral staircases. We climbed and climbed. Every so often, the guard stopped to allow me to rest. From the way he kept glancing back at me, he must have thought I did not have the strength to get to the top. He let me get my breath back, then on we went. How much further? How could I convince my knees to support me a little longer? At the top of every set of steps there was a room. As I paused, I managed to see inside some of them, but most had their doors shut. I do not know if it was because I felt so exhausted or because of the twists and turns of our climb, but I could not understand how the House of the Stars was built, especially since it grew narrower and darker with every step. Were we penetrating inside the hill? If that was the case, how was it that I could see the sky through narrow slits in the walls? After a while I ceased to care. The guard and I continued our climb. There were no more resting places or rooms; the walls closed in on the stairs, which grew steeper and steeper. And poor Cucub here was longing for the open air. "We've arrived," was the last thing I heard. I was exhausted after several days' walking and the endless stairway: I collapsed.

'I came to in a large room, with protruding window openings. Once I had properly regained consciousness, I realized I was in an observatory. What I had taken for windows were in fact observation points. I would love to describe all the details of that magnificent place for you, but I can see that Wilkilén has already fallen asleep, and my experience as a story-teller suggests I need to be brief.

'I told you I found myself in an observatory. I should add that the only person with me, watching me come round, was Zabralkán. He and I had never come face to face before. Let me explain that there was nothing unusual in this, because it is the custom in Beleram for musicians, jugglers and story-tellers to congregate on ceremonial days on the enormous platform that runs round the House of the Stars. These were splendid celebrations when Zabralkán, one of the greatest of the Supreme Astronomers, would honour me in particular among all the artists of the Remote Realm. How could I possibly forget those days? Hundreds of torches were lit along the main street to light the path of the night-time processions that wound their way down from the remote villages. Careful, Cucub!

You're falling into the temptation of trying to describe every detail again. If I do it once more, don't hesitate to tell me so.

'Did I mention that Zabralkán is the greatest of the Supreme Astronomers? What I am sure I have not told you is how embarrassed I felt comparing his proud bearing with my own ragged appearance after such a long journey. Yet I soon calmed down when I saw that Zabralkán was not interested in how I looked. Filling a bowl with sweetened pumpkin, the Astronomer offered it me. After the first few sips I felt restored. By the time the bowl was empty I felt capable of walking back to Centipede Yellow there and then. I told Zabralkán as much, and he smiled. But look at Kuy-Kuyen! She is smiling too... she must be having a pleasant dream. Even so, as I can see that there are still more people awake than asleep, it is worth my while continuing.

'The Supreme Astronomer was pacing round a big rectangular stone block in the centre of the observatory. The block stood let's say a handspan from the ground. It was three times longer than it was wide, and was covered in carvings. You can imagine how many of them there were if I tell you that I started at the drooping head of a snake at one end and, although I did my best to follow its body through images of birds and deer, stars and moons, as well as indecipherable signs and garlands of flowers, I soon lost track of it. Weary of watching my attempts, Zabralkán told me to desist. "You can look for the serpent's tail later," I remember he told me. "Now we must talk of important matters." He began to explain what all of us here are well aware of: that there was important news to communicate, which was destined for only a chosen few to hear; that messengers were to be sent out... that great events were imminent, and so on and so forth. That I should be back in time for the Great Council... and that I had been appointed as a messenger!

'Do you recall, Dulkancellin, that you asked Kupuka why you had been chosen to represent the Husihuilke people? Well, I asked the same question of Zabralkán: why choose me as a messenger? The only reply either of us received was an order. And after that, many more. First, that I was not to leave the House of the Stars until the day of my departure for the Ends of the Earth. It's true that I was looked after most exquisitely. I slept in a soft bed and was well fed; but I was also given endless instructions. Hour after hour of explanations, details of my journey, warnings. Afterwards, poor me! They made me repeat everything to make sure I had properly understood. Then the next day, we started all over again. They often changed something from what they had told me the previous day, to be sure I was paying attention. They made false statements and asked trick questions; they presented complex problems and absurd solutions. On and on, until they finally accepted that Cucub was ready to face his demanding mission.

'I learnt that in the same House of the Stars, perhaps close by me, other messengers were undergoing the same training, and yet I never saw any of them. I also learnt from Zabralkán that one of them was heading for the Land Without Shadow to look for the Pastors of the Desert. I thought that as we were travelling the same path, we could go together. I would have been pleased to have someone to share songs, bread and fear with along the way, but it was not to be. Did he leave before me? Or after me? I have no idea. All I can say with any certainty is that only my soul and I travelled from the staircase of the House of the Stars to this hut.

'I left Beleram at first light one morning. I remember I saw several men raking the games court, and some stallholders just arriving at the market. I have to admit I paused at a food stall to buy a tortilla. That pause was not part of my itinerary, but how often the smell of that tortilla gave me the strength to carry on!'

Cucub's story gradually filled the room with apparitions. When the Zitzahay mentioned the tortilla, they all licked their lips at the thought of the perfumed delicacy. When their mouths were dry again, their ears were deafened by the sound of thousands of birds from the most beautiful valley in the world which came to revive the flagging fire. When the Zitzahay spoke of the hair of the fish-women in the wind, the men conjured them up in their minds. When he recalled the sun in the desert, they all loosened their cloaks. The flock of llamels Cucub rounded up with his words took a long while to leave, crammed as they were into the small wooden house. In the end, an eagle came and perched on Kush's pile of blankets, then vanished again. But the forest at the Ends of the Earth was still there, and seemed more familiar than ever thanks to the Zitzahay's words.

'The landscape guided me so well,' Cucub went on, 'that I started to sing as I walked, just like I used to do in my own land. Thanks to that, I was able to tell quite clearly at every moment how far the Husihuilke villages were from me. Although I never saw them, I could stretch my arm out and point to them: one here, another over there, calculating the distance they were from my song.

'The Supreme Astronomers told me many things about the Ends of the Earth. For an unknown reason, some came back to me more than others as I travelled through the forest. "The Marshy River separates the Land Without Shadow from the Ends of the Earth. That is where the Husihuilkes live and die. Their villages are grouped around a family clan. Each clan has the same founding ancestor who unites each family through blood and war. These family clans are all Husihuilkes. But these ancestors also make them adversaries..."

'I am repeating here exactly what I was told by the Astronomers, without adding or omitting anything. Often when I rested, their words came back to me. As I sat high in a tree, searching the sky for a familiar star to light the way for me, I could hear the voices of Bor and Zabralkán: "The Marshy River separates..." And during those nights, even though it may be hard to believe, I thought of Dulkancellin. That's right, warrior,

I thought of you, and wondered what kind of man you were. Not just any man, obviously, if you had been chosen to represent your neighbours and your adversaries at the Great Council.

'As I understand it, there are clans linked by honour or family ties between their original leaders. And there are others which, despite having been bitter rivals, have put an end to the wars by marrying their sons and daughters. But it was also explained to me that some clans will not accept any alliances beyond that of their blood mingling on the battlefield, or any pact apart from the truce agreed so that each side can carry off their dead.

'Dulkancellin will have to take weighty decisions in the name of everyone. This man I have come to find, I remember telling myself whilst waiting for sleep to come, this man will have to be able to do so without disregarding anyone.

'The first part of my journey, from the dawn when I left the House of the Stars until the moment I crossed the bridge over the Marshy River, took me thirteen times ten days, plus another nine. Each day was a notch on my belt. The next stage, from the southern end of the bridge to the door of your house, took me only half that time. Not that the distances were very different, because the river is almost halfway here. No, it was because it was so much easier to make progress through the forest than through the desert.

'It was no lie when I said that my journey through the forest was untroubled. Despite this I could tell you any number of stories about things that happened on the way, finishing off with the tale of how I rested very close to here to check that the Kukul feather was where it was meant to be. But I will not go into all that. I'll omit those details, and come quickly to the point where the warrior opened the door to me, and after having travelled for two hundred and nine suns when all I had seen was my own reflection in water, I saw another human face once more.

'You are mistaken if you think I have lost interest in telling you more

about my journey. I'm not ending here because I have no wish to continue...
but I am stopping because of Piukemán. For a long time, the lad resisted
falling asleep, pinching his hands and changing position on his rug. But
now he is sleeping. I look round and consider what I see. Who is still
awake? Kush, Dulkancellin, Thungür, and of course, the Zitzahay here.

'I have learnt that nothing happens by chance these days. That is why
I interpret their falling asleep not as an insult to my art but as a valuable
opportunity I have no wish to squander. If I had any doubts about revealing certain secrets whispered to me in the House of the Stars, this has
removed them. The little ones are sleeping. The three who are still awake
are those who can and should know about ancient events, which are the
origin of what will happen both today and tomorrow.

'Dulkancellin will learn of them the moment we arrive at the House of
the Stars. But the sooner he hears about these events, the longer he will
have to reflect on them. As for Kush and Thungür... I imagine Kupuka
intends to inform them of everything when he returns. My question is:
what if Kupuka is not able to return? Let us not forget for a moment that
we are living in uncertain times. In every part of the Fertile Lands there
is talk of inexplicable occurrences. Among them, several disappearances.
Will the Earth Wizard return? If he does not, and if Dulkancellin and
Cucub do not come back either, at least two people among the Husihuilkes will know the facts and be able to decide what to do next. This is what
I think, and I trust I am not wrong.

'Before I begin, though, I think it would be better to carry the children
to their beds; I imagine they are quite clever at waking up without anyone
noticing. If you will allow it, I think I am strong enough to carry Wilkilén.

'Oh! and Old Mother Kush, perhaps you could bring us some warm
milk and some corn bread.'

10

ANCIENT EVENTS

When Dulkancellin, Thungür and Cucub returned to sit by the fire, the bread and milk were already laid out for them.

'Drink while it's hot,' Kush told the Zitzahay. 'Your voice will thank you for it.'

'Thank you,' replied Cucub, with a slight bow.

There was no sign of the storm abating. If anything, the freezing wind grew even stronger, and the sky fell into the marshes.

Cucub had learnt to trust the roof above his head. When he had first arrived, he thought it would not be long before that wooden hut, with its straw and tar roof, let in the rain. He had recalled with nostalgia the stone walls of the Zitzahay people. But now, dry and sheltered, sniffing the sweet smell of herbs from the chimney, he told himself that Old Mother Kush's house was the best place in the world in which to listen to the rain.

'Zitzahay, we will go on listening to you because you have promised to tell us valuable things,' said Dulkancellin. 'But night will soon be turning to dawn, and we all need to rest a little. Tomorrow is the day before we set off, and there still is much to do. I beg you not to say more than you have to.'

'I will not waste a word. But let me warn you, whether there are few or many words, you will hear and forget them unless you see the need to remember them.' The story-teller paused for effect. 'On the day I arrived, I spoke as if in passing of something that is essential to know in order to understand how murky are the events we face. At that time, Kupuka was the only one who understood the importance of my comment. I could tell that from the troubled look he gave me. This time I will be more explicit, not to trouble you but to alert you. The coming events have succeeded in confusing our Magic. Trying to understand the strangers' real reason for travelling to our shores, and of course the decision to be made as to whether we should receive them with bread or battle, has drawn a line. On either side of it, our Magic interprets the same signs in different ways. Everything is confused. Where some read night, others read day; no one can remember anything of this kind happening before. To my humble way of thinking, I predict that if this does not change we are running a very great risk. If the Council is mistaken in its conclusion, if our actions are not well directed from the start, something terrible will happen to us.'

'How is it that you can understand that, and even I can understand that, but the Magic cannot?' asked Dulkancellin.

'Of course it can!' Cucub replied. 'But it cannot find a way to deal with it, nor to arrive at a definite conclusion. I trust that there is no pettiness or arrogance in our Magic. Nor betrayals. There is Wisdom that has not yet been attained. That, and only that, is what I pin my hopes on. Perhaps by the time we reach the Remote Realm we will find that the movement of the stars in the heavens, the prophecies, the sacred dreams, the calendars, the visions of the initiated and the messages from the earth will all have been interpreted in a single fashion.'

Dulkancellin waved his hand to show he had understood. Then he encouraged the Zitzahay to get on to the important matters.

'Zitzahay, you have been brief. But now tell us if you can exactly where this line you speak of is drawn.'

'Your question anticipates what I was about to tell you,' said Cucub, annoyed at the warrior's impatience. 'Since you so desire, I will convey this to you in a few words. Some believe it is the Northmen who are coming. Or rather, who are coming back. Others fear – may the stars align in our protection! – that it is the shadows of Misáianes who are on their way, as our ancestors were warned long ago.'

Cucub paused, sure that the Husihuilkes would ask him to explain further. To his astonishment, Old Mother Kush said:

'The first name you mentioned is not unknown to me. Northmen… I heard about them when I was as small as Wilkilén. It was from the mouth of one of my grandparents, on a night very like this one.'

'That is possible,' Cucub admitted. 'Many people heard talk of the Northmen. And some elders can dig deep into their memories and bring back what they were told. You, Old Mother Kush, must have heard of their red hair and colourless skin. But it is more difficult for you to know what they did when they were among us.'

'You are right. I close my eyes and hear the voice of my grandfather describing those men. I also remember he told us they had never before reached the Ends of the Earth. But that is all I can remember.'

'Sister Kush, there is no way you can recall what you do not know,' said the Zitzahay. 'We would have to go back not to one grandfather but seven of them, if we wanted to reach back to the time when the Northmen visited us. And their coming was as secret as it was remote in time. The truth about those events was preserved in sacred books that only a few could read. And so it remained, awaiting the right time to be revealed. That time is now upon us, and we are the first to be aware of it. Is this destiny of ours a good or bad thing? I am not sure.'

'Tell us what we need to know,' insisted Dulkancellin.

By now, Cucub felt completely at ease. He went on:

'One day in the far distant past, the Northmen disembarked in the Remote Realm. At that time, very little was known... or I should say, very little was remembered about them: we knew they lived in the Ancient Lands, on the far side of the ocean. And that they were the direct descendants of a timeless, noble race of men. The expedition of the Northmen brought bad news. Worse than anything that had ever been heard in our lands. Our leaders listened to them. And as I said before, everything the Northmen related was written in hermetic language on folded bark parchments that were placed in lacquered cases, then stored in a stone chest, which was hidden in a private place, and...'

'Wait a moment, Zitzahay!' Dulkancellin objected. 'Try to get to the essential! Please tell us why you said "bad news".'

'Who said "bad"?'

'You did!'

'Me?'

'Yes, you!' the warrior insisted, obviously annoyed.

'In that case I did not succeed in expressing my real thoughts,' said Cucub. 'I should have said "terrifying news". Or in other words, news that would turn the world upside down. Glimpses of the end.'

'Zitzahay, in honour of the gravity of what you are talking about, forget your artistry for a moment and tell me clearly: what are you referring to? What news are you talking about?'

Dulkancellin's manner brooked no contradiction.

Cucub blushed with silent embarrassment. And the Husihuilkes waited in silence for him to recover from his feeling of shame.

'I was working up to that,' muttered the Zitzahay, as if excusing himself. Then he began his answer, with the sincere intention of not letting his tongue run away with him any more. 'A war was beginning in the Ancient Lands; a war so absolute, so different from any that had gone before that the Northmen crossed the ocean to bring us news of it. From the Ancient Lands to the Fertile Lands. No one would run such a risk simply to inform us about a war like all the others. Our ancestors were warned by those Northmen: "Brothers of the Fertile Lands, the motive for us coming here could not be another battle between Creatures, however important that might be. We have come to tell you that in the Ancient Lands the final war is about to be fought. We are facing someone whom his own mother baptized Misáianes, which in distant languages has the meaning "Eternal Hatred". The Northmen said Misáianes had been created in the bowels of Death itself. Created and trained to unleash the power of fierce cruelty against our world.'

When Old Mother Kush, Thungür and Dulkancellin heard these words from the Zitzahay, they sensed that Misáianes was a name capable of dividing Time. A shudder ran through the room, fluttered and settled on their souls like a bird of prey.

'The books I referred to,' Cucub went on, 'faithfully reflect what the Northmen told us. I can remember some of the fragments most frequently repeated by Zabralkán during the time I spent in the House of the Stars, and I can think of no better way to conclude what I have to say: "It is for us, the inhabitants of the Ancient Lands, to undertake the first battles against Misáianes. That is as it should be, because Misáianes was born and grew on a mountain in our continent. And that is where he is concentrating his forces. We will fight to the last drop of blood of the last noble Creature, but that may not be enough. For now, this part of the world is still safe. We and the ocean are a shield for you. Preserve this place and this life of yours! Protect yourselves, and protect the children we will leave among you! It is in them that we are depositing our hopes for the future, even if the Ancient Lands should fall. If we are victorious, we will return to search for our descendants. You will see us come back over the sea. And then we will pass bread from hand to hand round the ceremonial pyre. But if we are defeated, it will be They who appear. Misáianes will gather strength in the Ancient Lands. Then he will dispatch his armies to devastate this continent, because that is his intention: not to leave a single tree in blossom, not a single bird singing. We know that when this moment comes you will fight as we are doing now. But that moment, if it does come, will only arrive after many, many years. This war will stretch beyond the span of human life: that is why you must ensure you keep the memory of these words alive and protected. No matter how many years go by… When the arrival of a new fleet is prophesied, there must be some of you who can remember all this in order to decide whether it is the Northmen who are on board, or if it is Misáianes who is drawing near. Them or us. Life or Death. That is all. And make sure that our children multiply!'

The Husihuilkes were beginning to understand.

'I can see you are starting to understand,' said Cucub. 'Is it the Northmen who are coming, or Misáianes? Instead of illuminating us, the signs only make the question more obscure. Everything presenting itself to the eyes of Magic can be read in two different ways, and the result is uncertainty.'

'We have never heard anyone spoken of in the way you described Misáianes,' said Dulkancellin. 'Tell us, Cucub, who is he?'

The Husihuilke warrior's question had its reply in the sacred books. Testimonies written in a holy tongue. Tales of a war as yet unfinished, that cast its shadow over the present.

Many years earlier, the ages of seven grandfathers, the Astronomers of the Remote Realm had asked the Northmen the same question that Dulkancellin did of Cucub.

And when we, the Astronomers, asked about Misáianes, the Northmen replied in the way we have transcribed here. We took down the words exactly as they spoke them, without adding or omitting anything. These are sacred books that we will keep safe until the new arrival of the ships.

The Northmen named Misáianes. They called him the Ferocious One, the one who should never have been born. That is what the Northmen said. We fear Misáianes, the one who saw the light of this world because his mother went against the Great Laws: that is what they told us.

Death, condemned not to give birth to mortal or immortal creature, wandered through eternity demanding progeny. She sobbed and begged, but the prohibition was absolute. A refusal that would never be reversed. So Death rebelled. She moulded an egg from her own saliva, then produced it from her mouth. She secreted juices and fertilized it with them. And so from this revolting substance her son was born, protected by the solitude of a forgotten mountain in the Ancient Lands.

This being, born from Disobedience, brought horror with him; and horror was not merely a part of him, but his essence. The son brought with him evil such as not even his mother could imagine. That is what the Northmen told us. This happened because the Great Laws were broken – that is what they said.

When this happened, a wound was opened. And Eternal Hatred, lurking beyond the edges of the world, found this opening. Eternal Hatred found its way in through this wound of Disobedience. It was formed inside the egg, and came into being. Thanks to the son of Death, Eternal Hatred took shape and found its voice in this world. This is what the Northmen told us. Its lizard soul came crawling out. The Evil One.

Then Death saw what she had done. She saw her progeny was the flesh of Eternal Hatred, and sought to rip it to pieces with her teeth. The first day, she did not succeed. Nor could she destroy it the following day. On the third day she felt proud of the beast, and called him Misáianes. On that third day a new era began, an era of mourning. But nobody knew.

Misáianes grew. He became master over a multitude of Creatures and extended his empire. You should know that the son of Death will never show his face. So the Northmen told us. It is written that his features will

93

be concealed until the last days. So they said.

What Misáianes, the son of Death, says is like the truth, and confuses anyone who stops to listen. He knows how to praise the powerful and seduce the weak; he knows how to whisper and set brother against brother. The danger is great. He can seem to us like a glorious master, our new teacher. He can seem like the counsellor of the sun. So the Northmen told us. The danger is great; this they said. Many will run in whichever direction he points. Many in this world will worship him.

Hear this and remember. Misáianes came to destroy the time of mankind, of animals, of water, of living green and of the moon, the time of Time. Many will be intoxicated by his poison; many more will fall in battle. Better to fall in battle. So spoke the Northmen. Do not forget this, they warned us.

Misáianes, the Ferocious One, is the end of all light. Misáianes is the beginning of inbred pain. If we are defeated in this war, Life will fall with us. If we are defeated, light will be condemned to drag itself over ashes. And Eternal Hatred will stride through the twilight of Creation.

This much we have written of what the Northmen told us. We will keep the sacred books as they asked us to. The day will come when someone speaks the name of Misáianes once more. They will name Misáianes and ask where he comes from. And whoever asks shall find an answer.

11

FAREWELL!

It was the morning of their departure. During the night the rain had eased until it had almost ceased, but with the dawn it began to fall heavily once more.

Everything needed for the long journey had been ready since the previous day. Despite this, Dulkancellin carefully checked every item again. When he was sure everything was there, he turned to face his family. He wanted to speak to them, but his throat was dry, and so many confused thoughts were running through his mind he could barely order them.

'This is the moment of departure. You know I have no choice but to leave you and undertake this narrow path. Take care of yourselves, and wait for Kupuka. He will bring you news.'

The moment for them to leave had come. Dulkancellin, who did not know how to shed tears, went up to his daughters. To avoid crying, Kuy-Kuyen tried desperately not to blink. Wilkilén dried her tears noisily. Their father leant down and kissed them both on the forehead.

'Farewell.'

Then he hugged Piukemán. The boy would have liked to prolong the embrace, to confess he was afraid. But his father's eyes prevented him.

'Son, you must help Thungür in his tasks, and obey him.'

'Yes, Father,' replied Piukemán.

Thungür and Dulkancellin said goodbye clasping each other's forearms, in the manner of warriors.

'The golden oriole's prediction has come true. As you can see, my son, the forest is never wrong. As soon as I cross that threshold, you will be the head of this family.'

'Against my wishes,' said Thungür.

'Hunting and fishing, decision-making, the life of the village; all of that will continue while I am away. So should all of you.'

'What are we to say when people ask after you, Father?'

'Tell them I have gone on a journey. Nothing more. Kupuka will explain the rest when he judges the time to be right.'

Dulkancellin gazed at his mother. She came over and took his hands in hers. Old Mother Kush was thinking of Kume.

'Dulkancellin, do not leave this house without embracing another of your sons. Do not increase the pain.'

'Old Mother Kush,' the warrior replied, 'it seems as though the years are clouding your mind. I have four children, and have said a sad goodbye to each of them.'

They all stared at Kume, who sat apart from the group, threading leather thongs. The boy did not raise his eyes from his task, but Kush could see him clench his teeth. *He is the most handsome of them all*, the old woman thought, trying to find consolation in the thought.

'Hurry up, Zitzahay,' said Dulkancellin. 'We need to be going.'

'Wait a moment,' was Cucub's reply. 'I have to repair a hurt.'

It was plain the Zitzahay was referring to Kume, and so Dulkancellin tried to stop him.

'We don't have time, Cucub. We have to go—'

'Husihuilke, I have respected the laws you live by,' Cucub said firmly. 'Now you should respect mine. We should be as close to one another as are grains of sand. Any discord will be used against us. That is what I think, and I will behave accordingly.'

He went over to Kume, who had risen to his feet.

'There will be so great a distance between us that we are unlikely to meet again. I am not to blame for what is happening; I had no wish to burst into your forest. I would have preferred to stay singing my songs under the sky I am familiar with, but that was not to be. I salute you, and offer you my friendship.'

Kume's black scowl became moist. The wetness around his eyes sprang from somewhere deep inside him, a place where he was always sad. All of a sudden, he stiffened once more. Smiling disdainfully at Cucub, he left the room without a word.

'Let's go,' said Dulkancellin.

'Whenever you wish,' Cucub replied, glancing down at his empty, extended hand.

At the door the two men gathered up their bags and drew their cloaks tight. Dulkancellin knew everyone was waiting for him to say a single phrase: I will return. But Dulkancellin, who did not know how to shed tears, did not know how to lie either.

'Farewell!' was all he said.

They had only gone a few steps before the pouring rain rendered them invisible. Five pairs of eyes sought them out: they all wanted to see them one more time. To smile at them and keep back the grief.

'Farewell, Dulkancellin,' said Old Mother Kush, knowing this was the last time she would see him.

It was Cucub's song that led their way through the labyrinths of rain. The Zitzahay was singing:

> I crossed the other man
> And the river took care of me
> And I had no river bank...

Part Two

12

HEADING NORTH

The two men set off from Whirlwind Pass heading for Beleram, the city where Cucub lived. This was also where the House of the Stars, excavated into the side of a mountain, concentrated its Magic. They knew the points of departure and of arrival, but the path between was uncertain. The two travellers had to invent it each time water destroyed the usual tracks, fallen trees blocked the way, or marshy ground meant they had to make long detours.

They also had to seek shelter each night. Dulkancellin was expert in finding the protection the forest offered hunters and the lost. Protection which marked the rhythm of the first days of their journey. One day, shelter appeared too early, when they still had the strength to go further. The next day, it would be far off, and the distance they had to cover would test the limits of their endurance.

When they first started out, they spoke of unimportant matters. Neither of them wished to mention the reasons for their journey, or to speculate about what might happen. The warrior was interested in knowing what life was like in the Remote Realm. Cucub was happy to respond to all his questions, raising his voice so as to be heard over the noise of the rain in the forest. When Dulkancellin had no more queries, the Zitzahay sang.

The following day, the Husihuilke spoke no more than was necessary. And the Zitzahay's song sounded weary.

On the third day, they began to feel irritated. Their swollen feet in muddy leather boots, their constantly soaked clothes, and the sweaty smell of their bodies made them ill at ease. Because of this they were sure that anything they said would be misinterpreted, and so said nothing at all. A long time later, Cucub recalled that part of the journey as a prolonged silence in the rain.

The very same cave where Shampalwe had cut her last flowers gave them some respite. It was there, thanks to the Zitzahay's insistence, that they stopped for their first meal. They had not brought an abundance of food with them, but it had been chosen to help them resist the arduous climate and their difficult march. Properly rationed, it would see them through the period when the pouring rain made hunting difficult, if not impossible.

Cucub separated two portions of dried figs, and offered Dulkancellin his share. The warrior rejected them without even looking.

'You should not refuse to eat,' said Cucub. 'Have some, even if you are not hungry.'

'I'll do so later,' Dulkancellin replied. 'But don't try to copy me! Eat until you're licking your fingers. You need it more than me.'

Cucub, who had no wish to copy behaviour that would make life harder for him, went inside the cave to enjoy his meal. Since this was the first day of their march and he was still singing, he hummed between every mouthful.

Seated at the entrance, Dulkancellin watched the rain fall on Butterfly Lake. He knew that before long its waters would rise to the foot of the rocky outcrops that bounded the lake to the west. And that to the east, it would become a dangerous muddy swamp.

The warrior did not have the gift of imagination. He did not know how to daydream; still less how to invent things. But on that dark noonday, so close to where Shampalwe had cut her last bunch of flowers, he saw his wife more clearly than the landscape around him. The slopes running down to the lake were covered with the fresh green of summer. The summer when Wilkilén was born and her mother came here to fulfil the rite of motherhood. Dulkancellin saw Shampalwe dancing by the lake shore as the ceremony demanded. He saw her turn first one way, then the other: one hand at her waist, the other cupped by the side of her head. 'Turning with the steps of a partridge,' she would tell Kuy-Kuyen, to teach her the dance of the Husihuilke women. Shampalwe greeted the warrior with a smile that shaped her eyebrows into a single black line. From the mouth of the cave, her husband returned her greeting with a wave of the hand. Fortunately Cucub was so intent on devouring the last figs that he did not notice: if he had seen the warrior waving at empty space, he would have thought he had caught a fever.

'Cucub!' called the warrior, drifting back to the reality of the rain. 'Let's walk on. This is a region of caves. We will soon find another one where we can sleep.'

Although Dulkancellin knew every inch of the forest, he had to pay attention to their progress. He stopped every now and then to consider which was the best, or least risky, route to take. Whenever he did this, Cucub would look up at him like a child to his father. And when the Husihuilke set off again, the Zitzahay would follow him without a moment's hesitation.

They walked and walked. Many days went by in which the wind never stopped shaking the trees for a single moment. High above their heads, the branches groaned and bent in a threatening fashion. Frequently the threat was real enough, and enormous boughs came crashing down, far too close for Cucub's comfort.

Every so often, above the noise of the storm, they could hear the Earth Wizards' drums. The two men would pause and raise their heads, trying to determine exactly which direction the sound was coming from.

'It sounds as if they are following our footsteps,' Cucub would say.

Wherever the sound came from, and whatever it might mean, the beating drums kept the men company. The Husihuilke and the Zitzahay were comforted to know that Kupuka could not be far away. They renewed their march with a spring in their step.

Then one night, just after they had finished eating a hare Dulkancellin had succeeded in catching, something unexpected happened. They had found nowhere better to spend the night than a hollow trunk, where they were preparing to get some rest. Curled up at the back, Cucub was already almost asleep. Dulkancellin was trying to squeeze into a space that was too small for his big frame. All of a sudden, the warrior saw something that made him leap out of their den without bothering to protect himself from the rain. His sudden movement woke the Zitzahay.

'What is going on?' he asked, poking his tousled head out of the trunk.

'Come quickly!' shouted Dulkancellin. 'You have to see this.'

Cucub picked up the warrior's cloak and his own, then struggled outside.

'What is happening?' he asked again, throwing Dulkancellin's cloak round his shoulders as he did so.

Dulkancellin pointed towards the sea. A stream of lights like will-o'-the-wisps could be seen against the black night. Heading north just as they were.

'Lukus!' muttered the Husihuilke warrior. 'I wonder what made them leave their islands to travel in this rain.'

'There's an easy answer to that,' said Cucub. 'The lukus have also been called to the Great Council. The ones we can see are probably going to the House of the Stars. But there seem to be lots of them, and as far as I know, there should be no more of them than of us.'

'There certainly are many there,' said Dulkancellin.

'As you can see, most have reddish tails.'

'That means they are young, of fighting age.'

While Dulkancellin and Cucub were speaking, the lukus disappeared. They must have gone back into the thick forest.

'Let's go home,' the Zitzahay suggested, meaning the hollow trunk. 'We'll be able to think it over better there.'

They returned to the tree, where they spent most of the night searching for an explanation of what they had seen. Shortly before the dawn, none the wiser, they both fell asleep. They awoke stiff and sore, chafing in their damp clothes, and still thinking about what they had seen the previous night. Outside their shelter, the morning was the same as ever: cold and rainy. In order to save provisions, they set off once more without eating anything.

Over the next few days, they often saw the lukus again. Always after nightfall, and always heading north.

Almost a hundred of the creatures had left their islands and taken the western path, which for most of the way bordered the coastline of the Lalafke Sea. This was a great number, as the population of lukus was not large. If a hundred young lukus had left their islands to travel up a continent they hardly knew, then these were strange times indeed.

Men and lukus continued in the same direction, but by different paths. Several days went by with no contact between them. Some nights Dulkancellin awoke with a start, thinking he could hear the breathy whistling the creatures of the islands used to communicate with each other. He thought the lukus could be watching them, but knew he would not be able to see them until the lukus chose to show themselves.

Nothing else relieved the monotony of those days of their march. The northern limit of the Ends of the Earth was close. The climate was finally growing less harsh: the rain was easing off, and occasionally stopped altogether. The wind from the sea that had been constantly lashing them was now a plaintive moan.

It was on one of those nights without rain that the lukus showed themselves. Dulkancellin and Cucub saw them draw near: two red tails and a white one, and prepared to receive them.

The old luku was a few paces behind his young escorts. Men and lukus stared at each other without surprise.

The meeting took place in a clearing where Dulkancellin had succeeded in lighting a fire, which Cucub had managed to keep alight. The white-tailed luku spoke in the Natural Language so that the two human beings could understand him.

'Like you, we are going to the city of Beleram. We are to take part in the Great Council being held in the House of the Stars.'

The Husihuilke and the Zitzahay realized there was no point denying what the luku already appeared to know for certain, and so decided not to say anything.

'I was chosen to represent my people,' the luku went on. 'And I was told to travel along the coast of the Lalafke until I reached Umag of the Great Spring. There a guide from the race of human beings will be waiting to lead me for the rest of my journey.'

'But you are accompanied by many others,' Dulkancellin said.

'I am travelling with those who are most skilled in the art of war. Only a few others have remained on the islands to protect the weak.'

'Can you tell us why you disobeyed the orders and decided to send an army?' asked Cucub.

'Of course I can. That is the only reason for this visit.'

A star appeared in the sky. A glimmer of light that none of them saw.

'We do not think it should remain a secret that strangers are arriving in their ships,' said the luku. 'That is neither necessary nor acceptable for the inhabitants of the Fertile Lands. On the contrary, we are sure that these events should be proclaimed, because only an army of all our peoples will be able to face this new enemy.' As he spoke, the luku's appearance changed. A frown spread over his harsh features, and his words were mixed with strange whistles. 'We should not give these intruders any time. If we let them land, we will be lost. If they so much as leave the mark of their footsteps on our earth, then many generations will reap poison.'

'You say that the men arriving from across the sea will be our enemies. How can you be sure of that, when the Magic itself is not certain of it?' asked Cucub.

'Do not be so impertinent!'

The luku's neck stiffened. His two escorts looked to him for an order, but none came. Dulkancellin, who knew the inhabitants of the islands well, prepared to defend the Zitzahay. But the luku's neck gradually sank back into its shoulders, and so he relaxed his grip on his axe. When the luku spoke again a few moments later, it was in a less hostile manner.

'For many generations, my people have had the White Stone in our possession. It came from the depths of the sea, and was in the islands long before we inhabited them. But the White Stone was put in our charge, and with it we received a prophecy: "When the White Stone changes colour, and turns from light to dark, this will mean the power of Life over Death has been vanquished. It will be because the reign of sorrow is commencing..."'

The Husihuilke warrior nodded. He had heard of the existence of the White Stone from the elders.

The luku searched for something under the long, flowing beard that hung from his chin. The lukus' hands were very useful to them when they ran, because they were short and strong, but they were not very agile. This meant it cost the old luku a great effort to pull out the small leather pouch hidden there. And an even greater one to remove the White Stone from the pouch and show it to the two men on his callused palm. The

Stone was perfectly cylindrical, and was a translucent white colour. Deep within it was an irregularly shaped dark stain.

'Here it is!' said the luku. 'This Stone has always been pure white, without any kind of colour to it. Last summer, deep in its heart, a shadow started to appear. So tiny that many preferred not to see it. Now that winter has begun, nobody can claim the stain does not exist. The Stone is turning dark! The prophecy is being fulfilled! As you can see, Zitzahay, the magic of the lukus is also speaking: and it has no doubts.'

'But the Astronomers—' Cucub protested.

'The Astronomers are wasting their time debating contradictions,' the luku cut in sharply. 'We have no such doubts. We are going to the Great Council to show them the White Stone. We trust this will be enough for the peoples of the Fertile Lands to understand that the war has already begun. And above all, that Magic should take up arms without delay. If they do not, then we will deserve our defeat.'

'What will the lukus do if the Council does not support them?' asked Dulkancellin.

The luku shook his bushy white tail before replying:

'In that case, we will fight and die alone. You can be assured that the enemy will not find the lukus making garlands in their honour.'

'If you decide to go against the Council's decision you will be seen as traitors,' said Cucub.

Something flashed through the luku's mind. Something that he refused to express out loud.

'Whatever happens, we must now continue our journey northwards. We will only halt to talk to the Pastors of the Desert,' was his sole answer.

'Remember this is not the time to reveal any secrets!' Cucub warned him. 'But bear in mind we do not think as you do!'

The luku thrust himself forward defiantly, and raised himself to his full height. He tucked the stone back beneath his beard, turned on his heels, and left without a goodbye. The two young lukus did the same, following him at a short distance.

Dulkancellin and Cucub were alone again. Wrapped in their own thoughts, they sat in silence as the fire died out. After a while, the Zitza-hay lay back with his hands behind his head.

'Look, Dulkancellin!' he said, sitting up and pointing to the sky.

He was staring up at the stars, the few stars twinkling high above the forest.

'We can sleep in peace, brother. Tomorrow we will be woken by the sun.'

13

THE CARPET ON THE SAND

The luku army sped onwards, soon leaving the two men behind.

Standing on its hind legs, an adult luku came up to the waist of a Husihuilke warrior. When erect, they advanced only awkwardly, yet if they used their paws, they could bound along tirelessly. Their shiny tails, which rose high above their heads, were lashes for any foe. Wherever they struck, they left a bloody wound. Then, thanks to the confusion this caused, the luku would return to the attack. If a luku succeeded in wrapping his tail round his adversary, the result was horrific. To emerge alive from a combat against a group of enraged lukus was rare, even for the warriors of the Ends of the Earth. But the lukus had enormous eyes, through which their souls were visible.

When the lukus crossed the Marshy Bridge, the same one Cucub had taken in the opposite direction on his way to Dulkancellin's village, the sky was blue; the sun was warming the sand. Unlike the Zitzahay messenger, the lukus did not try to avoid the Pastors. On the contrary, they deliberately sought them out. They had travelled for a day when in the middle of the desert they saw a line of high dunes. This seemed to them like a good place from which to reconnoitre the land. And so it proved. As night fell, the group of luku scouts who had climbed the dunes spied campfires in the distance. At first light, the luku army headed for them.

A few tents spread in a semicircle, an adobe hut used to store grain and other things, animal pens, a water hole... and scattered all around, pots, tools, piles of wood, men and beasts. The camp was a temporary one, which the Pastors would soon abandon, leaving only traces that the wind would soon erase.

The island creatures were warmly received by the Pastors. The main part of their army stayed on the outskirts of the camp, while the old luku was immediately taken, as he had requested, into the presence of the leader.

Their conversation was brief, and took place inside a tent similar to all the others in the camp. The Pastor chief was sitting on a pile of llamel skins. He listened to everything the luku had to say, which was almost the same as what Cucub and Dulkancellin had heard when they met in the forest. As he had done then, the luku was about to show the White Stone as proof of his words, but something stopped him. A vague feeling made him change his mind and tell the Pastor he had nothing more to add. The Pastor chief realized it was his turn to respond. The luku had to struggle to understand him, because not only did he speak the Natural Language badly, but he had the rough accent of those living in the desert.

'Not everything you have said is new to us. Some days ago, our Head Herdsman met a Zitzahay who brought a message with him. He spoke of a Council to be held in Beleram. He explained why it was being held, and said he wanted to take the man's first-born son with him. The Zitzahay said he would take him to the House of the Stars to represent the Pastors there. The herdsman watched his son leave with the Zitzahay, but was troubled by the news and did not delay in reporting it to the chiefs in the camps. Now you have arrived and shown that he was right to be concerned. I will have to find him quickly so that we can act! I will set out this very day. I will need to visit our camps to ask where he is, because at the moment I do not know. When I find him I will tell him the decision the luku people has come to. You go on ahead with your army. We will join you in the Remote Realm.'

The white-tailed luku felt that his message had been understood, and that they had sealed a pact of loyalty.

'Wait, luku! I will tell my people to prepare an offering in honour of you and your army. We have little more than maize beer, but I think it will be refreshing for you. Drink, it will give you strength for your journey.' The Pastor's smile revealed his black, decaying teeth.

The Pastors told the lukus they would take them to a place where they could celebrate. This was a piece of flat ground surrounded by dunes covered in thorn bushes. The only entrance was along a narrow path that the lukus found hard to walk down. On the sand in the centre of the hollow, the Pastors had spread a rush carpet. They placed bowls full of their maize beer in the centre. The sun beat down on the offering.

Exhausted from the heat and their days of travelling, the island creatures tasted the slightly acid maize beer with great pleasure: all the more so as it was cool from being kept in jars under the sand.

The Pastors did not join in the celebration. Drawn up in two lines on either side of the lukus, they watched them drink. They watched anxiously. They watched them...

After their encounter in the forest clearing, Cucub and Dulkancellin never saw the lukus again.

Now that the rain had stopped, their trek became easier, so that they soon reached the river on the border. They were at the edge of their territory, and the Earth Wizard had still not appeared.

'It's odd we have not seen Kupuka,' Dulkancellin commented to his companion. 'He assured us we would see him again before we left the

Ends of the Earth. And he would not go back on his word except for a very serious reason.'

'I agree with you,' Cucub replied, and was even more surprised at his answer than was Dulkancellin.

With the purpose of resting and waiting for Kupuka, the two men decided to halt on the banks of the Marshy River. They walked inland from the estuary until they came to clear water, and bathed for a long while. Then they washed their clothes in the river and spread them out to dry in the sun. Beside them they laid out all their belongings so that they could dry out too. This was a good moment to get some respite, because from now on they would have to redouble their precautions.

The Zitzahay looked for a strong branch, and sharpened one end. He waded back into the river up to his knees, then stood stock still with his improvised harpoon raised in one hand. Twice he plunged it into the river without success. The third time he speared a big fish. So big that after they had flavoured it with herbs and cooked it on hot stones it made a real feast. All this food left them feeling sleepy, and they decided to rest under the shade of a tree. When they awoke, the sun had set and Kupuka had still not appeared. The Earth Wizard was taking too long: the travellers knew they could wait no longer. Reluctantly, they put their dry clothes back on, swung their bags on their backs, and set off once more.

Dulkancellin and Cucub crossed the bridge under a full moon that shimmered on the desert sand.

They walked all through the night. At first light, the north wind brought bad news.

'There's a smell of death,' said Dulkancellin, sniffing the air. 'The wind reeks of death.'

As they walked on, the stench became stronger.

'It's coming from over there,' said the warrior, pointing to a circle of high dunes to the north-east of their path. The gaggle of carrion and their dreadful screeching told Dulkancellin that they had a lot to feast on.

'Cucub, we have to go and see what has happened.'

The Zitzahay tried to persuade him otherwise.

'What are you saying? We have to avoid the Pastors. That means we should aim back towards the coast. And if I am not mistaken, those dunes are in the opposite direction. If we do as you suggest it would be disobeying orders and running a terrible risk!'

'Even so, we have to do it.'

'Why do we "have to"?' said Cucub. 'Why go out of our way for a dead llamel?'

'The stench on the breeze cannot be due to one dead llamel.'

'All right,' Cucub admitted. 'Let's say there are lots of them.'

'I trust I am wrong, but I have the feeling this is something far more serious. Anyway, if you are right we will only lose the time it takes us to reach the dunes and return. They are not far off, so we will not be long.'

With this, the Husihuilke set off towards the dunes. The Zitzahay followed. He was muttering complaints and conjectures until the fetid odour silenced him too. As they drew nearer to the dunes, it became harder and harder to breathe. In a short while, they were struggling up a steep mound of sand. Cucub made no great effort to catch up with Dulkancellin, who had strode on ahead of him. Even though they were both protecting their noses and mouths with their cloaks, it was not enough. Cucub doubled up several times, overcome by the foul smell. Dulkancellin also had to fight against rising tides of nausea.

'Over here, Zitzahay! I've found a path.'

The path was a narrow gap through the thorn bushes, leading to the top of the dunes. From there they could look down into the hollow below. When they did, they immediately wished they had never come to this spot. Scattered all over the patch of ground, their bodies pecked at by hundreds of beaks, the luku army lay rotting in the sun.

Unable to bear what he was seeing, Cucub closed his eyes. His one thought was that he never wanted to open them again. Perhaps because he had often returned to battlefields in search of his dead, the Husihuilke warrior forced himself to be strong.

'Stay here,' he ordered the Zitzahay. 'I'm going down there to find out why all the lukus died. And if I can, I'll try to save the White Stone.'

Dulkancellin rushed down the slope through the thorn bushes. His presence disturbed the birds of prey, though they merely flew up and circled overhead, waiting for the first opportunity to renew their banquet.

It was midday in the desert. In the burning heat, the Husihuilke searched among the dead bodies for the luku elder. Some of the corpses lay with their faces to the sky. Others had fallen face downwards, or were piled up in a heap. Dulkancellin pulled them from each other, trying to find the luku with the long beard he had met only a few days before. But all their faces were grimaces of pain, too similar in death.

Feeling giddy and sick, Dulkancellin carried out his task as if in a dream. He had not achieved anything, apart from confirming that the lukus had not died fighting. At that moment, a noise made him raise his head. Along the top of the dune he saw two lines of Pastors, already drawing back their bows. And they had Cucub with them!

14

TAKEN PRISONER

Cucub walked in front of Dulkancellin, with the Desert Pastors urging them on as quickly as possible.

The Pastors resting in the shade of their tents were amazed to see two strangers arriving, flanked by the desert guards. They ran out to meet them. Neither Cucub nor Dulkancellin could understand either the questions asked or the replies given, because the Pastors were speaking in their own tongue. They imagined, however, that they were to be taken to see the chief. And they were not wrong.

The group came to a halt outside a tent that was no different to any of the others. Two Pastors who, to judge by their bearing, must be in positions of command, disappeared inside and did not reappear until several hours later. By this time it was growing dark in the desert; the wait continued by the light of the first campfires. Cucub held his head in his hands, dejected at the result of what he saw as their disobeying of the orders they had received. Faithful to his habit of only being concerned with the present, the Husihuilke warrior was busy studying the area in which they were being held captive.

All of a sudden, the tent flap opened. One of the men inside poked his head out and shouted an order. The two strangers were immediately bundled inside. The roof of the tent was so low that Dulkancellin could not stand upright. Perhaps for this reason, or because this was the custom, the man who appeared to be the chief signalled the two men to sit on a mat. He himself remained seated on a high pile of llamel skins. Perched there, and with a cloak covering his entire body, he looked far more imposing than he would have done standing.

'The lukus came here to tell us of their fears over what is about to happen. Now my men tell me they have found them all dead in the desert. And that you, stranger, were searching among their bodies. The lukus were our guests. Now they all lie dead in a hollow... Who are you, and what do you know about these deaths?' The Pastor chief spoke the Natural Language unclearly, mixing it with the guttural sounds of his own tongue.

The two men were sure that the lukus had told the Pastor about the Great Council soon to be held in Beleram, and of the warning from the White Stone. They also knew that if they were not completely honest they would never reach the House of the Stars in time. What then of the command to keep the true reason for their journey a secret? Was that not one of the strictest instructions they had received?

Cucub and Dulkancellin exchanged glances. The secret was already fatally wounded. They, though, could still reach their destination. The Zitzahay, who was more skilled at speaking, took the lead and explained who they were and where they were headed.

'We too spoke to the lukus,' he said, by way of conclusion. 'In the forest, two days' march before the Marshy River. Later, the stench of death led us to the place where we found them. My companion was not rummaging among their corpses. He was searching for—' All at once, Cucub decided not to mention the White Stone. 'He was searching for the cause of their death. It seems as though there is someone roaming these deserts. Someone apart from you and us.'

Unfortunately, this revelation did not produce the result Cucub and Dulkancellin had been hoping for. The reply they received seemed friendly enough, but it was not what they would have liked to hear.

'I believe what you have told us, stranger from the Remote Realm. I think it is true you were sent to take this Husihuilke to the House of the Stars by the Astronomers. I believe you... but I must tell you it is our Head Herdsman whom you have to convince. He is the one who must decide if you will be allowed to continue with your journey. We know he is on his way, and trust he will soon be here. But until he does we will keep you with us.'

'Please understand! We must make all haste. We are already late, and many people are awaiting us. Let us be on our way!'

Cucub's urgent appeal had no effect.

'That cannot be. But do not worry, the Head Herdsman will be here soon. I promise to speak on your behalf. When he gives his approval, we will supply you with llamels to cross the desert more speedily.'

With that, the chief spoke to the other Pastors in the tent in their own language. Afterwards, to show his consideration, he explained what he had told them.

'I have ordered these men to search. I've told them to try to discover what happened to the lukus.'

Dulkancellin understood that for the moment there was no point insisting. He contented himself with asking a favour on behalf of the dead lukus, towards whom he had a longstanding debt.

'I beg you also to order a proper burial for them,' he said.

The Pastor chief settled on one elbow. His silence could have been taken as agreement.

'That silence troubles me,' said Cucub.

'That silence...' Dulkancellin could not forget it either.

The two men were talking together. They were shut in an old building

119

that served as a grain store, a barn when the flocks were having their young, and a shelter against sandstorms. It smelt of damp and manure. The only light came in through a small opening near the roof.

'We have been here too long,' said Dulkancellin.

'Four suns. The one beginning to appear outside now will make it five,' Cucub replied.

The warrior paced up and down the floor of their prison.

'I dreamt of the lukus again last night,' he said. 'At first it was just as before. They appeared in my dream in the same way as they appeared to us in that hollow. I went down towards them... but before I could touch them, I awoke with a start. This time, though, the lukus waited for me to fall asleep again, then came back to my dreams.' Only then did the warrior seem to remember he was not alone: 'Listen, Cucub! The only wounds I saw on the lukus' bodies were made by those birds. Death did not come from outside. It came from within, and caused them great pain. They must have swallowed some strong poison.'

'You've said the same thing countless times in these past few days,' Cucub complained. 'Don't you have anything new to add?'

'I could add that this second dream left me feeling very uneasy.'

Cucub began to pay more attention.

'What do you mean?' he wanted to know.

'I dreamt that the lukus were drinking maize beer. A rush carpet was spread out on the sand, with bowls filled to the brim placed on it. The lukus seemed contented. So did the Pastors, but they were not drinking... they were waiting.'

'What were they waiting for, Dulkancellin?'

'They were waiting to see the lukus die.'

This jolted Cucub fully awake.

'Brother warrior, tell me what you are thinking.'

'I think we need to save ourselves. We are not to blame for what happened to the lukus. And I am beginning to think that no one here is really interested in finding out either. We must flee this place, and if we live long enough, we can come back and discover the truth.'

'Speak for yourself,' said Cucub. 'If I succeed in getting out of here, I never want to return.'

The sound of the bar on the door being lifted interrupted their conversation. One Pastor entered with their food; another stood on guard at the entrance. The breeze wafting in through the opening gave the two men more satisfaction than the scrap of dried meat and warm gruel they were given each morning.

'Is this the Pastors' hospitality?' said Cucub, not expecting any answer. 'Tell your chief from me that in our Remote Realm we treat our guests far better.'

The Pastor did not respond, but placed the clay bowls on the ground and left. No one would come again now until sunset. When Cucub and Dulkancellin were alone, they renewed their conversation.

'The Pastor who brings the food is easy to overcome,' said the warrior.

'Don't forget the one at the door.'

'Of course not!' said Dulkancellin impatiently. 'We only need to think of an excuse to bring him inside as well. I can take care of both of them. Then you and I can escape.'

'As far as I can see, all you are taking into account is your own strength,' said Cucub.

'What else should I be considering?'

The Zitzahay made as if he were looking all around him.

'That window, for example.'

'That sounds like nonsense to me. No one could fit through it.'

'That's true,' Cucub agreed. He dropped back onto the straw pallet, then went on: 'No one who was not the acrobat who enthralled entire villages in the Remote Realm.'

Dulkancellin knelt beside him, waiting for the Zitzahay to explain more fully.

'From the first moment we were put in here, I've been using my brain. I have an escape plan that has several advantages over yours. To tell you just one: it depends on a clever trick.'

'I can see that. What else?' asked Dulkancellin, unable to believe Cucub was talking seriously.

'We won't run the risk of an unequal fight between you and two other people.'

'I'm willing to take that risk.'

'I knew you would say that!'

'What other advantages are there?'

'We will not have to cross the camp with the Pastors all around us. The best thing is they will not know we have gone until several hours later. Do you accept that this would considerably reduce the risks?'

'The risks aren't that great. We hear every morning when the Pastors leave with their flocks.'

'We also hear the ones who stay in the camp.'

'That can only be a few of them.'

'And there will only be a few risks if for once you just listen to some-body other than yourself, Husihuilke of the Ends of the Earth!' Cucub took a deep breath and controlled himself: 'Besides, and this is important, my plan will give us a whole night to get ahead on our journey.'

Dulkancellin knew that the most difficult thing about their escape was not getting out of the camp but managing to put as much distance as possible between them and the Pastors. He was also aware that the lack of a sentry at the entrance to the store would not go unnoticed for very long.

'Tell me what you have been thinking,' he asked.

Soon afterwards, the details of their escape plan were complete.

The Pastors changed the guard four times a day, but only opened the door twice. At first light the man with the meat and broth came in. At sunset they were brought a pitcher of milk. This was when life returned to the camp, as the Pastors came back from grazing their flocks. Then there was a smell of cooking, the noise of games, songs, laughter. To try to get away then was unthinkable.

That evening was the same as usual. They were given their milk, the flocks returned, food was cooked over the fires, the men played games and sang. Cucub and Dulkancellin paid particular attention to this routine; and when the last sound of laughter and talk died down and they were sure everyone in the camp was asleep, they set to their task.

Dulkancellin knelt down and Cucub climbed on his back. Dulkancellin stood up, and the Zitzahay clambered onto his shoulders, then also stood up. This brought him to the edge of the opening, which he clung on to. Dulkancellin stepped back, but immediately rushed again to his original position, arms outstretched. It was impossible to get through that narrow gap! The little man could not hold on for long. Certain he would drop from the ledge, the Husihuilke prepared to catch him before he hit the ground. But Cucub hauled himself up, and succeeded in getting head and shoulders through the opening. Dulkancellin had to accept that for the moment his strong arms were not needed.

Cucub took a deep breath. He had very little room and had to take advantage of every nook and cranny. He pushed himself out further, and slowly turned his body. With a further effort, he heaved himself up so that his legs were still inside the store, but his back was out, facing the desert. The worst was over. He pulled on the rope tied round his wrist, and when it came tight, toppled over backwards. The rope was made up of bits and pieces of thongs and belts. Dulkancellin kept a firm hold on one end of it, while Cucub wriggled out of the opening and used his feet to climb down the outside wall, until finally he was standing on the ground. There were only three people awake in the camp: the guard, who was yawning and staring into space; Cucub, who managed to relax his face muscles; and on the other side of the wall, Dulkancellin, who smiled at the rope he was still clutching.

In the darkness, the unmistakable hiss of the most feared snake in the desert could be heard close by. The guard shuddered, desperate to know where the sound came from. The hissing started again. 'It's over there,' the guard whispered to himself. It seemed to be coming from the northern side of the store, where there was a small window. Machete in his perspiring hand, he walked towards it, carefully watching where he put his feet. *It would fool me too*, thought Dulkancellin.

When the guard went past the window, Cucub was hiding beyond the next corner. He pursed his lips and made the snake hiss once more. The guard strode towards the sound: it did not seem quite as close now as before. Cucub quickly turned the corner of the store until he was on the southern side. He curled up his tongue and imitated the snake again. This time the hissing brought the guard up short just before he reached the corner.

The war between the snake and the Pastors was a long history of hatred, in which it seemed that running away was not important. If the guard killed this one, the next day he would be a hero. The thought made him grasp the machete more tightly. Be careful now, thought Cucub. He was retreating with his back to the west. The next hiss seemed to be mocking the Pastor guard. He swore that after he had killed the snake he would cut off its head and hang it at the entrance to his tent. *If your sisters come to pay me a visit, they will see what happened to you, and will be afraid of coming near my mattress.*

Cucub pulled back again, feeling his way along the southern wall. His fear made it seem endless. At last he touched the rounded end of the building, and felt the western wall against his back. Cucub took a moment to calculate the risk. The door was close by; so was the guard. Cucub could hear him drawing nearer. Only fresh hissing from the snake could make him halt, and give the Zitzahay the time he needed. But Cucub's mouth was as dry as dust, and he could make no sound. He reached the door, laid his hand on the bar. But his mouth was still too dry.

No longer hearing the snake, the Pastor hurried on. He was facing the sea, but his face showed disappointment. *It must have seen the machete and gone back to its nest.* He lowered his weapon, and decided to return to his post. Just as he was doing so, the snake found its voice. A long, loud hiss paralysed the Pastor and concealed the noise of the bar being slid back. The door edged open, and Dulkancellin slipped out. The next hiss was so fierce that it covered the sound of the bar being dropped back into place. Recovering his breath, the guard leapt back. Cucub and the warrior vanished round the north-western corner of the store, and found themselves beneath the window once more. When the guard returned to his post after stalking his invisible enemy round the entire building, the door was as it should have been, with the bar properly drawn across it. The guard looked out into the darkness, and yawned again.

Helped by a cloudy sky, the Husihuilke and the Zitzahay made their way through the camp. Some of the fires were still lit, but snores from the Pastors asleep in their tents, oblivious to what was going on, were the only sound to be heard.

Near the animal pens they found some llamels grazing.

'We mustn't let this opportunity slip by,' Dulkancellin whispered in Cucub's ear.

The llamels were tame animals, used to all the chores their masters imposed on them. Dulkancellin mounted first. Once he was astride the enormous hairy beast, he helped Cucub get up on another one. The llamels and their riders set off towards the north.

They started out with no belongings or weapons, as all of them had been taken from them when they were shut in the grain store. And because of their haste and the risk they were running, they had no supply of water either.

'A performance like that would have won me a good few gourd seeds back in the Remote Realm,' Cucub said triumphantly.

'You were very good,' Dulkancellin admitted.

Cucub took a deep breath, then proudly blew out the air.

'Let me remind you what you said to Kupuka. And correct me if I'm wrong,' said Cucub. This time it was his companion's voice that he imitated: "'I'm not going to need the Zitzahay on the journey.'"

The Husihuilke's only reply was to kick his mount to make it go faster.

'Let's go!' he said, 'there's no time to lose.'

15

THE DAY THE SHIPS SET SAIL

For an entire day, the llamels made their way across the desert almost without any rest. The two men had to choose between the uncertain safety the coastal route offered them and the possibility of finding water and food in parts further from the coast, where patches of green promised some nourishment. But this was where the Pastors were lords and masters. In the end, they took the inland path, despite the risk of coming across the Pastors. The next dawn found them in the midst of some thorn bushes, digging in the soft, dry earth for anything of use to them. They emerged with real treasures: two shoots from a giant cactus that they stripped of spines and hollowed out to make bowls. Two stakes they could sharpen. A pliable reed to take the place of Cucub's staff, and several stones to use as tools. Even though there was no sign they were being followed, they wrapped all this in the Zitzahay's cloak, climbed back on their mounts, and set off again.

They were anxious to get on, but increasingly found they had to call a halt to their journey. The scorching sun at the height of the day, the freezing cold at night, as well as the llamels' weariness, all slowed them down. Yet it was thirst, the need to drink and the certainty they would soon feel thirsty again, that was the worst thing their bodies and souls had to suffer.

Four of them needing to drink. Four, if they wanted to continue to ride. Four, all of whom had set out without water supplies. So far, they had only found one spring a short distance from the camp, where the llamels had drunk enough to last them a few days. After that there was only water from the cactuses that the men could sip. As they went on and on, they were desperate to be able to drink their fill. They were exhausted, their muscles weary, their lips cracked and their eyes smarting. When the land began to rise and fall in front of them, they sat on their mounts, their minds numb, and let the animals seek their way.

Day was dawning. A dry, chill wind made them draw closer still to the animals' bloated stomachs, trying to find sleep that refused to come, or only fitfully. That was why when Cucub suddenly spoke, Dulkancellin thought the Zitzahay must be talking half asleep.

'It's her! It's her!'

An eagle was circling high above Cucub's excited outburst. Cucub sprang to his feet, but the bird flew away.

'Don't worry, she'll be back,' he said. And to show he himself was not worrying, he sat down again.

Dulkancellin remembered Cucub's description of his journey to Whirlwind Pass, and the friendly eagle he was so grateful to.

'Are you sure this is the same bird?' he asked.

'As sure as I am of my own name, brother. Let's continue on our way, and you'll soon see the eagle will bring us comfort.'

What he said soon came true. First they found some of the fleshy leaves that had refreshed Cucub on his outward journey. Then, before too long, the bird guided them to the water holes the desert kept for those whose dwelt there. And she flew in a looping zigzag that led them well away from the Pastors.

At night they could see points of light which made them think their pursuers could not be far behind, and were just waiting to lay hands on them. But the days went by, and nothing happened.

'We are coming to the end of this sad land,' said Cucub.

The constant difficulties they had to face simply in order to survive and make their slow progress northwards meant they forgot the ultimate reason for their journey. Urgent matters kept all thought of this at bay, until the Zitzahay's words suddenly brought it sweeping back. A pitcher of water spilt on the sand suddenly made them think of who they were and what they were doing in the desert. They were being pursued, and had to get to the House of the Stars. They were two people who would never have met had it not been for the fact that an ancient prophecy was about to be fulfilled. *The ships will come back across the Yentru Sea. Either we or Misáianes' army will be on board. This will mean the survival or the end for all that lives on this earth.* That ancient pronouncement of the Northmen, forgotten by all but a few, was leading them to a shared destiny.

The eagle reappeared early the next morning. It came from the sea, and as soon as it spied the two men began to fly backwards and forwards above them, telling them they should also head for the coast. Cucub and Dulkancellin hesitated: they could see the end of the desert in front of them. There was no sign of the Pastors: no shadows or campfires. But the eagle flew so insistently over their heads that in the end they followed her. Every step they took that was not towards the north seemed doubly tiring. Even Cucub went along protesting about his winged friend's puzzling ways. Yet, as had so often happened in the past, he soon had to bite his tongue: they got to the top of one of the many sandhills, and suddenly there was Kupuka. Possibly it was the brightness of his clothes' colours in the midst of the dull brown of the desert that made him seem like a miraculous mirage. They closed their eyes; opened them again. The Earth Wizard was still there, beckoning to them.

When they drew close, they could see how weary he looked. Kupuka had come from far away, from long voyages and hard tasks. It was plain it had been a great effort for him to come and meet them. In all this strange solitude, Kupuka was a true friend, and they greeted him as such.

'How did you manage to get here?' asked Dulkancellin.

'There is always a way.'

The Wizard smiled down at his wet feet, and the two men remembered the fish-women. But they never found out if they were right, because Kupuka changed the subject at once.

'The eagle knows things and has told me them. What do you two have to say to me?'

A lot. So much had happened, from Kume and the feather to their escape from the Pastors' camp. The three men sat in the shade of a rocky crag, that shrank as the sun rose in the sky. Since there was so much to tell, Cucub related most of it, Dulkancellin rather less. As they spoke, they handed round a wineskin that Kupuka had brought, filled with a health-giving water that was bittersweet at first, and left a taste of salt in the mouth. The further they got with their story, the darker the Earth Wizard's face grew: he became lost in thought. He listened to everything they had to say, and since it was a long tale, the three men eventually ended up huddled against the rock to take advantage of the last of the shade.

Kupuka began to draw in the sand. Cucub and Dulkancellin saw him grow more agitated with each line he traced. Then he rubbed the drawing out and began all over again, slightly changing the position of the figures. Kupuka drew big and small circles, stars, triangles, spirals that joined with wavy or broken lines. He walked around, taking a few steps away and then coming back to draw more shapes with anxious fingers. He was muttering snatches of words, and answering his own unfinished questions. It was all the more surprising to see him in such a frenzy because the sun was beating down so fiercely it was all the others could do to breathe. When the Earth Wizard began to dance around his drawings, the two men realized these were random thoughts he had set down, and that now Kupuka was in a world of visions that would help him organize them wisely. Sweating profusely, Kupuka returned to his work, rubbed it out determinedly once more. His next attempt was very different. His hand knew what it was doing: when it drew a shape, the Earth Wizard left it. He came to a halt, observing the result of his trance, raining drops of his own sweat on the predictions he had traced. His eyes closed, and he fell fast asleep on the sand.

'Who knows how long he will sleep,' said Cucub, wondering how they could protect him from the sun. 'Perhaps between the two of us we could lift him onto a llamel, then lead him to that patch of vegetation over there. There's not much of it, and it doesn't offer much shade, but it might bring us some relief.'

Dulkancellin brought one of the llamels over. But before they could start to lift him, Kupuka woke up as full of energy as if he had slept a whole day beneath a fragrant bush. He got nimbly to his feet, then even more agilely climbed on to the llamel.

'Climb up behind me, Cucub. We'll go over to that patch of vegetation: there's not much of it, and it doesn't offer much shade, but it might bring us some relief.'

'Do all Earth Wizards have your strange way of sleeping?' asked Cucub.

'Do all Zitzahay have your strange way of talking?' Kupuka replied.

Dulkancellin smiled with satisfaction, glad that Cucub had met his match.

As soon as they had reached the vegetation and dismounted, Kupuka called them to him. His face had darkened once again. He spoke quickly and in a low voice, as if afraid someone might be listening in that vast emptiness.

'What you have told me, together with all the things that have been happening, plus the further news I have received: all this has come together in my mind. Today, I have realized what it all means. In its ancient wisdom, the earth has clearly revealed to me what I must do. I am leaving now. You are to follow your path, and do as you have been commanded. As long as I still have the strength, I will fulfil my part.'

'Again you are leaving us without any explanation,' said the warrior.

'Any explanation from me at this time would be nothing more than stones in your sandals.'

The first sign of what was about to happen was a sudden darkening of the sky, as if a passing cloud had appeared overhead, although everywhere still seemed clear. Kupuka, Cucub and Dulkancellin stood waiting. They knew this was only the start of something far greater… and that something soon occurred.

Surrounded by a ring of darkness, the sun shrank until it was nothing more than a whitish hole helpless against the dark. A wan sunset quickly replaced the bright midday.

The llamels began to trot up and down aimlessly. Every so often they kicked out or rubbed their heads in the sand, as if oppressed by their own weight. They raised their muzzles to the sky as though they wished to become birds, light and airy enough to escape from the earth.

In the midst of this sombre twilight they heard a crying sound. It was not carried by the wind; it did not seem to come from any particular place. It neither grew nor died away. It was hoarse, and so ancient and weary that the blood of the Wizard and the two men ran cold. As if they were hearing the cry of the earth.

While they stood there, as caught up in the enchantment as the llamels, an inexplicable shadow appeared in the distance. At first, all they could see was a growing, indistinct cloud on the ground, as if a dark cloak were being spread over the sand. It was coming from the south, and heading towards them at great speed. When it was close enough for them to distinguish the dark stain more clearly, it no longer looked like a shadow, but revealed its true nature: it was made up of hundreds, hundreds upon hundreds, of flying creatures. Cucub wanted to run away, but Kupuka took him by the arm and prevented him doing so. It would have been impossible anyway: the creatures would engulf them, if that were what they wanted.

'Stay still, Cucub,' said the Earth Wizard, 'this is nothing to do with us.'

Kupuka knew that such a huge exodus must be connected to something far more important than three men and two llamels. He pulled the terrified Zitzahay towards him, burying his face against his chest. The swarm came ever closer, a mass of hairy claws, writhing tentacles, leathery hides and slimy skins, knots of spiders, lizards crawling over mounds of shells. Whatever the Wizard said, Cucub felt sure he would die from their fetid poison. Kupuka watched the vast cloud of vermin approach, muttering a spell over and over again.

The Earth Wizard was right, however: the swarm of creatures passed close by them without deviating from its path. Something far more powerful was drawing them irresistibly to the north.

As they disappeared into the distance, the creatures once again resembled first of all a cloak, then a shadow, and finally a black line that gradually faded from view. It was only now that the howling stopped, and the all-powerful sun returned to the midday sky.

Cucub was the first to speak; ashamed of the way he had reacted, he tried to apologize.

'I think I need to go to the sea. I must bathe myself,' he stammered, pointing down at his soaking clothes.

'You can do that later,' Kupuka replied. Then he added: 'Don't feel ashamed. Think what would happen to Dulkancellin if he had a flute instead of a weapon, and one of your best audiences instead of his worst enemies.'

Wise words indeed! The Zitzahay felt he had never heard anything more true in his whole life, and breathed a sigh of relief. Dulkancellin preferred not to say anything.

'What we have just witnessed,' said Kupuka, changing the direction of his thoughts, 'was the confirmation that the visions I saw were correct. Today is the day that the strangers have set sail. From now on, every moment will bring them closer to us.'

The Earth Wizard was anxious to be gone, and did not hide the fact.

'Come on, come on! We have to leave: you towards the north, me to the south.' He was searching in his pack as he spoke. 'I am afraid to tell you I will be taking with me something that has been very useful to you. The eagle will be coming back with me. There is something I have to give her to do, because she will accomplish it far better than I can. That is, if there is still— No matter! She is no use to you any more. Nor am I...' He finally found what he had been looking for. 'Instead, I am leaving you this deer sinew. Take it, Dulkancellin! If you find a suitable branch, you can make a bow again. And you, Cucub, can keep the wineskin. One sip of that concoction restores as much as many drinks of water.'

Dulkancellin and Cucub knew it was no use asking the Wizard how he was going to travel. The three of them walked towards where the llamels were grazing. The beasts had recovered their usual calm and were dozing standing up. By the time they were properly awake, their riders had mounted and were ready to set off.

'I do not think the Pastors will appear,' said Kupuka. 'But if they do, head quickly to the north-east until you come to some wide salt flats. Do not try to cross them on the llamels; leave the animals behind and continue on foot. You can be sure that the Pastors will stop at the edge of the salt. Their llamels cannot walk across it because their hooves crack so badly they cannot go on.'

'Why would the Pastors not simply leave their llamels too?'

'No, Cucub,' the Earth Wizard interrupted him. 'The Pastors would never go on without their animals. Not so far from their camp. It does not seem as if they want to catch you anyway, otherwise they would have done so by now.'

'If we have to travel across the salt flats we will reach the sea a long way from where the Zitzahay landed,' said Dulkancellin. 'What will happen then?'

'It does not matter where you appear on the coast. Just as they did with the Zitzahay, the fish-women will bring you a boat to take you across Lalafke sea.'

'And when we reach the far shore everything will be easy and enjoyable!' exclaimed Cucub. 'We will be in my Remote Realm.'

'Don't be so sure,' said Kupuka, patting him on the back. 'Everything is changing in our lands. Even our own houses are strange to us now.'

Their conversation was over. Dulkancellin did not want to say goodbye again, and so was the first to turn away.

'Wait a moment!' Cucub stopped him. 'Remember we need to go towards the sea.'

'I remember that you need to go to the sea,' the warrior corrected him.

Kupuka was left on his own, watching them ride off. If they continued to the west, as they seemed to be directing their mounts, they would soon come to the waters of the Lalafke. The Earth Wizard shielded his eyes to see them better. How slight Cucub looked compared with the Husihuilke warrior! And how exaggerated his movements appeared!

'Listen, Dulkancellin,' Cucub was saying, arms whirling. 'Think about why it is that I have to go to the sea. I mean, put yourself in my place. Or better still, see it as Kupuka saw it, and convinced me of the same... think about it... that's all I'm saying.'

16

IN A STRANGE HOUSE

They were all sitting around the same carved stone that had so astonished Cucub, placed in the exact centre of the observatory. Bor and Zabralkán were closely following the newcomers' account.

'The truth is, the last part of the desert was much easier,' Cucub was saying. 'No Pastors, no salt flats, no flying creatures. We left Kupuka, and a few days later came to the Mansa Lalafke. Just where we needed it we found a well-equipped raft, so we set sail. We landed in the Remote Realm sooner than we expected. My eyes saw Thirteen Times Seven Thousand Birds again!'

Cucub was enjoying his return. He felt shielded from all harm, and treated the Supreme Astronomers with a familiarity he would not have dared adopt before. He was a Zitzahay back among his own people. Perhaps that was why he felt he could ignore Kupuka's final warning.

'The Wizard told me my own land would seem foreign to me. I think he was wrong! Ever since I returned to Beleram it feels like home!'

Cucub surveyed the high stone walls, the jade instruments the Astronomers used to read the sky with, and the horn they blew to the four points of the compass to announce ceremonies and feast days. From where he was sitting, through the opening which allowed the Astronomers to observe the setting of the sun in the summer, he could see a corner of the wide games court, a paved street he had been up and down hundreds of times, and the edge of the jungle. Like the carved stone, everything was as he remembered it. How he would love to go down to the market for an intoxicating drink and a slice of agouti meat soaked in its own fat! Cucub was bubbling with confidence, and felt emboldened to continue.

'I think Kupuka was blinded by his own visions. I think he came to conclusions that were far too gloomy. I must admit I myself fell victim to a pessimism that now, seeing what I am seeing, seems to me exaggerated.'

Dulkancellin could not believe his ears. The little man's foolishness drove him wild yet again. His stomach churned with a desperate desire to remind Cucub of something he had neglected to mention. *You are quick to dismiss the person who shielded you in his arms and restored your courage. You accuse him of being blinded and of jumping to the wrong conclusions. But although you talk and talk, you say nothing of the panic that made you soak your clothes.*

Dulkancellin was about to voice something similar to these thoughts, when Zabralkán himself interrupted the Zitzahay.

'We are pleased that you feel at home once more,' said the Astronomer. 'Now we must do all we can for the Husihuilke representative to feel the same way.'

The warrior must have appeared hesitant, because Bor spoke up to support his fellow Astronomer.

'That is our wish,' said the taller of the two Astronomers, in a reedy voice. 'We would like our home to feel like yours.'

'I thank you both,' murmured Dulkancellin, but his thoughts were elsewhere.

How could this stone palace, that smelt of stone, possibly feel like his tiny wooden house? What were the similarities between the imposing vestments of the Zitzahay, with all their feathers and precious stones, and the simple garments the women of the Ends of the Earth wove on their looms? And Cucub's exaggerated gestures, so distant from the Husihuilke reticence, also seemed to find an echo in the Astronomers' behaviour. The differences between them were obvious, but not what they might have in common.

Dulkancellin recalled his arrival at the House of the Stars. The first thing he remembered was their decision to wait until nightfall before entering Beleram, so that a Husihuilke should not be seen walking through the city, and still less entering the House of the Stars. 'If you agree, we'll wait here on the outskirts of Beleram until it grows dark,' Cucub had told him.

The area surrounding the city was planted with fruit trees. The creepers covering most of the ground and wrapping themselves round the tree trunks had orange flowers on them. Together with the ripe fruit, they filled the air with sweet scents. As it grew dark in the jungle, a heavy dew that was almost like drizzling rain made the colours of the vegetation even brighter. Great and small birds came in search of food. However heavy-hearted he felt, the Husihuilke warrior could not deny it made a marvellous sight.

The cultivated fruit trees merged quickly into thick jungle. Beyond the orchards, the vegetation was so thick it was impossible to find a way through except along the paths the Zitzahay had cleared with their machetes. 'We have made paths to connect our villages. Others take us to where we can find water, wild animals to hunt, or medicinal herbs.' As Dulkancellin recalled these words from Cucub, he realized that this was the moment when his companion had regained his sense of pride.

Dulkancellin and Cucub had already taken one of those paths: the one linking Centipede Yellow with Yellow of the Swallows, and both villages with Beleram. The sun was setting as they embarked on the final stretch. According to Cucub, at that time of day nobody would be coming into Beleram, although it was possible that some people might be going the other way, leaving the city after their day's work. With this in mind, they kept a sharp eye out on the path ahead of them, and several times when they saw others approaching, ducked into the undergrowth.

As Cucub had suggested, they waited outside the city until night fell. It was only when the artisans had left their workshops, the market traders had packed up and gone, and the streets were deserted, that Cucub and Dulkancellin ventured through the city.

The Husihuilke warrior's first sight of Beleram was by the light of the stars and the torches burning outside the important buildings. These seemed quite spaced out, and if they were put there according to a plan, he could not discern it.

Dulkancellin realized that these constructions, each of them built on top of a pyramid, were not where the Zitzahay lived. *'Of course not. That is where the Astronomers live and have their observatories. Down here is where we make things and buy and sell. Over there is where we hold our games.'*

Beleram was a city free of vegetation. Stone upon stone upon stone, keeping the jungle at bay.

The road leading to the House of the Stars was the broadest in the city. Narrow alleyways led off it on both sides. *'Look, Dulkancellin, if you go down this one you reach the market,'* Cucub had whispered on the silent street. But the warrior was interested in something else...

The construction at the end of the avenue had to be the House of the Stars. There was no need to ask Cucub to be sure, although the distance and the flickering torch light did not allow him to get a clear view of it. Even so, he had to keep telling himself it was not a dream. Thanks to the glow from the torches, the warrior could see its intricate outline: the towers and platforms made it very different from the geometrical precision of the other buildings.

'Will you admit it is more beautiful than anything you have ever seen before?'

Dulkancellin would have liked to tell Cucub that it was both more and less than beautiful at the same time. He would have liked to say he wanted to reach it as soon as possible, and yet also hoped that it would take them a long time. But Dulkancellin was no great talker, and so all he said was: *'It's as beautiful as... it's very beautiful.'*

Thanks to burning lamps placed after every ten steps, the warrior could continue his examination of the House of the Stars as the two of them climbed the endless staircase. Halfway up, he could make out the figures sculpted on the frieze surrounding the building. They were so big they could only be seen properly from a great distance. *'These images make the Astronomers immortal. When they die, Bor and Zabralkán will have theirs too.'*

A voice was calling him. There was a hand on his shoulder.

'Come back, Husihuilke!' Voice and hand belonged to Zabralkán. 'Your thoughts have led you far from here.'

'Not that far. I was climbing the stairway, and had almost reached here.' As he said this, Dulkancellin realized he had spoken without thinking. He felt ashamed. He had had no idea his mind had wandered, but he immediately saw his reply was out of place.

'You had a hard journey. You both need rest,' said Zabralkán, ignoring his interruption. 'We will call for someone to go with you.'

Zabralkán's abrupt way of ending their conversation made Dulkancellin forget his embarrassment. He did not want to leave without bringing up the matter that most concerned him.

'We know that a representative of the Pastors of the Desert has arrived at the House of the Stars, and is to take part in the Great Council. What do you intend to do with him?' Dulkancellin felt he should be more precise: 'What do you intend to do concerning the death of the lukus?'

'Nothing. Absolutely nothing,' replied Bor. His tone, and the fact that he immediately stood up, made it clear that to insist would be an impertinence.

But the warrior did not back down. Nor did he pay any attention to the Astronomer's impatient gesture for him to withdraw. Choosing his words carefully, he said:

141

'I mean no disrespect. I mention this because I think that the death of the lukus cannot... should not be silenced. And also because I believe that the sign from the White Stone—'

'You may believe what you wish, Husihuilke,' said Bor, returning to his place at one end of the rectangular stone. 'But remember that there are some decisions which cannot be changed. This is one of them!'

Dulkancellin looked across at Zabralkán just in time to catch a note of hesitation in his gesture. This gave the warrior the slight opening he needed.

'Am I to understand that you have decided to forget the death of someone whom you yourselves chose as a representative?'

The Husihuilke had no chance to discover what Bor's reaction to his insistence might be, because Zabralkán immediately spoke again.

'Your wisdom is well known to us, brother Bor,' the Astronomer said carefully. 'That is why we make so bold as to beg you to explain to the representative of the Husihuilkes the reason for our decision.'

'And we are well aware of your wisdom and your kindness, brother Zabralkán,' said Bor, making to rise to his feet again. 'But we also know there is no time to explain everything to everyone. We are who we are, and we do what we must do.'

'Please remain seated, I beg you. Let us end this conversation with an explanation that will reassure us all.'

There could be no doubt that Zabralkán had some kind of authority over Bor. The warrior did not know if this was due to his age, his rank, or some other quality. Whatever it was, his polite request led to a change of heart.

'Listen carefully to what I am about to say,' said Bor. 'This Council has no competence to judge disagreements or conflicts among the peoples of the Fertile Lands. No matter what they may involve, or however great they are. Would the Husihuilkes allow us to intervene in the wars that have always divided their clans? We are not here to condemn the harshness with which the Lords of the Sun treat their slaves. Or to decide whether the House now ruling them are usurpers, or if their rivals to the throne are the ones in the wrong. In the same way, nobody should act as judge in the bitter dispute we Astronomers have with some families of the Owl Clan. We have called the Council to consider something more important than our petty quarrels. Think what would happen if, instead of concerning ourselves with something that threatens every one of us in equal measure, we wasted time and effort over our differences. The strangers will not be waiting for us to reach an agreement. Their ships will soon be here, and we do not know their intentions. You have heard enough about Misáianes to know that if it is his armies who are arriving, it is likely none of us will survive to continue to fight our neighbours. What we mean by this is that if there were conflicts between the lukus and the Pastors, they should not be brought into this.'

Once again, Dulkancellin glanced over at Zabralkán in the hope he would understand. But the Astronomer stared back sternly at him, showing he agreed with every word Bor had uttered.

'The lukus and the Pastors have never had any dispute between them; in truth they have hardly ever had any contact. But is it conceivable that the death of the island creatures is in no way related to the arrival of the ships?' Dulkancellin was speaking as much to Cucub as to the others. 'Remember, they were bringing the White Stone as proof.'

'It seems to us you have not yet fully understood,' said Zabralkán.

'Let us try another way,' said Bor. 'Pay attention, Husihuilke, and answer our questions.'

At first, Dulkancellin did not fully realize what the Astronomer meant.

'Did you see the slaughter of the lukus with your own eyes?'

'No.'

'Did anyone else you can trust see it?'

'No.'

'Can you be sure it was the Pastors who put the lukus to death?'

'I believe so, because—'

'Could you swear it and shed your blood to defend your view?'

'No.'

'Do you not think the Pastors were bound to be suspicious of two strangers they found close to the disaster?'

'Yes, I suppose so.'

'Were you mistreated by them? And please, don't mention the food. We have already heard enough about that from Cucub.'

'Not exactly mistreated, no.'

'Were you pursued?'

'I don't know.'

'At least they never caught up with you, did they?'

'That's true.'

'Could not the lords of the desert have caught up with you if they so wished?'

'Yes.'

'Husihuilke, do you really want to put the Fertile Lands in peril by causing the failure of a Council that will decide the destiny of all those who live here? And all for a supposition you have?'

'There is a lot of evidence—'

'Evidence of the sort you had when you wanted to put Cucub to death? What if this was another hidden Kukul feather?'

The warrior was confused. All of a sudden it seemed that right was on the side of the Astronomers, and his own protests were like those of Wilkilén. Thinking of her made him smile, and because he did so the others thought he had accepted Bor's argument.

'Good! You must have many things to do, and I have business I need to attend to,' said Cucub, thinking he could spend the rest of the night somewhere close to the market and several hot tortillas. 'Brother Dulkan-cellin, it was a pleasure to accompany you, but now I must leave you.'

'Where do you think you are going?' asked Bor.

'To the market,' replied Zabralkán, to avoid Cucub launching into a lengthy explanation.

Cucub's face fell when he heard that he would not be able to leave the House of the Stars until the end of the Great Council. This was a new order from the Astronomers; as usual, there were sound reasons for it.

'You have seen and heard many things,' Bor explained. 'Much more than any of the other messengers. Then again, you are not one to hold your tongue. We cannot risk letting you leave here. Anything you said to people in Beleram would be ill-advised.'

Zabralkán asked Bor to step aside with him. The two Astronomers got up and walked over to one of the openings in the wall. They spoke to each other in a low whisper.

While the Supreme Astronomers were deliberating, Cucub was think-ing of the rewards he had been hoping to receive for all he had done. To remain shut up, even in the House of the Stars, seemed like a harsh punishment to someone accustomed to roam freely, to leave a rainy village for a sunny one whenever he felt so inclined. For his part, the Husihuilke warrior was intrigued, trying to follow the body of the snake through the intricate patterns on the stone. When he and Cucub saw the Astronomers coming back over to them, they abandoned their own thoughts and wondered what they would be told to do next. Zabralkán, who was in the lead, said to Cucub:

'Good news for you! We have decided you should pay a visit to the market in Beleram, because there is something you can do for us. People from all the nearby villages gather there. Not only do you know many of them, but most know and trust you. Go there and find out what they are saying. Ask them in particular about anything you find strange, because it's important for us to find out about things they may not realize the significance of. Everything you have told us, in addition to what the lukus said and what Kupuka fears may happen, means that we want to know from our own people if they have seen any unusual signs. Go and do as we ask. Afterwards, you are to come back to the House of the Stars and stay here as long as is necessary.'

Cucub's face reflected his changing reactions to Zabralkán's words, and finished by showing his delight at having regained much of what he had thought was lost.

'I will do as you command. If you agree, I will return tomorrow before the sun has reached the centre of the sky.'

None of them wanted to prolong the discussion any further. Zabralkán beat twice on a gold disc hanging from the wall. Dulkancellin and Cucub made ready to leave the observatory.

'One last precaution,' said Bor. 'Tell us, Cucub: what will you say when anyone asks why you have been absent for so long?'

'I will say… Yes, I will answer: it seems as though no one wants to be married, be born, or to die without me and my music being present!'

'That will sound convincing coming from you,' Zabralkán said.

'But looking as you do, no one will believe you have come from any kind of ceremony.' Perhaps Bor was not so sure about the permission they had given Cucub to leave. 'Before you go, you will be shown where to bathe and be given fresh clothes.'

Their escorts were waiting outside the observatory doors. Two of them led Cucub off down a stone corridor; the other two stood waiting for their orders concerning the Husihuilke.

'These men will take you to the room set apart for you. There you will find all you need to restore you after your journey. Very early tomorrow we will open the Great Council.'

The escorts, wearing short red and green tunics, showed him the way

146

without saying a word. As they walked along, they went past many closed doors and only a few that were ajar. Dulkancellin noticed spacious rooms with servants scuttling to and fro filling vases with aromatic oils, spreading mats over the floors, or lighting candles. Despite the late hour, many people were busy in the House of the Stars, yet no sound could be heard.

Dulkancellin lost interest in the majestic luxury all around him: he found it oppressive. To calm himself he thought of Kupuka. The Earth Wizard always walked barefoot through the forest. He had no servants, and his home was a cave somewhere in the Maduinas Mountains. He carried a bag worn from use over the years, had a sense of smell that allowed him to know past and future, and eyes that could follow a trail left several winters earlier. Dulkancellin reflected that he respected no one so much as gaunt, stern-faced Kupuka, who knew the mysteries of the earth and was a friend to thorns and thistles. *'Here I am, heading for Kush's bread,'* the warrior heard him say.

When Dulkancellin came out of his reverie, he found himself outside an open door. Two escorts were standing on either side of it, waiting for him to enter.

17

THE MEETING OF THE GREAT COUNCIL

Tapestries hung from the high walls of the chamber where the Great Council was
to be held, and nine mats were spread on the floor. That was all. Eight of
the mats were in a semicircle; the other was placed further away, to one
side. Each mat had a leather cushion on it.

The representatives were led in very early the next morning. They were
brought in one by one, at regular intervals. Each of them was accompanied
by two escorts. They were shown where they should sit. Once everyone
was assembled, Bor greeted them. He wasted no words in presenting them.

'Zabralkán, Supreme Astronomer and first among the Brotherhood of
the Open Air. Molitzmós, from the land of the Lords of the Sun. This is
Dulkancellin, representing the Husihuilkes. And this is Nakín, from the
Owl Clan. Elek, from the offspring of the Northmen we know as the
Stalkers of the Sea. Illán-che-ñe, who will speak on behalf of the Pastors.
And I am Bor, Supreme Astronomer of the Zitzahay people. The empty
mat is where the representative of the lukus should have sat.'

Dulkancellin peered over at the representative from the desert to see
if he showed any disquiet, but Illán-che-ñe betrayed no reaction to the
Astronomer's final words.

'Dear brothers,' Zabralkán began. 'It is essential you hear with your own ears and your understanding the document we have inherited. You will hear everything the Northmen told our ancestors, words which they kept in sacred books for the day when they had to be spoken once more. You will hear of the warning the Ancient Lands gave the Fertile Lands five hundred years ago, according to the sun cycles, but eight hundred and eighty-six if we follow the cycle of Magic. We must all listen, because therein lies the answer that the heavens are hiding from us. The events occurring now have their explanation in these books. We must discover it quickly, and then be able to act accordingly.'

The man sitting to one side on the ninth mat laid out nine cloths of embroidered wool on the floor. On top of them he carefully and ceremoniously placed the sacred books, their protective covers already removed. These were seven books made of bark in which was written all that the Northmen had brought with them across the ocean. News of a war that in those faraway times was being fought in the Ancient Lands against the power of Misáianes. The man began to read from the books in the order he had displayed them. His voice betrayed no emotion, almost as though he did not understand what he was reading. Yet he spoke in such harmonious phrases that after a while all his listeners could have sworn he was singing.

As Dulkancellin listened intently, he gazed round at the others.

'"When they spoke to us, we set their words down, without adding or omitting anything. These are the sacred books we will preserve until the day of the ships. The Northmen named Misáianes, calling him the Ferocious One...'"

Bor and Zabralkán were wearing more majestic robes than on the previous evening, but these could not compare with the splendour of Molitzmós's attire. The representative of the Lords of the Sun was adorned with gold and turquoise – arm-bands, necklaces, and hoops in his nose and ears – and wore long plumes on his headdress.

Dulkancellin's spare clothes had been left behind in the desert. As a result, the Husihuilke had arrived dirty and dishevelled at the House of the Stars. In the room he had been given he had found water to bathe in, and fresh clothes to put on, similar to those the men of the Ends of the Earth usually wore.

"'And so Death rebelled. She moulded an egg from her own saliva, then produced it from her mouth. She secreted juices and fertilized it with them. And so from this revolting substance her son was born, protected by the solitude of a forgotten mountain in the Ancient Lands.'"

Nakín, from the Owl Clan – if Dulkancellin remembered correctly, that is what Bor had called her. She was the only woman taking part in the Great Council, and looked as small as a child. Just like a child, apart from her weary-looking face. She wore her hair to one side, kept in place by several ribbons. Her bare forehead and thick eyebrows caught his attention. The Husihuilke knew that the Owl Clan lived in the Magic Time. And that it was so hard to enter or leave there that they were the only ones who could withstand the ordeal. Perhaps that was the reason why the skin beneath her eyes was so much darker than the rest.

"'This being, born from Disobedience, brought horror with him; and horror was not merely a part of him, but his essence.'"

Never before had Dulkancellin seen a man with hair the colour of pumpkin flesh... this was Elek, the descendant of the Northmen. As he sat, his body rocked ceaselessly backwards and forwards. *Like the sea,* thought Dulkancellin.

"'Then Death saw what he was. On the third day, she grew proud of her creation and named him Misáianes. Misáianes grew, and became master over a multitude of creatures. Beings of all kinds render him homage. Because Misáianes, the son of Death, speaks words that sound like the truth...'"

Despite all Bor had said, the man sitting opposite him, the one called

Illán-che-ñe, aroused deep-seated misgivings in Dulkancellin. He was the youngest of all those present. A young Pastor who could not have lived through many more rainy seasons than Thungür. The warrior looked away, and for the rest of the reading stared intently at the place that should have been occupied by the luku with the flowing beard.

'"Keep the memory of this, they told us. Misáianes is the beginning of inbred pain. If we are defeated in this war, Life will fall with us. And Eternal Hatred will stride through the twilight of Creation. This much we have written of what the Northmen told us."'

The reading from the sacred books had finished. The man on the ninth mat carefully wrapped them up again. Placing the books in the centre of the semicircle, he bowed to each of the representatives in turn, then left the room.

Zabralkán was the next to speak.

'We shall now open the Council, conscious of the fact that this is the most important one ever to be held. There is no record of anything like it, either in living memory or in our written histories. Magic has brought you here, as representatives of the Fertile Lands, because we all share the same fate. Whatever resolution we come to, never forget it: it will have repercussions for every last fish and blade of grass. Beyond these walls, our Magic is delving into the four elements in search of unequivocal signs. There is no wind from the north that has not been questioned, no birds are migrating without carrying messages and requests, there is no movement in the sky or on land that has not been closely observed. Yet all the answers we have received are either empty or obscure. Within these walls, we have only a few days to decide. We must be capable of transforming confusion into decision. Afterwards, we will be responsible for what happens. Brothers, we are all aware of the immensity of our task. First we wish Dulkancellin to inform us of certain facts of which not all of us are aware. Following him, each of those present is to share their news with the rest of us. Husihuilke, you may begin.'

Dulkancellin spoke of the lukus: of their meeting in the forest, the White Stone, of their dead bodies strewn around the desert hollow. He mentioned being held by the Pastors, without adding his own conjectures. Finally, he justified his escape with the only reason that everyone there would recognize as genuine: 'We were being held too long. And we knew the Council could not wait.' As Dulkancellin spoke, Bor nodded with satisfaction. It was clear that the Husihuilke had understood the need to silence his own fears, and avoid everything not directly related to the Council's deliberations. Dulkancellin went on to mention Kupuka's unexpected appearance in the midst of the desert.

'Brother Husihuilke,' said Molitzmós, one of the Lords of the Sun. 'Could you explain more clearly what the person you call Kupuka saw in his visions?'

'I will try, but it will not be very different from what I have already said. Kupuka received such visions from the strangers that he could tell it was the day and time when their ships set sail towards the Fertile Lands.'

'There have been several indications of that,' added Zabralkán. 'We also fell asleep in the sun that same midday and dreamt that a path was being forged through the sea.'

'This is valuable information,' said Molitzmós in an encouraging tone. 'But did Kupuka say anything about what the visitors were like?'

'Nothing at all.'

'You said he left in haste,' Molitzmós insisted. 'Do you know what Kupuka was intending to do?'

'He told me nothing, and in all truth I am not even sure if it had anything to do with the events that have brought us here,' said Dulkancellin. It was obvious that he was learning. 'All that is certain is that he headed south. The rest is supposition.'

'My name is Elek. I belong to the Offspring of the Northmen, and would like to tell you of something that is happening among my people. It began some time before the messenger came to seek me out. At first, there were no more of them than the fingers on one hand. But soon, many more adopted this new habit of staring at the Yentru Sea for day after day.'

'But is it not an ancient tradition of your people to stare at the ocean?'

'Not in this way.' Nakín's question had been a friendly one, and so was the answer from Elek. 'We are tied to the sea. Our life is ruled by its cycles. Hardly a day goes by when we do not go down to the shore of the Yentru. That is our usual place for reflection and repose; we look to the ocean for our sustenance and for answers. But what I have mentioned is different. Something strange is driving many of my people to stand motionless gazing at the Yentru, not eating or drinking, until their strength fails them. I have seen them collapse to the ground while they stare at the horizon. Some of them cry; others smile. All of them are waiting. When they are asked who they are waiting for, all they mutter is: "The Fathers are coming." That was what was happening among my people when I received the order to come to the Remote Realm. And it may still be going on now.'

'What you said seems a good sign,' said the woman. 'If the Offspring call the strangers "Fathers" that must mean—'

'Let us not be hasty,' said Molitzmós. 'We should not let one good sign make us forget all the others!'

For some reason, Dulkancellin had not been expecting the representative of the Lords of the Sun to say anything like this. He was pleased to hear it, because he thought the same. He raised his hand in approval, and was rewarded with a grateful smile.

'I saw nothing where I live,' said Illán-che-ñe, who had difficulty speaking the Natural Language. 'I saw nothing, and nor did the others.'

For some time now, the use of the Natural Language had been dying out among the Pastors of the Desert. Although the other peoples of the

Fertile Lands considered it a duty to pass the language on across the generations, the desert tribes neglected it.

'Remember, Illán-che-ñe left his land before the luku army arrived,' Zabralkán reflected. Then, since a prolonged silence indicated that no one else had anything to add, the Astronomer raised his voice once more: 'We have waited as long as possible for an unmistakable sign. But as you have seen, all have been obscure and contradictory. Whoever may be coming has already set sail. Our time is up. We have to decide on what we must do without possessing any certainty about the strangers. All that remains is for us to strive our utmost over the coming days, even if we have to admit that most of the time we will be acting like blind people or children.'

'Tell me if I have understood correctly,' said Molitzmós. 'This Great Council has to draw up a plan and set it in motion. We all knew this before we came. What is new is that we will have to do this without any clear idea about the identity of those who are coming, or what their true intentions are. Am I right?'

Zabralkán nodded. Then he and Bor launched into a lengthy summary that left all the others with gloomy forebodings.

'There has been no revelation, and so we have no clear knowledge,' the Astronomers said. The many conflicting signs did nothing more than create confusion. And no one, not even Magic itself, was able to find an answer. 'The sky and its stars are not speaking clearly,' said the Astronomers. There were few records of anything similar ever having occurred before. It was happening now, and any mistake they made would mean the end of all hope.

'We had been hoping to greet you all with the name of the strangers,' said Zabralkán, 'but that was not to be. There is something more we should like to say before we hear your opinions: even if it were certain it is Misáianes' army which is drawing near to the Fertile Lands, even if that were certain, it would still be a difficult decision. How could we confront the power of Eternal Hatred? We do not have sufficient forces to do so, or any strategy that does not bring misfortune in its wake. This being the case, how much more difficult it will be to decide when we are not sure of the truth. The Northmen or Misáianes? We must try to be certain that our decision has the feet of a deer so that it can leap from side to side, causing the least possible harm.'

All at once, as if they had finally understood how much was at stake, everyone wanted to speak, to give their own view. Zabralkán had to intervene on several occasions to keep order.

'How long will it be between when the ships appear on the horizon and when they reach our shores?' Nakín wanted to know.

'Less than two suns,' Zabralkán replied. 'But if we understand your meaning, we will have to ignore any banners the ships may be flying, or any message they send us. How could we trust them if we do not know who they really are?'

'Could it be there is no better alternative than a surprise attack?' asked Bor.

'To attack them before giving them the chance to let us know who they are could mean an unjust death for the Northmen,' said Elek.

'We would regret their death in many ways,' said Nakín of the Owl Clan. 'Would they not return to seek revenge? We would spill the blood of the Northmen, and then they would spill ours.'

'What will happen if it is Misáianes' army which takes us by surprise?' said Dulkancellin.

'The Husihuilke has anticipated my own thoughts,' said Molitzmós. 'If we have to choose between complete devastation and a mistake, however serious it may be, I choose the mistake. I choose war.'

'Will we be able to defeat Misáianes with spears and arrows?' asked Nakín.

'That's a good question, beautiful owl woman,' Molitzmós said again. 'We are talking about a war against Misáianes as if it were like the wars we know. But be warned! Let us not forget that this is something more than throwing our spears and fighting to the last drop of our blood.'

'We shall fight to the last drop of our blood,' said Elek, 'that is what the Fathers did. And that is what they said we should do.'

'If it is Misáianes who is on his way, that means your Fathers were defeated,' replied Molitzmós, Lord of the Sun. 'Are we to follow in the footsteps that led the Northmen to their extinction?'

'We have reached the most difficult point of our deliberations,' said Zabralkán, 'and we are pleased to have done so quickly. We all understand that war is the only reply the Fertile Lands can have to Misáianes. But it is possible that when we say "war", not all of us are thinking of the same thing.'

Their spirits were aroused: gestures and words became heated, and the representatives split into opposing groups.

'Do you remember what the sacred books say? They say: "Misáianes speaks words that sound like the truth—"'

'Which means that until the very last moment they could seem like Northmen,' warned Molitzmós.

'The books also tell us: "They will come to devastate this continent, because that is their aim—"'

'That does not authorize us to spill the blood of the Fathers,' Elek protested.

'They also say that at the start Misáianes will try to seduce the powerful and strong—'

'Which means he will conceal his true intentions. And that he will have chosen ones... who will be exalted—'

'Chosen ones who could be amongst us here,' said Molitzmós.

'Chosen ones whom he himself will one day destroy,' said Zabralkán.

'"Not a single flower, not one bird left to sing—"'

'Misáianes needs eyes and ears in every corner of the world. Eyes and ears to help him rule for ever. This earth is vast and full of hidden corners; the seas and the winds are also vast. Misáianes knows that Life will look for the tiniest of places to hide in: any fresh blade of grass, any hidden newborn creature where it can lodge and start again.'

'Let's put our faith in what a blade of grass can do then!'

'I did not say that!'

'So we should let them put out the sun, and light a fire under the rocks!'

'I did not say that!'

The day was drawing on. The people of Beleram went about their usual tasks, not imagining what was going on at the same time in the House of the Stars. There, since dawn, seven people were meeting who had to bear the weight of a momentous decision. The differences between them seemed insuperable. Arguments broke out; anger coloured both questions and answers. All the while, Zabralkán contemplated them serenely, as if he had known this was going to happen, and was waiting for the storm to blow itself out.

And in fact, from this tough but honest disagreement it was inevitable that the path of understanding should emerge. The first points of agreement were vague. When one of them tried to be more precise, they soon lost their way again. They drew closer, only to move apart once more. Yet every distancing was less extreme than the previous one.

It was at this point that Illán-che-ñe asked to speak. He signalled this to Zabralkán with an almost imperceptible gesture. Anxious to hear what the Pastor had to say, the Supreme Astronomer immediately granted his request. The young man representing the Pastors was seated on his mat in the way the men of his people always sat: with his legs together and bent at the knee, leaning his chest on them, his hands on the floor. It was some time before he spoke, probably because he had to search for the words in what little he knew of the Natural Language.

'Everyone says of the Northmen... They say the Northmen told them, the Northmen commanded them to... but Illán-che-ñe wants to ask you all why you believe and obey these people. Nobody asks if the Northmen intended to deceive, and were lying about what was happening in their own lands.'

The silence that followed was a weary one. Illán-che-ñe's comment forced them to return to the beginning. It left them once more at the start of the day, exhausted by the thought they had to start all over again.

In their minds, each of them went over the question put by the Pastor. Each of them thought that there must be a conclusive answer to it. It did not matter that none of them could find the exact words. Someone must be able to. Zabralkán would surely do it...

18

THE SIDERESIANS

They were bringing the storm with them.

A fleet was crossing the Yentru Sea towards the Fertile Lands: many
small ships with triangular sails that appeared on the crests of the waves,
dropped into the troughs, and then bobbed back up again. The cloudy,
moonless night sky was black; black the capes covering the men on board.
And black, jet-black the dogs with frothing mouths that were crammed
into cages on their decks.

On one of those decks, a man strolled slowly, beating the palm of one
hand with the leather glove he had just removed. Leogrós, admiral of
the Sideresian fleet, paced up and down without looking round him. He
completely ignored the crew, who shrank back to leave him a free path,
holding their breath. These beings mattered to him little more than the
scraps of food he kicked towards the side of the ship. It was only when he
met Drimus, who was heading in the opposite direction holding a bunch
of living mice between his fingers, that Leogrós deigned to nod his head
slightly in a sign of recognition.

Leogrós had to accept the Doctrinator, without really knowing what his
powers were. He had to be content knowing that Misáianes had appointed

him to command the three ships that were to aim straight for the port of Beleram. Although Leogrós was repelled by this misshapen being who knew nothing of weapons or wars, he did not try to oppose him, nor would he have been able to. So far, Drimus had not confronted him in any way. And yet a certain haughtiness about the way he behaved suggested Leogrós should beware of him. No one would have dared mention it, but everyone knew that the Doctrinator was protected by and obeyed One who was not on any of their ships. He and only He was Drimus's master.

The Doctrinator walked to the stern of the ship. This was where he spent most of his time, curled up among the cages, feeding the black dogs. As soon as they saw him coming, the animals stirred. Backs bristling, jaws slathering, without even so much as growling, they kept a close watch on the man bringing them food. They knew the banquet was never enough for all of them, that only the quickest and fiercest would enjoy the taste of hot entrails. Today, however, the man was in a playful mood. He walked round the cages slowly, a smile on a face as lopsided as his hunched body. Picking one out of the bunch of mice he was now clutching to his chest, he held it up by the tail and swung it in front of the dogs. They all followed its movements intently, fascinated by the smell of fear.

'Oh, my little ones! Your hunger will soon be sated, because all flesh that opposes Misáianes will end up in your guts.'

Drimus the Doctrinator threw the mouse into a cage. The dogs fought a short but vicious battle over it. The winner stalked off, clutching the prey between its teeth. The others prowled round, waiting for the next opportunity. Drimus did not renew his game until the first victor had rejoined the others.

'He might win again. Yes, it could be, because he has the taste of fresh blood in his stomach. Oh, my poor little things! You'll have to fight for them!'

The same bloody game was repeated several times, more or less identically. The last mouse twisted and turned between Drimus's fingers. He watched it struggling for life while he decided its fate. Which cage should he choose? He was hesitating too long, and the dogs began to whine. Eventually, the Doctrinator put the mouse on the deck and opened his fingers.

'There it goes! There it goes, my little ones! You will soon be free to chase after it!'

The dogs flung themselves against the bars of their cages, desperate to catch the escaping prey. The stormy wind carried the sound of their howls into the distance. More black dogs joined in from the other ships. Soon their noise drowned out the sound of the sea.

The game was over. Drimus squeezed his way between the cages. He took a few more steps, then sat down on the wet deck. Raising his hands to his nostrils, he smelt them: they smelt of fear, and he had no intention of wasting that. He stretched his arms out towards the two cages, thrust his hands through the bars, and offered them to the dogs to lick. His head drooped slowly forward until it hung from his skinny neck. The rain started to beat down again, but the Doctrinator sat without moving while the beasts fed themselves from his fingers.

The Sideresians did not come from the same land, did not speak the same language, were not even from the same species. They had never existed until Misáianes had called them to his shadow.

Misáianes' legions were recruited among all the species that inhabited the earth in those ancient times. It took the Uncreated hundreds of solar years to bring them together, train them, remove all trace of pity they might feel, distance them from any love. Misáianes delved deep into the Creatures' bitterness; he exacerbated their anger and hate to set them against each other, because he knew that out of this he could create his army. Then he blew in their ears, and many swore their loyalty to him.

Misáianes never left the mountain where he had been engendered. Others were appointed to come and go from his dwelling place with the threads of his vast web. Thick fog hung in the air of his territory. Death upon death, cold and darkness spread from there to threaten the world.

The vassals clamouring around him were of opposite kinds: the lowest of the low, and the chosen ones. The Master kept close to him a multitude of beings incapable of the slightest understanding: brutish slaves stripped of all feeling, who carried out the most menial tasks he commanded. There were others, though, who were allowed to draw near to his breath. These were Misáianes' favourites, the prolongation of his fingers, of his will. They were the ones he sent out into the world, pushing forward the darkness. And far from that desolate spot, where the sun still shone and life went on as normal, there were many more who adored and served him. This was because his words sounded like the truth.

Misáianes turned brother against brother. He whispered in the ear of the arrogant, and turned them against the arrogant; he kissed the forehead of the weak and turned them against the weak. He furthered his plots through murmurs and lies, so that everyone believed they knew what only He knew, and so that those condemned to die thought they had been blessed. Misáianes' power was concealed by cunning and disguises. In this way, many followed him without suspecting it. In a war that only He, from the depths of his impiety, could have conceived.

This was the origin of the Sideresians.

A fleet was sailing towards the coast of the Remote Realm. And although some of the ships had sunk because of the terrible winds, there were still a great many of them.

Since dawn, there had been a bustle of activity on the ship where Leogrós and the Doctrinator sailed. The same was true of the other ships. The crew came and went from deck to hold; Leogrós and Drimus went over the details of the plan once more. The moment had arrived for the fleet to split into two. This was still several days before the Sideresians caught their first glimpse of the coast of the Fertile Lands.

Only three ships, under Drimus's command, would sail into the harbour at Beleram. They would be carrying many more gifts than weapons. The others would head north until they reached the ports abandoned during the great migrations that had taken place when the local peoples headed south in search of warmer climes. Ever since then, the far north of the continent of Fertile Lands had been uninhabited. The distant north. The north beyond the Border Hills, the gateway to the land of the Lords of the Sun; further north than the Golden Valley, where their golden cities flourished; further north than Claw Canyon, where their slaves were sent to die. The north far beyond the last inhabited place.

This was where Leogrós's fleet was bound. His ships were laden with weapons that no one who lived in the Fertile Lands would have been able to recognize. And with visible and invisible evils. Even ones that entered the nostrils of the Creatures and killed them with sickness.

The Doctrinator clambered down into the boat that was to transfer him to his new ship. Leaning over the side of his own vessel, Leogrós watched him leave. As soon as he saw that the hunchback had reached his destination, he gave the order and the fleet divided in two.

The three ships heading for the port of Beleram set course due west.

The others turned their prows northwards. Some of them were heading for the Border Hills, where they would land in the uninhabited region that stretched between the last villages of the Offspring of the Northmen and the first cities of the Lords of the Sun. The others were to continue without nearing land until they were level with the abandoned ports, when they would set course to the west.

The storm left together with the fleet. Leogrós's ships took it with them. Their advance was cloaked in a dank, misty rain that accompanied them throughout the rest of their crossing. The sky above Drimus's three vessels was a clear blue.

19

THE FEET OF THE DEER

'Look at the sky!' exclaimed Nakín, pointing towards the coast. 'It seems as though the storm has decided to veer off north and leave us this beautiful blue sky. That usually heralds the arrival of good friends.'

To Dulkancellin it appeared as though the Owl Clan representative was trying to find confirmation of her own feelings. He also thought that although rest had restored her beauty, she still looked weary. It was plain that to spend so much time in the solar world was a great effort for Nakín.

They were walking together round the interior courtyard of the House of the Stars, which was shielded from the prying eyes of Beleram by high stone walls. The other representatives, together with Bor and Zabralkán, were doing the same. The Council had been meeting for seven days now, and this was the first time they had all been allowed to go outside. The Husihuilke warrior was overjoyed when he heard this from Zabralkán. Although they were accustomed to being given a rest after they had eaten, this was the first time they could do so in the central courtyard. They all gladly accepted the proposal.

It was so pleasant to see the sky not through a wall opening, to breathe in the warm, moist jungle air. Even so, it was not enough to free them from their concerns. Each of them was going over the results of the latest discussions in their mind. Whenever two of them met on their walk, they would immediately begin talking them over.

The Great Council had been in session for seven days – seven days of proposals and arguments. And still no decision had been reached.

It appeared, however, that there was a general agreement, although this still met with resistance from some of the representatives, especially Elek. An attack before the strangers could say a word was beginning to seem like the only means of defence left to the Fertile Lands. This position, initially proposed by Molitzmós and Dulkancellin, was gradually gaining ground among the others. If they were to make a mistake, better an unjust battle than the end of Life itself. They were all aware that a mistake of this kind would bring down the Northmen's wrath on their heads; and that sooner or later all the peoples of the continent would have to face the consequences. The risk was enormous, and yet the Council seemed to be edging towards it. So it was that even while the Council was still deliberating, preparations for war were being made.

None of the peoples of the Fertile Lands was expert in naval warfare. The small fleet that the Offspring of the Northmen had constructed thanks to their inherited knowledge was made to transport goods, or at most take people up and down the coast. This meant that the war had to be fought on land. The Zitzahay army would not be able to resist any attack from the strangers for long; therefore everything was put in place to call on the forces of the Lords of the Sun, who had a large army that could reach Beleram in a matter of a few days. Although the Husihuilke warriors were the most feared, it would take them too long to arrive.

'Let's walk over to that staircase,' Dulkancellin suggested.

He had just recognized Cucub. The Zitzahay was seated at the foot of one of the many stairways that descended to the interior courtyard.

He was so absorbed in his own thoughts he did not even seem to notice what was going on around him. Dulkancellin had not heard anything from him since the night when Cucub was sent to the market to get news and tortillas. The Husihuilke did not want to waste this opportunity, which might possibly not come again, and so he asked Nakín to go with him to the staircase where Cucub was resting, his eyes fixed on the cobblestones.

'Wake up, Cucub!' shouted Dulkancellin as he drew near.

Looking up, Cucub tried to smile from ear to ear and with all his heart, as he usually did. Dulkancellin could see, however, that this was not the same smile that used to annoy him so. The Zitzahay got to his feet, greeted them both with a nod of the head, and tried his best to think of something amusing to recount. Fortunately for him, he did not have to keep up the pretence for long, because Nakín quickly realized that the two men wanted to be alone. When she saw Elek passing by on his own, she excused herself by saying she wanted to talk to him, and parted from them to catch the Offspring up.

'Well? What's wrong?' asked Dulkancellin, always one to come straight to the point.

Cucub sighed and sat down again.

'If you sit here beside me, I'll try to explain,' said the Zitzahay. He fell silent for a while, then began: 'You, brother, were with me when the Astronomers allowed me to go to the market, provided I stuck my nose into what the people of Beleram were saying. And you will recall, because it made you angry, that I was in an excellent mood, and left the House of the Stars full of optimism. It was such a shame that my happiness proved so short-lived! It began to fade even before I reached the market. And it disappeared completely as soon as I tried the cane-sugar honey.'

Dulkancellin was on the point of standing up, furious at having allowed Cucub to entangle him in yet another of his ridiculous tales. It was only the memory of the little man's sad smile that made him keep his patience.

'I know the honey that comes from the cane-fields in my jungle,' Cucub continued. 'I can recognize its taste among thousands. When I was at the market, I tasted the honey from one pot and then another; but however many I tried, the old taste had vanished.'

There could be no doubt Cucub was talking seriously. Dulkancellin tried to understand what he meant, but the Zitzahay's growing anxiety only complicated matters.

'Calm down, and try to find some other way to explain what you mean.' Dulkancellin's advice only made the Zitzahay more anxious.

'There is no other way! There isn't! I'm telling you that the taste of honey has disappeared! Something must have terrified it for it to decide to abandon us.'

Dulkancellin laid a hand on Cucub's shoulder. At the very moment when he did not comprehend him, when the Zitzahay's brain seemed clouded by nonsense, the Husihuilke felt he was truly his friend.

Cucub gave up. He had known from the start it would be hard to make himself understood. Now he felt it would have been better to say nothing at all. What he had to do was to change topics, so that his distress would be forgotten.

'Who is that man in magnificent garments walking with Bor?' he asked offhandedly.

'That's Molitzmós, one of the Lords of the Sun,' replied Dulkancellin.

'I don't like him,' said Cucub instinctively.

Molitzmós never wore the same garments twice, and they were always sumptuous. The clothes he was wearing shone like jewels in the sun as he walked with Bor in among the jasper fountains.

'Everything often becomes unclear to me,' Molitzmós was saying. 'I don't feel I understand anything.'

In the Council, the representative of the Lords of the Sun had often stood out because of his keen intelligence. Not a session went by when Molitzmós failed to win the others' admiration for his wise interventions, and it was Bor in particular who showed himself enchanted by the insight he evinced. So now the Supreme Astronomer found it hard to believe what he was hearing.

'How can someone like you be saying that?'

'There are thoughts I would have preferred not to have, and yet they have come to me. Fears I would have liked to ignore, but found that impossible,' said Molitzmós.

'What are you referring to?' asked the Astronomer.

'I am referring to certain facts I learnt long ago, and which have come back to me now. In recent days it has been impossible for me not to recall the time when Magic was split by a feud – so much so that it divided into two Brotherhoods. One of them, perhaps the more numerous, remained in the Ancient Lands. The other embarked on the long journey to the Fertile Lands.' Molitzmós looked over at his companion. 'But look who I am telling all this to! You must know every last detail of those events.'

'That doesn't matter; go on... please, go on.' Bor was beginning to be disturbed by the direction their conversation was taking. 'Follow your train of thought, and say what you have to say.'

'If you insist,' said Molitzmós, 'although I already feel I have gone too far. As I was saying, after the split, the two Brotherhoods put an ocean between them. I was told that those who came here did so across the strip of land which in those days united the two continents.'

'So it was,' Bor agreed. 'Our ancestors reached the Fertile Lands from the far north, bringing with them an invaluable inheritance; and to do so they used the land bridge you mentioned. Then—'

Bor fell silent.

'Were you about to mention what happened to that strip of land?' So

Molitzmós also knew about that. 'Tell me, is what they say about it true, or merely a legend? Is it true that the Brotherhood who came to the Fertile Lands sent that bridge to the bottom of the Yentru Sea, in order to sever all links with their fellow Wizards on the other shore?'

'It is completely true,' replied Bor, sure by now that Molitzmós was aware of far more than was any of the other representatives. 'The land bridge joining the two continents was buried deep under the ocean by the Magic of the Fertile Lands; and it was said it would remain there for ever. But you were the one who was talking.'

'So,' Molitzmós continued, 'Magic went in two opposing directions. And I think it was enmity rather than the sea that caused the great gulf between them. The cause of their feud is plain to see from the names the two kinds of Magic adopted.'

'The Enclosed Brotherhood and the Brotherhood of the Open Air,' whispered Bor. 'Both adopted their name with pride.'

'As it was bound to be,' replied Molitzmós. 'The Enclosed Ones, as those who stayed in the Ancient Lands chose to call themselves, declared it was their duty and their right to watch over Creation. They created and strengthened an empire of Wisdom. Its aim was to devote itself to the Creatures, but never to discuss anything with them, or to consult them when important decisions had to be taken. Still less, to allow them to sit in judgement on their rule.'

Bor considered it his duty to clarify the statement that the representative of the Lords of the Sun had made.

'It is true: the Enclosed Brotherhood proclaimed that their Magic should rule alone over the Creatures. They insisted that the gift of Wisdom was proof that they should be the masters. Only the Wise have a natural, innate talent for selfless devotion. Therefore the Magic that possessed Wisdom would never misuse its power. They said that Wisdom makes the best rulers, because a Wise man can only be content when he is being generous. But those of the Brotherhood of the Open Air saw things very differently.' Bor paused to see Molitzmós's reaction, then went on: 'This Brotherhood left the Ancient Lands with the hope of re-encountering here what they felt had been lost there: the true source of Magic. In their view, all that the Enclosed Brotherhood considered natural, and called their "duty to watch over the Creatures", was in fact no more than arrogance. The Brotherhood of the Open Air considered that Magic in the Ancient Lands was straying from its origins, and so one day its light would die out. This conviction was what drove them to cross the sea and start again in the Fertile Lands, far from the walls in which the others enclosed themselves. Out in the open air.'

'Far from any walls... out in the open air. Only you can say so much in so few words!' Molitzmós praised him. And Bor, who was not deaf to words of praise, thanked him with a gratified smile.

'We are talking of the distant past,' the Astronomer reflected. 'With the passage of time our differences were smoothed out. The enmity which split us no longer exists.'

'However that may be, some are still in the Ancient Lands, and others here. The land bridge between the two continents has never resurfaced. And as far as I can tell, contacts between them and you are still few and far between.' Molitzmós knew he was touching on a wound and tried to put things gently. 'Would I be wrong in thinking that the differences have not disappeared altogether? Do not the Enclosed Brotherhood and the Brotherhood of the Open Air still behave in different ways?'

The Supreme Astronomer tried very hard to conceal his unease.

'It is obvious that the Magic of the Fertile Lands has never stifled the voice of the Creatures. On the contrary, we have drawn close to them and listened, as you can tell from this Council itself! Did we not send for you all so that together we could take such a vital decision? But if you mean that in the Ancient Lands, Magic proceeds in the opposite manner, we have to admit that this is possibly true.' Bor took a deep breath before he went on. 'But tell me, Molitzmós, how it is that we have reached this point? Explain what path led your thoughts back from the Council to the ancient schism within Magic.'

As they walked past, Molitzmós reached out to stroke the jasper of the ornamental fountains. Sometimes he came to a halt, fascinated by the veins of colour in the stone.

'I think it would be best to forget this conversation,' he said.

'Why should we do that?' the Astronomer protested.

By now they had reached the central pond. Elek and Nakín were standing beside it, competing to see who could make more of the calls of the birds swimming on it.

'It will do them good to play for a while,' said Molitzmós as the two men moved on.

'Indeed, but don't you play the game of having forgotten what I asked you.'

There was no way out for Molitzmós. He had to finish what he had started.

'As I said at the beginning: there are thoughts I should have preferred not to have, and fears I should have liked to ignore. There is no worse doubt than the one a person feels when everyone else is in agreement about something: that kind of doubt leads to loneliness. That is why I am making so bold as to talk to you, to unburden my heart.' The representative of the Lords of the Sun spoke quickly, as if seeking to rid himself of something that was weighing down too heavily on him. 'The Magic of the Fertile Lands, inheritor of the principles of the Brotherhood of the Open Air, treats all the Creatures as if they were its brothers. It talks to them, consults them, even accepts their judgement. A few days ago, for example, the Husihuilke spoke about the Earth Wizard so familiarly it was as if he were an old neighbour. That is how it has always been between you and us. Yet now, when the times demand the splendour of Wisdom, it is as though Wisdom itself has gone to sleep. The best or the worst is about to happen to us. The best or the worst? There have been signs, but nobody in the Fertile Lands is able to interpret them. Magic's eyes are shrouded... might this not be because it has mingled so much with mankind, the lukus, the birds...? I heard Zabralkán speak of confusing messages: what if on the other hand it is Magic which has lost the ability to read them? This is the fear I would have preferred not to know of. I am afraid that part of the truth has remained within those walls of the Ancient Lands. I am afraid that, in its desire to become a brother to all Creatures, Magic here has left them unprotected. You may be amazed that it is I who am questioning the Brotherhood I should support. Someone like me, a simple Creature who, thanks to that Brotherhood's beliefs, can talk to you as an equal. Believe me, I too am amazed. But if the survival of Life in the Fertile Lands depends on Magic taking command over us, we would be very happy to see Magic wield its power. And we would accept the empire of Wisdom without demur. I shall never speak of this again. Forgive me, and forget, I beg you, this impertinence of mine.'

Bor's hair was standing on end, and with good reason. Molitzmós had just expressed exactly what he had often thought in the middle of the night. Whenever ideas of this sort came to him, the Astronomer was robbed of sleep. Instead, he would wander the corridors of the House of the Stars, or climb to the topmost observatory, and stay there until day began to dawn. But neither his pacing up and down nor the pattern of the stars could give an answer to the question that had kept him awake: what if the Brotherhood of the Open Air had taken a wrong turn? Only seven days earlier, when Cucub and Dulkancellin had reached the House of the Stars, his doubts had resurfaced and troubled him again. How hard he had found it to give the Husihuilke warrior those long and delicate explanations! Yet it was Zabralkán who had asked him to do so, and so he had been obliged to comply. It had annoyed him that a Supreme Astronomer, who ought to be devoting himself to acquiring Wisdom, had to justify his decisions to a Husihuilke, born and trained for war. Now Molitzmós was saying the same thing in no uncertain terms. Bor was astonished at the daring of the Lords of the Sun's representative – he himself, despite his position, had never dared communicate his own thoughts to Zabralkán. If occasionally he had hinted at them, the other man had responded with a silence that left no doubt about his attitude.

'Do you think it will be hard to overlook my boldness?'

The Supreme Astronomer understood he would have to say whatever was necessary so that Molitzmós would not suspect he shared his fears. He was about to speak when Zabralkán suddenly appeared, and saved him, for the moment at least.

'I think Zabralkán is looking for you,' said Molitzmós with an almost imperceptible smile.

'So it seems.'

Zabralkán caught them up, and, after greeting the two men, addressed Bor directly.

'Brother, we need to talk on our own for a moment.'

'With your permission, I am going to continue my walk,' said Molitzmós.

The Astronomers disappeared into the House of the Stars, while Molitzmós went back the way he had come.

On the way he passed the pond. Elek and Nakín had finished their game and were talking as they sat by the pond's edge. Molitzmós thought how good they looked together. Elek, pale-skinned and with his hair twisted halfway down his back, moved and behaved like an animal cub. Dark-skinned and tired-looking, Nakín seemed never to be fully awake.

Molitzmós stopped to look back at them from a distance. When he had observed them long enough, he continued on his way. He left behind the pond and wandered along the path between the jasper fountains. After that he crossed the bridge over the canal that brought water to the House of the Stars. The sound of water beneath his feet reminded him how thirsty he was. He needed a drink, but there was no slave near by to carry out his wish.

Molitzmós had been reluctant to travel to Beleram without his personal slaves. But however much he insisted, the messenger remained faithful to the instructions he had received from the Supreme Astronomers: 'Only bring the person we have sent you to fetch to the House of the Stars.' All the messengers had received the same instruction. So what was that little man doing with Dulkancellin? Who was he? To judge by his appearance and clothing, he must be a Zitzahay. But why was someone who was not part of the Council accompanying the representative of the Husihuilkes? Molitzmós stepped aside to intercept them.

'Greetings under this sun, brother Dulkancellin!' Then he turned to Cucub. 'And greetings to you, brother. Even though I do not know your name, or what you are called.'

'Brother is a good name,' replied Cucub. 'And may you receive many more greetings, Molitzmós of the Lords of the Sun!'

Dulkancellin was taken aback by his friend's impudence. Molitzmós, who had no idea who this insolent fellow was, took care to hide his anger.

'We are heading for the pond,' said Dulkancellin, trying to change the conversation.

'You'll find Elek and Nakín from the Owl Clan there.'

They nodded to each other, then continued in opposite directions. Suddenly Molitzmós recalled something that made him stop and turn round.

'Wait, Dulkancellin! I wanted to tell you that you should visit the jasper fountains. Look at them one by one! It's not often one has the chance to see such beauty.' He turned once more to Cucub. 'I will not recommend

177

them to you, because I suppose you know them better than I do.'

'You suppose correctly,' replied the Zitzahay.

Once they were some way away from him, Cucub began to imitate Molitzmós's way of walking.

'Look how the Plumed One walks!'

'How quickly you forget your worries!' The Husihuilke was concerned that Molitzmós might turn back towards them. 'And stop doing that; he might see you.'

'I haven't forgotten my worries,' said Cucub. 'And I still don't like that Molitzmós.'

Nakín saw them coming and waved. She did not know who Dulkancellin's companion was either, but Elek, who had often seen Cucub perform, quickly explained to her. Within a short space of time they were all conversing easily, although since Cucub was present they tried to steer their conversation away from the Council's deliberations.

'I see I was the only one to arrive here without a guide,' Nakín said with a smile.

'Why was that?' asked Dulkancellin, who knew very little about the Owl Clan.

'Because there is no path between the Magic Time and Solar Time. There is no track to follow, or river to canoe down. There is only a gateway somewhere in the world.'

The three men liked to hear her warm voice, and the childish way she chose and ordered her words. They asked more questions, simply so that she would go on talking.

'Tell me, Nakín, how you cross through that gateway,' asked Cucub, although he knew the answer from memory.

'Oh, it's hard work,' she said, raising both hands to her forehead. 'You have to perform a lengthy ritual. One day you drink the juice from a mushroom, which puts you to sleep. The next you chew some seeds, and dance. And so on, and so on... And when the person watching over you says you have reached the end, you sit and wait. Then slowly, very slowly, you leave one Time and reach the other.'

'What do you mean when you say "slowly, very slowly"?' asked Dulkancellin.

'The first thing that happens is that you turn very pale. Then you hear the others as if they were talking to you from a long way off, and it is the same for them. Everything is still where it should be, but gradually loses its colour. Little by little you slip out of one Time, and reappear in the other one. There the same thing happens, but in reverse. And it takes a long time for you to recover the colour in your cheeks.'

'Well, you have now.'

The voice was that of Molitzmós, who had crept up on them without anyone hearing him.

'Come and sit with us, brother,' Elek invited him.

Molitzmós accepted the invitation and sat on the rough edge of the pond, ignoring any damage the gold adornments on his cape might suffer.

'I wonder if any of you have seen Illán-che-ñe,' he said.

They all shook their heads. All except Cucub, who had never even heard of him.

'His wish to be alone is typical of his people,' said Molitzmós. 'That is how the Pastors of the Desert are.'

Terrified at hearing that name again, Cucub shuddered from head to toe. This confirmed Molitzmós's suspicions. He must be the messenger who had accompanied Dulkancellin from the Ends of the Earth. And if Molitzmós's memory served him right, his name was...

'Brother Cucub, perhaps you can confirm what I have said,' Molitzmós continued, with a mocking smile.

'I believe I can.' Cucub felt as humiliated as he did when he lost at the ball game.

Dulkancellin was the only one who understood what had just happened, and he thought the Zitzahay deserved it.

A horn sounded from one of the towers of the House of the Stars, announcing that the Council was to reassemble.

'How quickly this time in the sun has passed,' sighed Nakín.

The representatives all stood up, said farewell to Cucub, and left him.

The Zitzahay was alone once more. He would have liked to ask his friend not to leave him. Instead, he leant over the pond and began to pull faces at his own reflection. Whenever he had done this in the past he always ended up laughing out loud. But his easy laughter had disappeared as surely as the cane-sugar honey.

'Where can it have gone?' Cucub asked himself.

After the Astronomers, Illán-che-ñe was the first person to reach the Council chamber. The others quickly followed. As soon as they came into the room, they all understood that something had changed, and that to judge by Zabralkán's face, the change was for the better.

'Good news, brothers! Good news for the Fertile Lands!' His enthusiasm led him to lose his usual reticence. 'There are three... only three of them!'

None of them understood what the Supreme Astronomer meant.

'Each of us,' Bor continued, 'had begun to accept the idea that we should mount a surprise attack on the foreign fleet. We were resigned to accepting this as a first line of defence for our peoples, even if it turned out to be a terrible mistake. What we have learnt will lead us to take a step back from a course of action about which we all had grave doubts.'

'We will take a step back if everyone here agrees that is what we should do,' Zabralkán reprimanded him, although making it sound as if he were not doing so. 'You must listen to our news, and then we will decide. The gulls have flown in from the sea. The Yentru's Boatman sent them to us with a message: the foreign ships have been sighted.'

A murmur ran round the room. Everyone sat up straight, their eyes fixed on Zabralkán.

'They are still on the high seas, several days from our coasts. It's true that they reached here far more quickly than we were expecting. But the number of their ships is much smaller. The Boatman tells us there are only three of them. Only three small ships are headed our way!'

Now they could understand why Zabralkán was so elated. It was unlikely that Misáianes would think of invading the Fertile Lands with such a tiny fleet: how many warriors could there be in three ships? How many spears and axes? How much pain?

Illán-che-ñe, Elek and Nakín were of the opinion that the idea of attacking should be abandoned, at least as it had originally been conceived.

'It is the Fathers!' Elek asserted. 'There can be no greater proof than the number of ships in their fleet.'

'Three ships cannot declare war on an entire continent,' said Illán-che-ñe.

'Those are good seagulls to bring us the news we wanted to hear,' said Nakín of the Owl Clan.

Dulkancellin did not seem to completely share his companions' optimism.

'I would like to remind you of what Zabralkán said on the first day of this Council,' said the Husihuilke. 'He told us: "Our decision must have the feet of a deer so that it can leap from side to side, causing the least possible damage." It appears as though our visitors are the Northmen; and if that is so, I am as glad as the rest of you. But I say we should also take steps to protect ourselves. Let's not remove the deer's ability to leap, if it should come to that. A deer with injured feet is a dead animal.'

The Husihuilke warrior again! Bor found it hard to contain his exasperation. His eyes met those of Molitzmós, who was staring at him. The Supreme Astronomer felt ashamed that someone had been able to read his innermost thoughts.

The session lasted until the end of the night. The debate was long and tough. By the time day dawned over Beleram, the Council had decided unanimously on what actions should be taken.

Dulkancellin and Molitzmós would head for the Yentru Sea coast. Molitzmós would command a hundred and twenty archers and guard the northern approaches to Beleram. Dulkancellin would lead a much smaller force that was to hide among the rocks of the coast and keep a close watch on the strangers' movements. The others were to remain in the House of the Stars.

The Zitzahay people knew little of war. The last battles they had fought were in the distant, almost forgotten past. Even so, the House of the Stars maintained a legion of warriors who should be sufficient if necessary to confront the crews of three small ships.

The arrival of the foreign fleet could no longer be kept a secret. In a few days' time, the ships would be visible from the beach. Before this happened, the inhabitants of Beleram ought to be warned. What should they be told? Once more, the Council found it hard to reach a decision. As had so often happened, it was the arguments of Molitzmós, backed up by Bor and with Zabralkán's tacit approval, that won the day. The Council resolved not to tell everyone the whole truth. With the foreign ships so close to shore, this would only spread panic. And fear could cause irreparable harm. If the fleet were friendly, or so few in number it could easily be defeated, then there was no need to run the risk of revealing everything so suddenly and in such an alarming way.

The Council decided that the truth should be told only to those who needed to know. The villages, the people in the market, the artisans, would hear only a part of it: 'Visitors are coming from the Ancient Lands... Let the women and children braid flowers for them. And let all the people of Beleram make ready to receive and honour them in our best manner.'

20

THE RETURN OF KUPUKA

The Earth Wizard paused to observe things from afar. As he feared, the disasters he had seen throughout the Husihuilke territory were to be found here too. Evidence of how poor their people had become could be seen from Whirlwind Pass all the way down to Old Mother Kush's house. Kupuka had not been absent for long, which meant that these evils travelled more quickly than him… and he could not remember the last time he had got any sleep!

No sooner had he entered the Ends of the Earth and reached the first villages than many people came up and told him what was happening. 'Our squashes rot before they become ripe… our goats die as they give birth. Our eggs become as wrinkled as nuts… Our hunters return empty-handed, and our women wake crying in the middle of the night.' Some of them showed him proof of their misfortunes, but their haggard features spoke even more clearly than the rotten fruit they displayed. And everyone who talked to Kupuka, without exception, said that things were worse in neighbouring villages.

The laments Kupuka heard in Sweet Herbs were the same he heard later in The Partridges. And in Wilú-Wilú and The Corals. The Earth

Wizard had swept like a whirlwind through the most important villages: from the seashore to the Maduinas Mountains, from the Marshy River to Kush's hut. That was where he was now, staring sadly at the vegetable garden which was no longer Kush's pride and joy: gone were all its abundant crops of squash, potatoes, or maize. *I have been away too long!* thought Kupuka.

He walked across to the dwelling and halted at the front door. He was about to announce his arrival with the loud sharp knock he always used. In that way things would return to what they had once been, if only for a moment. But even that proved impossible, because before he could do so, Thungür pulled open the door. His hostile attitude soon disappeared when he recognized the old man's beloved face. *The son is the same now as his father*, thought Kupuka. The moment for the greeting ceremony had arrived: at last they could recover something from the good old times.

'Greetings to you, brother Thungür, and I ask your leave to stay in this, your land.'

'Greetings to you, brother Kupuka. I give you my permission. We are happy to see you well. We thank the path that brought you here.'

'Wisdom and strength be with you all.'

'May the same be with you, and more.'

All the family except Piukemán was there to receive him. Old Mother Kush was the first to come up. She took Kupuka's hands and held them firmly in hers. 'Tell us, tell us,' were the only words she managed to say. After her, it was Kume's turn. To the Earth Wizard it looked as if instead of growing up, he had grown old.

The length of time that had passed since the day he left seemed longer or shorter depending on which of the warrior's daughters he was gazing at. Little Wilkilén appeared almost exactly the same as the image he had in his mind. Kuy-Kuyen on the other hand had become a young woman.

'The moon has entered Kuy-Kuyen's body, and look how beautiful she is!' Kush said by way of explanation. 'When I see her around the house I think it's her mother.'

'They will soon be asking you for her hand in marriage,' said Kupuka.

'They already have!' replied the old woman. 'A few suns ago some of Shampalwe's family came to see us to ask on behalf of one of their sons.'

'And what reply did they receive?' Kupuka asked.

'None as yet,' said Kush, hugging her granddaughter, who was already taller than she was. 'She has not finished protesting about it.'

'But she ought to accept the offer.' Thungür had obviously learnt to take command. 'She is old enough. And possibly in Wilú-Wilú she will receive the nourishment we are increasingly unable to provide here.'

'Don't be so sure,' replied Kupuka. 'I have visited many villages on my return journey, including Wilú-Wilú, and they are all suffering the same hardships.'

The Earth Wizard wished to complete the plan that had been taking shape in his mind as he progressed through the Ends of the Earth, as quickly as possible. But he noticed Piukemán was not there, and so asked after him.

Old Mother Kush glanced at her eldest grandson. He nodded his approval. Taking Kupuka by the hand, she led him into the next room. Piukemán was there, curled up by the fire where Kush did the cooking. He was scratching at his own eyes, and had wounds on his arms. Kupuka immediately identified the look of terror on his face.

'It's the torment of the Ministering Falcon,' he whispered.

'It's the torment of the Ministering Falcon,' the old woman confirmed.

'Leave us, Old Mother Kush. Leave me with him.'

Kupuka recalled the young boy he had left. He gazed again at the youngster opposite him, destroyed for ever by the curse of the Ministering Falcon. He cried the bitterest tears he had ever shed. Fortunately, there was no one to witness this: Kush had left the room, and Piukemán could not see him. When he was sure his voice would not betray his grief, the Earth Wizard spoke.

'Here I am, O disobedient one!'

When he heard the old man, the boy sat up. Desperately, he opened his eyes wide to try to see Kupuka's face again. But his sight was fixed on other things.

'Be still, my boy,' Kupuka told him, sitting down beside him. 'That day when you crossed the Owl Gateway, taking Wilkilén with you, I was afraid your curiosity would lead you to a place of no return. Now I see that exactly this has happened.'

Once a year, immediately after the end of the rainy season, the Ministering Falcon called his family together. When the moment came, falcons flew into the air from all four corners of the sky. Some of them flew alone, others in great flocks. They were all heading for the same place: the region of the great nests, high in the Maduinas Mountains.

The Husihuilkes did not know for certain what brought the falcons from everywhere to meet the Ministering Falcon. It was rumoured that this was when the Ministering Falcon challenged all the young male falcons who wished to dethrone him; it was said there was a bloody struggle for the succession, and that almost always it was his own sons who killed him and took his place. This was what was told and retold, but no one knew with any certainty. Yet the Husihuilkes did know some things about it. They knew it was forbidden for them to witness this ceremony. They also knew that all those who had tried to do so were found out and punished. That was why on the day the falcons darkened the sky, they took great care not to go anywhere near the great nests.

Any human being who dared to see what was forbidden was punished through their eyes. The Ministering Falcon punished them by stealing their eyesight. Not to leave them in the darkness of being blind, but by transferring his own eyes to them. From that moment on, whether their

186

eyes were open or closed, they would see as the Falcon saw. If the Falcon was devouring its prey, the human being saw a bloody mess. And even if he screwed up his eyes, he was still forced to see it. If the Falcon began to fight, the human would see the terrified or terrifying eyes of his adversary. If the Falcon were resting in his nest, the man saw sky and rock. If the Falcon were flying in the sky, the man saw his beloved world from on high. When the man managed to fall asleep, he dreamt the visions of the bird. When the bird slept, the man saw his dreams.

Piukemán, the disobedient one, Shampalwe's curious son, had again defied the prohibitions. Just as on the day when he went beyond the Owl Gateway, he had wanted to see further than permitted. This time he had paid the highest cost.

'Once, the Falcon flew over our house,' Piukemán said between sobs. 'As soon as I realized it was coming in this direction I asked everyone to go outside, hoping the Falcon would look down and I would be able to see them again. I thought I saw Kush, but could not be sure… the falcon was flying too high and too fast.'

Piukemán had his eyes shut now: he was seeing Butterfly Lake.

'The Falcon has stopped to drink,' he explained to Kupuka. 'I can see the reflection of his face in the water, and the stones on the bottom.'

The Earth Wizard held Piukemán close against his chest.

'I saw the falcons fly by, and wanted to know. The same as that other time… I left without saying a word. I walked all that day and the following night. I ran towards where the birds were heading. At first light I reached the region of the great nests, and struggled so hard I found them. There was a ring of falcons with the Ministering Falcon in the centre.'

Piukemán suddenly jolted upright again. The Ministering Falcon had spied a squirrel it was going to hunt.

'Don't try to explain what I can already imagine,' said Kupuka.

The Earth Wizard had understood that another difficult moment was approaching. He held Piukemán tight until it had passed. After some time, the boy's body relaxed. The Ministering Falcon had devoured the squirrel, and was now surveying the treetops.

'Tell me, Kupuka, is there anything you can do for me?'

The Earth Wizard told him the truth at once.

'There is nothing I can do. Nor anyone else. You have two choices. One is that of death. It is a short path, and offers you quick relief. The other is the path to wisdom. That is a long, painful journey, but in the end you will find yourself in the best place on earth.'

'What must I do for that?' asked Piukemán.

'First of all, you must let your human body pass into that of the falcon. The more you are akin to the bird, the less you will suffer. The rest will come. You will see, it does come.' Kupuka stood up to leave. 'I have to go and talk to your elder brothers.'

'Wait!' Piukemán could see the treetops from high in the sky. 'Promise me you will seek out the Ministering Falcon, that you will stand in front of him so that I can see you.'

'I promise,' Kupuka said, and left the room.

Kush, Thungür and Kume were sitting on their rugs waiting to hear what Kupuka had to tell them.

'Now I am the guide and the messenger. I am the one who will lead you,' said the Earth Wizard. 'Tomorrow we must leave for the Remote Realm. And I must tell you that all the best warriors of the Ends of the Earth will join us along the way.'

'What are we going to do in the Remote Realm?' asked Thungür.

'We are going to fight a war,' said Kupuka. 'The hardest ever fought.'

The next morning, Kupuka and Old Mother Kush were talking. A fresh departure was about to take place. It had taken Kupuka the entire night to say all that he had to say. Now he was giving the old woman his final advice.

'The rainy season is drawing near once more. There is no one in this house to repair the roof. Ask the birds for help. They love you, and will do it for you.'

Kupuka was trying to ignore how sad Kush looked.

'Besides, you have to get ready to go and take part in the ceremony of the Sun.'

'Do you think that with all the misfortunes they are facing, the Husihuilke people will want to dance and sing?'

'They ought to celebrate all the more,' said Kupuka, a harsh note creeping into his voice. 'Did you hear me, old woman? More than ever!'

'I don't think I will be able to attend,' said Kush. 'Grief has left my soul empty. I'm old and tired... my only wish is to leave this world.'

The Earth Wizard tugged at Kush's long tress to reproach her.

'I am sorry, old woman, but you cannot do that. Clever Old Mother Kush has enjoyed herself in this world, yet when evil draws near, she decides to abandon it!'

Kush stared at Kupuka with the look of a frightened child. Never before had the Earth Wizard been so angry with her. Worse still, he seemed to be growing even more irate.

'You say grief has left your soul empty. I say to you: fill it with the grief of others! Remember that many mothers are saying goodbye to their sons. Everyone in the land of the Husihuilkes has precise instructions to follow. You must continue to hunt, sow crops, to spin and weave. And you, clever Old Mother Kush, cannot be less than your neighbours!'

The old woman did not dare say anything. Two tears, which Kupuka pretended not to notice, ran down her wrinkled cheeks.

'And especially you must take care of the three grandchildren who will be staying with you.'

On hearing this, Kush finally reacted.

'I wanted to talk to you about that,' she said softly.

'What do you mean?' asked Kupuka, calmer by now.

'I mean Kuy-Kuyen,' Old Mother Kush replied. 'She is a beautiful young woman, bathed in starlight. Shampalwe's family will soon be back for their answer. And I will have to let them take her away to be married. She is of marrying age now, so there is no reason to refuse. If I do, the family will be offended. Unless...'

'Unless what?' asked Kupuka.

'Unless you take her with you.'

Kush thought this would enrage the Earth Wizard yet again. Instead, he waited patiently for her to explain.

'I would like to see Kuy-Kuyen smiling and laughing from love, as her mother used to. I would like to see my beauty happy. And she will not be that if she has to stay here and is handed over to Shampalwe's family.'

'What makes you think she will be happy if she comes with us?'

'Well...' Kush hesitated before going on. 'Kuy-Kuyen often mentions the name of that Zitzahay messenger who came to fetch Dulkancellin. She mentions Cucub in her dreams and when she is wide awake. She often gazes northwards and sings sad love songs. Take her to where he is. Perhaps the Zitzahay will love her in return and will want to marry her.'

'But you are talking of weddings when we are going to war,' Kupuka protested.

'Look at it this way, brother: I am talking of love when death is drawing near.'

The Earth Wizard smiled. Human beings were the strangest Creatures!

'What will you do?' he asked.

'Don't worry about me. I have the experience, and Wilkilén the enthusiasm. As for Piukemán, I am sure he will choose the path of wisdom.'

Kupuka thought over what Kush was proposing. Kuy-Kuyen's journey might possibly have a meaning the old woman could not even imagine.

All of a sudden Wilkilén came running up and flung her arms round

Kupuka's legs. The Earth Wizard lifted her to his face and whispered in her ear.

'Yes, I'll look after her with all my soul!' she replied, giving away the secret.

The two old people stared at each other.

'So be it! I'll take her with me,' said Kupuka.

A few hours later, Kupuka, Thungür, Kume and Kuy-Kuyen started out on their journey. They took the same path that Dulkancellin and Cucub had followed at the beginning of the previous rainy season.

Kupuka strode off, muttering to himself.

'They must be about to disembark. If I have properly understood the dreams that have come to me, their ships must be very close to the Remote Realm. But it will not be too late.' He kept on repeating, 'No, it will not be too late.'

21

THE MARK OF THEIR FOOTSTEPS

It was still raining over the Remote Realm. The day the strangers disembarked, a thin, sharp rain was falling on Beleram. Like the thorns of a thistle.

The reception committee was waiting, formed up in the shape of a butterfly's wings. Molitzmós's warriors were surrounding the port. Dulkancellin and his men were watching the proceedings closely from the rocks near by.

The three ships moored in the bay. Shortly afterwards, the first strangers appeared. Men dressed in black and wearing black capes left their ship, came ashore on the only jetty in the harbour, and fanned out on both sides of it. The entire port was on the alert, ready for anything that might happen. An expectant silence, with the archers tensing their arms on their bows. Then another man appeared, also dressed in black, but mounted on an animal no one had ever seen before. He came forward a few steps from between the twin rows of his escort, then halted for a long moment, which some of those present measured in breaths, others in days. He came on. It was raining over land and sea. Rain like the thorns of a thistle.

Nobody there had ever seen an animal like this one: they had never even heard of its existence. Only two people had any memory of what it might be. One was Elek. He was in the first line of the welcoming party, and immediately recalled animals mentioned in his elders' accounts of the past. The other was Dulkancellin. From where he was hidden, the Husihuilke warrior could look down on the port. The animal he saw advancing reminded him of the one he had seen in a dream, the night before the ceremony of the Sun.

The majestic animal continued its majestic advance. But before it touched the soil of the Fertile Lands, the rider halted it once more. Some hearts beat so loudly they could be heard through the damp air.

The shoreline divided the day in two halves. On one side, the sea and black uniforms. On the other, jungle and brightly coloured tunics. All that united them was the rain, which continued to fall. Rain like the thorns of a thistle.

'*The mark of their footsteps on our earth and… remember!… many generations will reap poison.*' Dulkancellin suddenly recalled the words he had heard in the forest at the Ends of the Earth. The old luku's words took him by surprise. They seemed to him to come from a distant place that was not exactly memory.

The foreign rider paused at the end of the jetty. He took a long look at the waiting crowd. Digging in his heels, he made his mount rear onto its hind legs. From this height, the beast let out a long, strangulated bellow from its throat, which sounded just like the battle-cries of the local warriors. Standing close by, the members of the welcome party felt fear clawing at them. None of them moved, however, as their pride was greater than any fear. Behind them, the archers were ready to shoot to kill.

'Greetings, dear brothers!' shouted the stranger. His voice echoed all round the port. 'May the heavens look down on this re-encounter.'

The rider spoke the Natural Language fluently. When he had finished his greeting, he bowed his head.

194

Three of the lesser Astronomers stepped forward to receive him. One of them, who had previously been appointed to the task, was the first to speak.

'Stranger, we cannot return your greetings or call you brother until we know your name, where your ships are from, and the intentions of you and your companions.'

'My name is Drimus,' replied the rider. 'I come with my companions in the name of the leaders of the Ancient Lands. We have crossed the Yentru Sea to fulfil a promise made many years ago by my ancestors to yours.'

'You will have to repeat and prove all you have just said to the Supreme Astronomers and others. We will simply lead you to the House of the Stars.'

'This cold welcome does not offend me,' replied Drimus. 'It is what we were expecting. We are aware of the great concerns that have led you to take such precautions. We also know that as soon as you gain knowledge of our true intentions, your hardships will be at an end. But… everything in due course. For now, take us to the House of the Stars.'

'Not now,' replied the Zitzahay spokesman, still courteous but distant. 'It will soon be nightfall. The journey to the House of the Stars is not so short that it can be completed before dark. For now, you and your companions must return to your ships and not leave them until dawn. We will make sure there is abundant food for you all. Tomorrow at first light we will lead you and two others of your choosing before the Supreme Astronomers.'

'Brother twice over, I gladly accept your conditions: we would have had the same suspicions,' said the Doctrinator, enjoying the game. 'Even so, I would like to make two requests. First, that in addition to my two companions, I may be allowed to bring with me the many gifts that we have brought for the Supreme Astronomers. And secondly, let us leave the food for when we are all seated round our hosts' table. Prisoners lose their appetite.'

Raising his hand in a further gesture of greeting, Drimus turned his mount and returned to the jetty at a quicker pace.

That night the Zitzahay lit fires all along the coast, protecting them with a covering of branches and green leaves. For their own protection they built shelters with waxed cloths for roofs.

Dulkancellin and Molitzmós met to decide on what they should do the next day. They did not talk for long: Dulkancellin and his small band of men would watch the strangers on their way to the House of the Stars. Molitzmós's warriors would stay on the coast, keeping the fleet under surveillance.

The night was a long one for all those who could not sleep, and who alternately peered at the ships, then at the sky, then back again from sky to ships, fearful that something might happen at any moment. Yet nothing disturbed the calm. At last a misty dawn rose over the sea. The journey was meant to start at first light, but this had to be put back because of the mist.

Half a day's march from the coast, in the House of the Stars, Cucub was staring at the rain. When Zabralkán announced that the ships had arrived, Elek and Nakín were overjoyed. They ran after the Supreme Astronomer, anxious to hear the details. Cucub preferred to stay where he was, humming the song that Elek had not reached the end of. From that moment on, nobody saw him either eat or sleep. Nor did anyone hear him say a word. Watching the rain, Cucub cast off his sadness and left his fears for some other day, when the rain was over. And perhaps, who knows, that day would never come…

Cucub was so absorbed in his own thoughts that it took him some time to realize that the voice was talking to him. And still longer to understand what it was saying: that he should wake up? That he should hurry up? That Zabralkán wanted to see him at once in the observatory? Poor Cucub could not understand what they wanted him for.

As he followed the escort, his mind cleared, and by the final steps up the interminable stairway leading to the observatory, he had begun to ask himself what the reason might be for his being summoned in this way. On one step, he imagined one thing. On the next, something different. On the next, he was hoping they were going to ask him about the cane-sugar honey! Although he imagined many things, Cucub came nowhere near to guessing what finally awaited him in the observatory.

He saw her as soon as he crossed the threshold and his eyes grew accustomed to the strange light inside. He saw her and recognized her immediately, even though she bore little resemblance to the bird who had been his trusty companion during his long journey through the desert. She lay trembling against one of the walls, and looked exhausted and weak.

'Poor friend!' Cucub murmured, moving towards the eagle.

'You can look after her later,' said Zabralkán, intercepting him. He was holding something in his outstretched palm, and asked: 'Have you ever seen this before?'

'Of course!' said Cucub. 'And not long ago. It is the White Stone. Do you remember? The one the old luku showed Dulkancellin and me in the forest at the Ends of the Earth.'

'Are you completely certain?' asked Bor, not taking his eyes from the window that looked out over the main causeway of Beleram.

'I am, yes I am,' replied Cucub. 'No one could mistake a stone like that. Even though the stain deep inside it has grown a lot since that day.'

Zabralkán clutched the stone as if afraid it might disappear.

'The eagle brought it in her beak,' said the Supreme Astronomer. 'And it is plain to see that it cost her a great effort.'

'Poor thing, my beautiful friend,' Cucub said. The eagle, which had not taken her eyes off him, ruffled her feathers. 'I suppose she must have had to search long and hard among the bodies of the dead lukus to find it,

197

hidden as the stone was beneath the beard of a creature that had lost all its features and even its flesh.'

'But why would she do such a thing? Who could have told her to do so?' Zabralkán wondered.

'Wait a moment!'

Cucub's response was so emphatic that Bor left the window and came to join the other two.

'Now that I remember,' said Cucub, 'the Earth Wizard said something about this. It was in the desert, before he left Dulkancellin and me and headed south. He said something like: "I am afraid to tell you I am taking something with me that has been very useful to you. The eagle will be coming back with me, because she has to do something for me that she can accomplish far better than I can."'

Cucub's suppositions were not far from the truth. In his return journey to the Ends of the Earth, Kupuka had summoned the eagle and ordered her to search for the White Stone among the massacred lukus. 'As soon as you find it, take it to the House of the Stars. Fly without stopping, and leave it in the hands of the greatest of the Astronomers. You must do this quickly, sister eagle. There is no time to lose.' The eagle heard him, and obeyed so readily she risked her life doing so. Day after day, night after night, she used her eyes and beak in the ghastly task of trying to find a tiny stone in that mound of bones, hair and putrefaction. The sand carried by the wind, and the other birds still feeding off the bodies of the lukus, made her search even more difficult. Yet none of this could stop her. She searched and searched without resting, unable to eat anything except for the same rotten flesh she was busily sifting through. When she was about to give up, thinking that another bird must have swallowed it, her beak struck the White Stone, hidden among what was left of a flowing white beard. After that, she raced through the skies to the hands of Zabralkán. An exhausting race during which the eagle never thought of sparing herself. Now she lay close to death in a corner of the Supreme Astronomers' observatory. Kupuka would be proud of her!

'Thank you, Cucub,' said Zabralkán. 'Now please leave us.'

'Very well!' said Cucub. 'But allow me to take the eagle with me. She has saved my life more than once, and I will do my best to save hers.'

'If you are going to take her, do it at once,' insisted Bor.

Cucub went over to his friend. He had great difficulty lifting her and carrying her towards the door. Zabralkán was quick to open it for him.

'Good luck, Cucub.'

Bor and Zabralkán were opposed in mind and body.

'The strangers must not enter here,' said Zabralkán. 'We must avoid their coming into our House. For the present at least, until our brother representatives have heard this news.'

'There is nothing new,' retorted Bor. 'There is a stone, whose existence we already knew of. A stone of uncertain origin which cannot of itself tell us what the stars of the sky have not already revealed.'

'A stone which mobilized the luku people, which cast a shadow over Dulkancellin, and made Kupuka do things he was not prepared for.'

'The lukus... Dulkancellin... Kupuka...' Bor repeated. 'It seems as though the Creatures of the south have a great influence in the House of the Stars.'

'What do you mean by that?'

Zabralkán knew the answer, but he wanted Bor to hear himself.

'What is your meaning?' he repeated.

'My meaning is to remember our roots are in the Magic of the Ancient Lands, and not in some ignorant people of the southern isles. My meaning is that we should not forget we are the sons of the Great Wisdom of the north.'

'Our hope is that we are sons of the Great Wisdom of the world,' Zabralkán interrupted him. And without giving Bor any chance to speak, he added: 'The strangers will not enter the House of the Stars today. We will not discuss that decision now. We will do so tomorrow. And with all the other representatives. We will discuss all that is necessary. It is possible that, like you, they will disapprove of this decision, which may be the fruit of a misapprehension or deceit. Until such time, we will do all we can to prevent the strangers leaving any mark on our earth.'

'If that is the case, we must act immediately,' said Bor. 'The strangers are drawing near.'

The two Astronomers fell silent in order to listen. On the wind they could hear the sounds of celebration and astonishment that accompanied the arrival of the three strangers in the city.

There was no time to lose. Zabralkán left the observatory and set about the complicated descent to the main gate. He took short, rapid steps, completely forgetting the decorum usually shown by the Supreme Astronomer of the House of the Stars. He quickly left behind the highest staircases and long passageways. Apprentices and servants could not believe their eyes: Zabralkán raced through the rooms, appearing and disappearing at each twist and turn of the stairways, going down and down. Not at the usual slow pace of an old man and Astronomer, but with an urgency unsuited to his rank. Behind him came Bor, shouting orders to right and left in order to gather the retinue that always accompanied the Supreme Astronomers when they left their House.

Zabralkán was willing to rush out onto the platform in front of the building like any other human being. The guards at the main gate were taken by surprise by the group led by the old man. Their appearance was so sudden the guards barely had time to push open the heavy carved stone doors. Zabralkán was the first to emerge, followed by Bor, looking like thunder; and finally their escort, who had not yet managed to form proper lines. All of them reached the centre of the platform, then came to a halt. This gave the escort a chance to line up properly. Bor's face relaxed, and Zabralkán was a majestic old man once more.

The Supreme Astronomers stood waiting, their attention fixed on the confused clamour they could hear approaching along the paved main avenue. The strangers were there, at the gates of the House of the Stars, after having crossed the whole of Beleram.

Beleram, the capital of the Remote Realm. The city that their Magic had ordered to be built, the only sacred city, the one of which no one could dream, the one conserving the most ancient holy books, the one that observed the sky from its highest towers...

The entire population had come out to celebrate the arrival of the visitors. But as they drew near to the House of the Stars, the sounds were no longer those of celebration or open amazement. Instead, the crowd muttered darkly as the procession advanced.

At its head were the lesser Astronomers chosen to go to the coast to receive the strangers. Each of them was in a covered litter carried by four servants. Behind them came their assistants. A little further off were the strangers. Some in the crowd narrowed their eyes as if seeking to penetrate as far as the bones of the men dressed in black. Others were shouting, trying to name the strange beasts the strangers rode, which none of them had ever seen before. 'Animal with mane,' said someone. The name spread from mouth to mouth, until everyone was calling them that, and making them their own. Two of these animals, which instead of having men on their backs were covered by richly embroidered cloths, were being led by a Zitzahay. Dulkancellin's men had taken up their positions on either side and at the rear of the procession.

The procession came to a halt outside the House of the Stars. On their litters, the lesser Astronomers were astonished to see Zabralkán and Bor waiting at the centre of the platform. That was not what had been agreed, nor did it seem prudent. They quickly ordered their servants to set the litters down. If the Supreme Astronomers were standing, they could not remain seated, and much less look down on them. The servants carefully lifted the litters from their shoulders and gently placed them on the ground. Dulkancellin at once ordered the strangers to dismount.

Drimus understood that something untoward was preventing him gaining access to the House of the Stars. He deduced this from Zabralkán's gestures and from the way the lesser Astronomers turned to look at him. When the Supreme Astronomers sent for the Husihuilke warrior chief, Drimus realized that his mission might be under threat.

Among all of Misáianes' subjects, Drimus was the chosen one. Misáianes had chosen him to leave the first mark of the Sideresians in the House of the Stars. When that happened, the most important part would be accomplished! By the time Leogrós arrived, waging his campaign of slaughter from the north, he would find Magic's sacred place corrupted and sick. It would only take their dogs' fetid breath to dissolve its stone walls. Better than anyone, Drimus was the person who could confound the Astronomers, because he understood Misáianes' aims far beyond annihilation and slaughter. And because like them he spoke the languages of Wisdom. Drimus, glorious son of the Magic of the Ancient Lands, disdained all ambition for riches or the power of arms. The Doctrinator dreamt of an eternity that few could comprehend.

The same Astronomer who had greeted him in the port was speaking to him. He was saying he would not be received that day, but that he and his companions would be taken to a building close to the House of the Stars.

'Soon, possibly tomorrow, you will be visited by the Supreme Astronomers.'

Drimus the Doctrinator was forced to clench his soul in his fists in order not to show his fury. There was nothing he could do for the moment. Nothing but accept the order and wait. Wait until he had in front of him those who called themselves Supreme Astronomers, the descendants of the ones who had betrayed the Magic of the North. Drimus knew how to dig, to gnaw; he knew where it was hard and where it was soft. It would be easy for him to transform Bor and Zabralkán into two feeble old men who would fling open the doors of the House of the Stars for him.

'At least receive the gifts we have brought,' said Drimus.

'We cannot do that either,' he was told.

The Doctrinator wanted to know where they were to be taken. The building they pointed out was a grey pyramid, its base covered in red and blue figures.

The strangers climbed back on their mounts and set off, closely watched by the warriors. Drimus looked back towards the House of the Stars just as the doors closed behind the Supreme Astronomers and their retinue. He lowered his head to hide his expression, and began to whisper a litany forbidden to ordinary understanding. Slow incantations known only to the Wizards of the Ancient Lands...

22

ALONG THE PATHS OF THE FERTILE LANDS

In those days, two armies were advancing through the Fertile Lands. They did so along well-established paths and those long since abandoned; if necessary, they did not hesitate to hack new ones.

Both armies were marching towards Beleram and a clash with each other. A mighty war was fought when they met. The survivors waited until they had recovered sufficient calm to record these events and tell of them. When at last they could do so, they talked of streams of blood flowing down to the sea, of dead men burying dead men, of a lament heard for countless years. The Sideresians were coming from the north. Kupuka and the Husihuilke warriors from the south. The one to lay waste to Beleram. The other to defend it.

As the armies advanced, the shadow of a Wizard from the Ancient Lands darkened Beleram. But above all, it was the truth that lay under a dark shadow, so that the Supreme Astronomers could not recognize it.

From the north, the Sideresians. From the south, the Husihuilkes. And in between them, the House of the Stars, which could not see what was happening, because its gaze was turned inward on itself and the strangers shut up in the grey pyramid.

After the Doctrinator's three ships had left, the greater part of the Sideresian fleet continued on its way, intending to come to shore at different points on the coast to the north of Beleram. Their aim was to cut off the paths between one people and another so that they could not come to each other's aid. It would be a simple matter to overwhelm them, and then to fling their remains against the House of the Stars. 'Beleram buried under a mountain of dead bodies,' as Drimus liked to boast.

During the time the Doctrinator was being kept in the grey pyramid, Leogrós's fleet was reaching the coast.

The Husihuilke warriors had made a rapid advance and were almost halfway through the desert. From there on, things became more difficult. At night, attacks by the Pastors became increasingly frequent. The men of the desert raided without warning, then quickly retreated, protected by the contours of the wastelands they knew so well. The outcome of these brief skirmishes was not encouraging. Not simply because each nightly attack took its toll on the Husihuilke army, but because they slowed its advance.

And Beleram knew nothing of this! In the city and surrounding villages everyone went back to their daily tasks with reluctance, as if they realized that the strangers' arrival was not just of concern to the Astronomers but also affected their own small lives.

Zabralkán and Bor went daily to the grey pyramid, always accompanied by the other members of the Council. All except Molitzmós, who had been informed of the change of plans and remained on the shore guarding the ships. One, two, three days had passed since the arrival of the Sideresians in the city of Beleram. By now Drimus was on the point of fulfilling his mission: it was no coincidence he was Misáianes' chosen one. That night, for example, he was repeating to the Supreme Astronomers the same warnings the Northmen had given in that same city when the sun had been five hundred years younger. He repeated them word for word, without making a single mistake. All those who heard him were entranced, because the Wizard had the gift of enchantment.

The same night as Drimus was deceiving his audience by repeating the Northmen's words, a column of Sideresians was disembarking on the southern side of the Border Hills. Their ships moored in a cove where the jungle came down to the sea. Near by, the Offspring of the Stalkers of the Sea were sleeping peacefully under their palm-leaf roofs, in small family villages: Red of the Gourds, Red of the Fishermen, Small Red and, some way off, Distant Red. The descendants of the Northmen rested in jute hammocks whose swaying helped them dream of the sea. In their dreams, men, women and children were crossing the Yentru Sea back to the continent of the Fathers, and finally understanding where the colour of their eyes and hair came from. Lulled as they were by the high seas of their dreams, they did not hear the stealthy footsteps approaching their houses, or the gloved hands drawing back the flaps that served as doors to their huts. Small groups of Sideresians entered the palm huts, every single hut in every single village of the Offspring. Their glittering weapons slashed at the sleepers' dreams. Some managed to wake up before they died. Most preferred to go on dreaming that it was water from the Yentru that was soaking their tunics. At dawn, the hammocks were swaying with blue-eyed corpses.

Some hours later, the time it took the sunlight to move from the Yentru coast to the shores of the Lalafke, the Husihuilke army was preparing for another day's march. They had just thrown the body of a dead young warrior into the sea to save him from the desecration the Pastors would inflict on his remains. Kupuka sang the song that would accompany the young hero on his journey. Then they left him behind, because there were still many more nights to come in their desert crossing. And each would bring its harvest of death.

That same dawn, the one of the Offspring's last dream, the one of the young warrior being thrown into the sea, Zabralkán was observing an uneasy sky that changed each time he gazed at it. The Supreme Astronomer realized this situation could not last. Bor made little effort to hide his disagreement with the decision to keep the strangers away from the House of the Stars. Bor had no doubts: Drimus was a brother who had come in the name of other brothers.

None of the other representatives had opposed Zabralkán's decision. None of them, through what they either said or did not say, regretted the choice the Supreme Astronomer had made without consulting them. On the contrary, some seemed to rely on it. Despite this, Zabralkán was aware that the reclusion of the strangers was going on for too long, based on nothing more than his fears. What was wrong? Zabralkán could give no answer. Where did his spine-chilling dread come from? The strangers had arrived, and nothing terrible had happened. Why therefore was his soul so opposed to them? Zabralkán's thoughts had the feverish lucidity of someone who had not slept for nights.

The fact was that Zabralkán was the Supreme Astronomer of the House of the Stars. Even though Drimus wielded his centuries-old science in the service of Evil, Zabralkán felt a stabbing pain inside him that he could not and would not ignore.

The previous night, as always happened when he was in the presence of Drimus, Zabralkán's fears had evaporated. Even the stranger's appearance, which he recalled as that of a slimy little man with two overlong arms sticking out from his hunchback torso, changed when he was in the same room. On those occasions, Drimus's ugliness seemed to become legendary. He was not so much ugly as a weary scholar exhausted by his roaming through the Ages. Yet once Zabralkán was far from Drimus, his doubts assailed him once more. Whose voice was it foretelling death and desolation? It sounded like a remote echo reaching him from the depths of a cave. The Astronomer tried his utmost to understand what it was saying, but the echo was covered by the sounds of the world outside. What death did the voice mean? What desolation...? Through the window, the morning star found the Astronomer pacing up and down the observatory. 'Come to my aid, brother star,' Zabralkán implored him.

Far from there, the abandoned ports of the north were filled with noise. And the marks of unleashed hounds in search of food were soon to be seen on lands uninhabited for so many years. The fish-women, some of whom were passing close by on their way to Sad Island, concealed themselves behind a high promontory and saw what was going on. 'Let us swim south,' they said. 'We must tell the Astronomers what we have seen,' they said. 'We must tell everyone.' But an attack by carnivorous fish, unheard of in such cold waters, meant the fish-women could not reach their destination, and had to swim into deep waters, pursued by the predators.

A wind from the jungle, one of those moist, hot winds that herald wet evenings, decided to visit the Offspring's villages. It liked to see the redheads, who laughed when it blew in their faces, and came as often as it could. The wind was in a playful mood. It searched for tresses to undo and tunics to ruffle, but could not find any. The villages were deserted: there were no children threading seashells, or women cleaning fish. The wind pushed its way in through the flaps of the dwellings. Inside all it discovered were dead tresses and dead tunics stretched out on hammocks that barely stirred when it blew in. Horrified, the wind set off in the direction of Beleram with the sad news. But although it travelled in great haste, it never reached its destination. Before it could do so, another wind unknown in that region blocked its path and cut it to shreds.

In the other half of the continent, the Husihuilkes continued their advance, killing and dying each night. Whenever a dawn bird passed close by, Kupuka urged it to fly to Beleram with the news. Later he found out that none of them had arrived. Many people said they had seen lost birds flying round and round in circles, without finding a direction to head in.

As the morning sun turned red, Zabralkán was observing the city from on high. All at once, a movement caught his attention. Cucub was making his way across the platform carrying his friend the eagle. *He is going to bury her in the jungle*, thought the old man.

In those days, two armies were advancing through the Fertile Lands. They were destined to meet in Beleram, where they would fight the worst war ever known. From the north came the Sideresians. From the south, the Husihuilkes. And a Wizard from the Ancient Lands was casting a shadow over everything, so that the House of the Stars could not see what was happening. The fish-women could not bring the message, nor could the wind. Nor could the birds Kupuka sent.

From north and south. Drimus was readying them for the sacrifice. And Beleram knew nothing!

23

THE AWAKENING

'May your tiny eagle's soul join all the birds who no longer fly in this sky; and fly with them without ever tiring in the sky we living beings never see...' Cucub said this prayer as he buried his friend. Then he bowed deeply over her grave, and started back towards the House of the Stars.

He was about to leave the jungle without coming across anyone else, as was to be expected this early in the morning out here, when he heard footsteps coming along a path that crossed the one he was on. Cucub could have continued, thinking it was probably some early-rising hunter or a trader bringing his goods to market from a distant village. He could have done so, and yet he did not. Instead, he carefully hid so that he could see who it was without being seen. His caution was rewarded, because no sooner had he taken cover in the undergrowth than Illán-che-ñe appeared on the path. *What is he doing here?* the Zitzahay asked himself. It was very odd to see Illán-che-ñe heading out into the jungle, especially since he did not have permission from the Supreme Astronomers to leave the House of the Stars. *Perhaps I should find out where he is going and what he is doing,* thought Cucub.

The paths through the jungle were twisting and narrow, difficult to follow because they soon disappeared behind trees and undergrowth. Cucub soon lost sight of the Pastor. If he wanted to follow him, he would have to make up his mind quickly. It was not an easy task: the Zitzahay would have not to get too close, in case he gave himself away, nor stay too far off, in case he lost Illán-che-ñe at a crossroads or some turn in the path.

For the moment, the Pastor seemed content to stay on what was known as the Long Road, which Cucub knew by heart. This road in fact started in the centre of the city of Beleram. It began as a narrow but busy alleyway where stalls dedicated to selling leather goods were lined up. It went on and on, leaving the city as a bridge over a stream providing fresh water. The paving stones went as far as here; afterwards, it turned into a wide track of beaten earth. Shortly beyond, it split into two smaller paths. One of these turned west and reached as far as a range of mountains the Zitzahay called the Jaguar's Teeth. The other carried on northwards on the outskirts of the jungle. This fork in the Long Road linked Beleram with Red of the Gourds, the first Offspring village. From there it joined village after village until it ended up in Distant Red, the furthest of all the settlements of the Offspring of the Northmen. Shortly after the path divided, the northern one crossed a field of giant orchids. Then it bordered a lake of dark waters, where alligators and turtles lived. Beyond the lake, even though it was still on the edge of the jungle, the path became harder to follow.

This was the point where Cucub first saw Illán-che-ñe and began to follow him. When they had gone a little less than half the distance between Beleram and Red of the Gourds, the Pastor came to a halt. Without hesitation. Not like someone who has found a good place to rest, but someone who is taking up position.

Cucub did not move, his face pressed against the sharp smell of the bushes behind which he had quickly hidden to keep an eye on the Pastor. The little Zitzahay did not have much choice, because while Illán-che-ñe stayed where he was, he could not think of returning to Beleram. Not without the Pastor seeing him. The rest of the morning passed, and the sun moved across the centre of the sky. Cucub's limbs began to feel the strain of hiding without being able to move. The poor Zitzahay was starting to regret having followed the Pastor if it was only to witness what he was beginning to think was simply a harmless quirk of his race.

Cucub was still wondering about this when a new sound that had nothing to do with the jungle came to his ears. And, of course, to those of the Pastor. It was obviously not someone who was afraid of being heard. Someone who was running towards them. Or at least, trying to do so. A golden-haired youth suddenly appeared through the undergrowth. His eyes were fixed on the ground, trying to avoid any projecting roots, so that he almost collided with Illán-che-ñe. His first reaction when he saw the stranger was to run away, but the Pastor took him by the shoulders and tried to calm him.

'Be still... Tell me who you are.'

He was a young boy from the Offspring of the Stalkers of the Sea. By the look of him, he was exhausted from running, and terrified. His face was wild, his clothes torn. His sandals had been ripped almost to shreds, and his feet were so cut and raw they must have caused him terrible pain.

'I have to get to the House of the Stars,' the youngster managed to stammer, trying again to wriggle free from the Pastor's grasp.

'I am a friend of theirs... guarding this path on the orders of Zabralkán. If you don't tell me what news you are bringing, I cannot let you pass,' said Illán-che-ñe. 'Many strange people are roaming around the Fertile Lands. Most of them not from here, so we have to be on our guard.'

The flame-haired youth looked relieved.

'So you know then...' he murmured.

'Yes, we know,' replied the Pastor. 'But you know more. You have seen something, and must tell me. Then I will allow you to continue on your way.'

Cucub was expert at picking up whispers. Even so he found it hard to follow what they were saying, especially Illán-che-ñe, who had his back to him. The Zitzahay concentrated on trying to make out the faint, halting words of the Offspring boy:

'Some of us were sleeping on the beach last night. We have been doing this recently, waiting to see who it was that would arrive from the sea. I was on the shore with my younger brothers and sisters, but our parents were asleep in their hammocks,' said the youngster, his voice fading further and further as he remembered. Eventually he fell to his knees, so that Illán-che-ñe had to kneel down to keep hold of him. 'At first light we went back into the village because we knew they would be looking for us to start the day's work.'

The Offspring youth spoke slowly, delaying as long as possible the moment when he had to talk of death. But there was not much more he could say, and the look in his eyes showed he was now confronting the image of what he had found when he returned to the family hut. He described all he had seen in the only way possible: as if it had happened to someone else, a long time ago. As if he had dreamt it.

He told the story in the hope he would be told it was not true. But Illán-che-ñe could not tell him that.

'What happened to the rest of your people?' the Pastor asked instead. 'The ones saved from the death you speak of because they spent the night on the beach. Where are they?'

'People from all our villages got together and realized that the same thing had happened everywhere. When we saw none of the older generation had survived, the eldest among us took charge. No one knew what to do... the girls were shrieking in panic, we boys were afraid of another attack.'

Behind his bush, Cucub was trembling from head to foot like a dying young pigeon.

'Tell me this and I'll lead you to Zabralkán,' insisted the Pastor. 'Where are the rest of your people?'

'They stayed behind to bury our dead. Meanwhile someone had to go on ahead to warn the House of the Stars. I volunteered to do so. Everyone agreed, because I have been the fastest runner since I was a little boy. The rest of my people are following on behind; they must already be on their way.'

No one will ever know what the boy remembered next. Perhaps it was a day in his childhood when his parents were watching him run along the Yentru Sea coast. Perhaps it was a summer night... No one will ever know. Whatever it was, it drained the last of his strength, and he collapsed against Illán-che-ñe, sobbing.

Cucub began to think he should leave his hiding place. He was no longer bothered about Illán-che-ñe's strange behaviour, or what he was doing out here in the jungle. Cucub had heard enough to completely forget his distrust of the Pastor and understand that he should join him to work out what to do for the best.

The Zitzahay gave himself the time to take a deep breath before he emerged, still staring at the slumped figure and hearing his sobs. That was how he knew that what happened next took place in the space of a single breath. Illán-che-ñe seized a large rock from the ground and smashed it against the skull of the young boy slumped in his arms. The first blow was not enough; the second left the rock covered in blood. The remaining blows were the work of Misáianes, whose evil cruelty had reached the Fertile Lands long before his ships.

Never in his life had Cucub witnessed such ferocity. Sometimes he had seen the instinctive fierceness of the puma seeking the throat of its prey. But never anything like this. Recalling this moment many years later, Cucub still felt a lump in his throat and found it hard to draw breath. Years later, the tiny Zitzahay would go to his death without ever finding the words to describe the feeling that had paralysed him there in the jungle. Whenever someone asked about the event, all he could do was repeat what his greatest wish had been: *If only Dulkancellin were here, if only Dulkancellin were here.* Cucub was not a Husihuilke warrior. He was someone who knew how to sing; faced with a crime, he found he could not move.

Illán-che-ñe turned and peered into the undergrowth. It seemed he had noticed something... Cucub squeezed his eyes shut, willing himself not to see what was coming. He was convinced the Pastor had discovered him; but even though he knew he was about to die, he still could not move. The only thing Cucub wished at that moment was not to see the Pastor arrive carrying that rock, with that smile on his face. Simply not to see him. His arms wrapped round his head, he waited for the blow. But none came. Slowly opening his eyes, feeling a mixture of relief and shame, Cucub saw the Pastor was dragging the boy's dead body off the path. Illán-che-ñe disappeared, and for some time all Cucub could hear was him forcing his way through the undergrowth. A few moments later, the Pastor reappeared, wiping his hands on some wet leaves, which he dropped behind him. Then he set out back along the path to Beleram.

Cucub waited until he was sure he had gone before emerging from his hiding place.

A trail of blood made it easy for him to find the boy's body. He was lying on his back not far from the path. Cucub could hardly bear to look, frightened he might recognize him as one of the children who ran after him along the sandy streets and formed a ring round him whenever he took his songs to the Offspring's villages. When the Zitzahay tried to speak, a hoarse, unintelligible sound came from his lips:

'May your little white soul play in the sea you so loved...'

This was the second time in one day that he was saying goodbye to a dead loved one.

'And forgive me for not giving you a proper burial,' Cucub ended. 'There is no time. May Mother Neén protect your bones!'

Cucub finished his prayer and bowed his head in respect. Then, as if the dead boy had lent him his flying feet, the Zitzahay ran off far more swiftly than his short legs would usually allow. Sometimes he took short cuts he knew of, elsewhere he forced his way through the undergrowth, scratching and cutting hands and feet. He ran despairingly, the image of the crime he had just seen imprinted on his mind. Worse still, Cucub accused himself, it was a crime he had allowed to happen. He sped out of the jungle, and along the streets of Beleram. All those who saw him thought he must have gone mad, his face looked so wild and terrible.

Many years later, when he told the story, he assured his listeners he had no idea where he had found the strength needed to run as fast as he had, reach the House of the Stars, bound up the innumerable stairs, bang on the door with his fists and demand he be taken at once before the Supreme Astronomers. He had no idea. Nor did he care how he had done it. The Supreme Astronomers were not alone. Nakín of the Owl Clan, Elek and Dulkancellin were with them.

Cucub did not need to be very astute to see that something very serious was going on there too. Zabralkán looked exhausted from his concerns. All the others showed signs of torment. And these must have been hard to bear, because when Cucub appeared before them, they all fell silent.

'Tell us,' said Zabralkán. The Supreme Astronomer knew Cucub was somehow about to confirm all that he himself was afraid of, alerted by the voice of an ancient Wizard who had spoken to him in his deepest dreams.

Cucub felt he ought to address himself to Elek: after all, it was the villages of his people which had suffered the massacres.

Cucub used few words to tell him the news. Far fewer than he would have wished. By the time he finished, he was staring at the floor, and because of this could not see that the others were overcome with a similar sense of shame. Zabralkán finally understood what had been troubling him so much for the past few days; so did the others. Now Illán-che-ñe's absence was explained. Now Dulkancellin understood it had been Kupuka who had spoken in Zabralkán's dream. Now they understood about the cane-sugar honey, the death of the lukus, the constantly changing sky, the eagle's sacrifice. Now, when it was already too late.

'It is not too late for the Deer. The Deer will defend his blood and his territory,' said Zabralkán. And his will was unshakable.

Whenever over the course of the years Cucub was asked about that moment, he always spoke of five wills united as one to take decisions. He remembered and gave detailed descriptions of the orders dispatched in every direction, the plan for simultaneous, precise movements. But above all he liked to talk of a column of warriors which headed for the grey pyramid in search of the strangers. 'I was almost at the front, alongside Dulkancellin,' he used to boast. And he added that the Husihuilke had allowed him to go, to let him recover at least a little from his sense of guilt.

Even though the warriors were organized and set off as quickly as they could, they found the pyramid empty, strewn with dead guards. The only living beings they could discover were the animals the strangers had brought as gifts for the Supreme Astronomers, which they found tied up inside the walls. The men looked towards Dulkancellin, expecting him to order them to kill the beasts, but he had a different idea.

The strangers must have gone back to the coast, where their ships are, he told himself. Speaking out loud, he added: 'They are fleeing on the backs of their animals. We will never catch them unless we do the same. I will mount the one with patches. Whoever is willing can take the white animal. If the strangers can make these beasts gallop, we should be able to do the same. Anyone who has ridden a llamel should know where to start.'

Hearing this, Cucub quickly offered himself.

'Not you,' the Husihuilke replied.

Not all the Zitzahay had ever had the opportunity to see a llamel, much less ride one. Fortunately, several of the warriors present swore they had done so. In the end, after giving the necessary orders, Dulkancellin and one of his men galloped out towards the port.

They rode out, and a wind blew in. A dirty wind that darkened the night in the Remote Realm. Dulkancellin and his companion had to ride in the face of a gale that grew stronger and stronger as they neared the coast. This, together with the fact that the horses were nervous and they themselves only novice riders, slowed their journey. Even so, this was far better than to travel on foot, in such a gale.

Cucub told of these events often throughout his life afterwards, and he always ended by repeating the same sentence:

'I felt relieved when Dulkancellin decided that the animals with manes should stay alive. I had seen too much death for one day. And besides, as soon as I saw them I fell in love with those animals.'

Part Three

24

THE DEER AND THE FIRE

Dulkancellin pushed open the gate and entered the big fenced-in area. This rectangular corral, built in one of the side courtyards of the House of the Stars, was where they kept the two animals with manes already in their possession, as well as where they would put the others the Husihuilke warrior hoped to seize from the Sideresians.

His very first ride had made him realize the value of these animals. Convinced they would one day be indispensable, he set himself to learning about them and training them. The Husihuilke trusted them completely. The Zitzahay did not share his enthusiasm. Most of them feared or resented the animals the Sideresians had brought, and paid for this whenever they tried to mount them. Cucub was the only one of their people who did not share this attitude. For that reason, he was the only one who could come close to Dulkancellin's extraordinary skill in riding them. The animals patiently endured all the acrobatic manoeuvres to which he submitted their huge bodies. In return, they were given names:

'Greetings, Spirit of the Wind!' said Dulkancellin, to the white-coloured beast. The other one, which was his favourite, was walking round the far side of the enclosure. 'Greetings, Dusky One!'

'Greetings, brother Dulkancellin!' the voice of Cucub had replied.

The warrior looked all round, but could not see the little Zitzahay anywhere.

'Where are you?' he asked.

'Neither up nor down,' Cucub said.

'Will you never stop playing games?'

Dulkancellin was never one to be patient, so Cucub decided to quickly put an end to the puzzle.

'Here I am,' he said, appearing as if by magic on Dusky One's back. 'Now, watch this.'

As he talked, Cucub demonstrated to the Husihuilke that was he was saying was perfectly possible.

'I am mounted on this animal. You are quite close, and are looking at it. Yet you think the animal is on its own. But you're wrong... Dusky One is not advancing alone. I, a fierce warrior, am concealed on one of its flanks. And you over there, who are a Sideresian, do not realize it. Dusky One comes closer... unaware of the danger he poses, you are still not concerned. Then when we are within striking distance, I suddenly appear. I charge at you, giving you no time to react. Falling upon you and your strange weapons, I kill you three times over.' Cucub threw himself at Dulkancellin, pretending he had an axe in his hand. 'Once for the old luku, once for the fleet-footed young Offspring, and once for my friend the eagle—'

These memories made Cucub feel sad, and so he had no wish to continue with his game. Dulkancellin was able to push him off as if he were no more than a child.

'Do you think a man bigger than you could do the same?' he asked, interested in his companion's new trick.

'Yes,' replied the Zitzahay. 'Even you could do so, if we only find the way. Come on, let's try.'

The day Dulkancellin had mounted one of these animals with a mane for the first time, the same day that the strangers were called by their true name, was known as the Day of Shame.

When Magic woke from its lethargy and saw what was going on, it understood there was much sorrow that could not be remedied. The whole of the Fertile Lands was mourning its sons: green maize fields, trees as high as the sky, lukus from the southern isles, birds, men, rushing rivers, all had been equally beloved. But although it was late and much had been lost, Magic drew closer still to the Creatures. Together they undertook a resolute defence that sought to preserve the last heartbeats of Creation, even if they knew a world had been lost for ever, in the forever of every possible time.

That day the countless orders flying out of the observatory were carried out in a huge number of determined actions. There was much to try to remedy as Dulkancellin sped on Dusky One's back in pursuit of the Sideresians who had escaped from the grey pyramid. And when the warrior returned empty-handed, there was still more to do. On the heels of the messengers sent to the land of the Lords of the Sun, fresh runners were sent to tell them the latest news: it was no longer a case of attacking an unknown fleet by surprise; nor were they three brotherly ships which had come to share a triumph. Now it was an all-out war against Misáianes, a war that had begun very badly.

A column of men was sent out along the Long Road to meet the children of the Northmen, who must be close by. Two trackers were dispatched to find Illán-che-ñe. Many were set busy preparing water, food and medicine. A host of other tasks that had to be done left the surrounding villages deserted. The young men were recruited for battle, the older ones occupied workshops to sharpen weapons. The village women and children were given refuge in the city's many stone buildings. Beleram was crowded with people who still could not fully grasp what was going on. The same was true in the House of the Stars: everywhere apart from Zabralkán's observatory and a hidden room where the sacred books were kept was full of women and children, who took it upon themselves to carry out many of the preparations for battle.

'I'm glad we are all in Beleram,' Cucub was saying. The two men had closed the corral gate and were heading inside the walls of the House of the Stars. 'I'd be even happier if we could all be inside these walls. That way I feel nothing bad could happen to us.'

'You are speaking of yourself and your friends,' replied Dulkancellin. 'The people of the Ends of the Earth will be alone when the dark night arrives. Old Mother Kush and my children will be on their own.'

'Forgive me,' said Cucub. 'It's just that distance… the Sideresians are so close to us, and so far from the Husihuilkes.'

'Who knows? No one can be sure whether at this very moment the Sideresians are not entering our houses exactly as they did those of the Offspring.'

'But just think,' replied Cucub, trying to ease his friend's mind. 'In the Offspring's villages the Sideresians met with only a few gentle people, who were sleeping an untroubled sleep. Nothing like that could take place at the Ends of the Earth, where the most valiant warriors in all the Fertile Lands live. Warriors who always sleep with one eye open.'

'I, though, am wondering how those brave warriors could confront faceless death.' Dulkancellin was referring to the weapons the Sideresians had used against the men guarding the coast under Molitzmós's command. Weapons that had allowed Drimus and his companions to reach their ships safely and make good their escape.

'Tell me again what happened,' said Cucub.

'You know I was not there when it occurred. My ears heard the roar. My eyes only saw the results.'

'But Molitzmós gave you an exact description—'

'Haven't I done the same?' said Dulkancellin. 'Haven't I told you the story each time you asked?'

Cucub insisted he tell him again.

'One last time,' the Husihuilke accepted. He began: 'As I have already said, when we set off for the port—'

'Don't start by saying "As I have already said", because that detracts from the interest of the story,' said Cucub.

'Very well, Cucub. When we set off for the port in pursuit of the Sideresians—'

'I cannot forget that you set off with someone who was not Cucub… I wanted to go with you, but you forbade me.'

'Cucub, didn't you say you wanted to hear the whole story again?'

'I did and I still do. I won't interrupt you again.'

'Very well, Cucub. As I was saying, we left in pursuit of the Sideresians in the face of a gale that held us back the whole time. We could not keep our eyes open because of the stinging sand. But when we drew close to the port, we heard the explosions. Neither of us knew what had caused them. In fact, apart from hearing that they came from the harbour, we had no idea what was going on. It was then, as I told you, that our mounts escaped our control. I'm sure that was due to our anxiety rather than theirs. The fact is that they bucked and twisted so much they almost threw us off. It took a great effort to calm them and persuade them to carry on. Meanwhile, until we reached the coast, we heard nothing more apart from the howling wind. The delay meant we had no hope of catching the strangers, but we were still confident that Molitzmós would prevent them from reaching their ships.'

'You were mistaken,' said Cucub, stressing each word.

'We had no way of knowing then what was taking place in the harbour,' replied Dulkancellin.

'What state did you find Molitzmós's men in?' Cucub was deliberately speeding up the story to reach the part that interested him.

'What state…?' echoed Dulkancellin, then went on: 'I found them confused by what had just happened, and very frightened. Some were standing round their bleeding companions, without daring to touch them. They simply stood there, watching them die. You might have thought they considered them cursed—'

'Of course they thought they were cursed!' Cucub exclaimed. 'What else could they think of a death that comes from afar, in the midst of a huge roar and clouds of smoke? And the body that falls is wounded but there is no sign of any arrow.'

'That's right,' Dulkancellin admitted.

'What about the ships?'

'The three ships were heading out to sea. We had arrived too late. All we could do was watch them leave, taking our enemies with them.'

'And Molitzmós?'

'He behaved like a true leader. I saw him restore calm among his men.'

'The same as you had done shortly before with Dusky One.'

Dulkancellin knew that Cucub was expert in cloaking his most damaging insinuations in a show of innocence. And since this remark was obviously double-edged, he preferred to ignore it. But Cucub was not in the habit of giving up because of a silence, however much it seemed like disapproval. So he returned to the charge.

'I'm not asking what Molitzmós did, but what he told you about what had happened.'

Cucub was doing his utmost to delay their return to the House of the Stars, and to make sure the Husihuilke warrior stayed with him. This was because he realized only too well that once they were inside the House of the Stars, Dulkancellin would be far too busy to finish the story. Fortunately for him, the Husihuilke warrior himself came to a halt as soon as he began to recall the words used by Molitzmós to describe the flight of the Sideresians.

'Molitzmós told us that everything had been calm. Or so it seemed. The ships had not moved. There was no sign of life on them, apart from three black birds circling around, apparently hunting for fish. The first sign that all was not well was a wind that did not come from elsewhere. According to Molitzmós, it sprang up directly from the shore. He said:

"'The air began to twist between us and the coast, and a thin tower of air rose up like a column, growing bigger at every moment. Then we were all enveloped by a sandstorm. It was almost impossible to speak to each other or hear what was being said, and none of us could keep our eyes open if we looked towards the sea. In spite of this, we started to march towards the coast to prevent the strangers leaving their ships if they tried to do so. We struggled against the force of the wind. All at once there was a sound like the buzzing of bees, and the wind dropped. When the mound of sand it had lifted sank to the ground, we saw that the strangers had left the jetty and were spread out on the shore. We were still further from them than the bows of our best archers could reach, so I ordered my men on. Then something happened which we are still at a loss to explain... Brother Dulkancellin, the strangers' weapons can throw fire from a long way off, a fire that tears bodies apart. Three times in short succession they aimed those fires at us, and three times one of our warriors fell like a pigeon struck in mid-air. Fire, smoke, death... After the third time, I could not control their fear, and my men began to run away. Some riders appeared from the south, and the strangers welcomed them with battle-cries. The new arrivals responded in kind, raising themselves up on the backs of their mounts. They raced across the shore, and came to a sudden halt at the end of the jetty. It was only then that we could see there were two men on one of the animals. The four of them dismounted, and were immediately protected behind the other men's weapons. The last fires kept us at a distance while they all returned to the ships. The rest you know: the ships sailed off. By the time you arrived, all you found were laments and fear. Believe me, Dulkancellin, it all happened so quickly I have taken longer just telling it you.'"

The Husihuilke finished relating what Molitzmós had told him. Cucub, who had heard the same story several times, was amazed at the warrior's new-found ability. *Who would have thought that the Dulkancellin I met at the Ends of the Earth would be able to say so much, and to tell a story so well*, mused Cucub, although he was not entirely sure whether this was a good thing. Since the Husihuilke warrior did not seem to have noticed his amazement, he preferred to keep this observation to himself. Something told him Dulkancellin might not like to find out that he was acquiring Zitzahay habits!

'So there were four of them!' was what Cucub eventually said. 'Four men… I'm sure that, as you say, it was Illán-che-ñe who left with the Sideresians.'

'Everything points to that,' replied Dulkancellin, walking on again. 'Although Molitzmós said they could not recognize them because all four were wrapped in their cloaks.'

'Talking of Molitzmós,' said Cucub, coming to a halt once more. 'Wasn't it very fortunate that of all the fires directed their way, none was aimed at the warriors' commander?'

Dulkancellin finally understood where Cucub had been leading him. And since he believed that such doubts, in someone who had not been at the port and knew nothing of the weapons in question, could not mean more than an unreasoned dislike, he decided to bring their conversation to a close.

'Yes, it was indeed fortunate. Otherwise we would have lost a great leader,' said Dulkancellin, hastening to reach the House of the Stars.

Cucub watched him stride away.

'Oh, yes! A great, great leader…' he muttered under his breath.

*

In the days following the ships' escape, there was no further news of the Sideresians. No fish, swallows, jaguars, or owls could provide any information about them. It was as if the Yentru had swallowed them. Emboldened by this lack of information, some wanted to believe the Sideresians had been so frightened that they were now heading back across the sea to the Ancient Lands. Yet no one who properly understood what was going on, and was aware of the orders these strangers were obeying, as well as the vast strength of the Power that had sent them, could accept this version.

And so it proved. Before the moon had gone twice through its phases, the first reports came filtering back to the House of the Stars. Bad news, although it had nothing to do with the march of a large Sideresian army towards Beleram, as many of them could have wished. *Somebody to fight… An army facing our army… A war!* This was Dulkancellin's wish during nights when he could find no sleep.

The fact was that after his working tirelessly to prepare for the only war they knew, the war of mankind, these hidden attacks that his bow could not prevent left Dulkancellin frustrated. How could he fight against the evils threatening the Fertile Lands? Perhaps Kupuka could, and all the other Earth Wizards. Perhaps the Supreme Astronomers could. But warriors like him were powerless. The Husihuilke saw freshly sharpened spears and axes leaning against the stone wall, and longed for a war. *A war,* was what he wished for.

The moons waxed and waned… each day the House of the Stars heard of fresh tribulations and losses: that from Claw Canyon to the River Yum, to the west of the Central Mountains, huge tracts of forest were burning; that the children of the high villages were dying, their faces covered in blotches. And that at the opposite end of the Fertile Lands, the water from the Great Spring gave anyone drinking it terrible pains and black vomit. Despite the fact that Magic had recovered its light and summoned storms to put out the fires, as well as sending medicine and healing songs to steer the sick back towards life, a painful battle was being fought.

Yet in the Fertile Lands, which only a few moons before had been a plentiful, fragrant land, something far worse than the fires, sickness, poisoned water, or young born before their time was occurring. Voices reached the House of the Stars whispering of disloyalty. These voices said that many people were abandoning their houses and villages to go and join the Sideresians. 'They are powerful... they have been sent by an omnipotent Being and will bless all those who join their service,' those who left were heard to say. The Magic knew that to distinguish between Good and Evil could be as hard as telling two grains of sand apart. There were bound to be mistakes and confusion. A punishment of death was declared for anyone bowing down to Misáianes.

In the days that followed, some of the border guards reported seeing the Sideresians. None of them was completely certain about it. When questioned, they spoke of shadows in the undergrowth, or furtive movements along nameless trails.

The first real news of their enemy's position arrived at the House of the Stars one windy morning. A small band of Sideresians had been seen spending the night in the jungle, on a sandbank in the Red River With Feet Apart.

'At last!' said the Husihuilke warrior.

The meeting following this report took place in the observatory. Zabralkán and Bor were seated at opposite ends of the stone table. Crowding round them, filling the room, were a group of lesser Astronomers and the representatives at the Council. There were fewer of these now than there had once been. Apart from the old luku, who had never arrived, now Illán-che-ñe, who would never be forgiven, was missing, and so too was Nakín of the Owl Clan.

She had been given the difficult task of memorizing the sacred books sheet by sheet, word by word. To do so, she had to dedicate all her mind to it, without any distractions. Alongside her, the scribes were busy making copies of them on sheets of soft leather. As soon as these were finished, they were taken out of the House of the Stars. The copies were sent to different, almost inaccessible places in the Fertile Lands, in the hope that if everything else were lost, someone living in another Age might rescue them.

These sacred books contained ancient explanations about all that had been created and had taken place. At this time of war against Misáianes, Magic had to protect them in whatever way it could. It did not matter how many warriors they put to guard them, every one of them could be killed. Every wall could be knocked down, every chest be broken into. That is why they scattered the sacred books all over the continent, and hid them where no one would think of looking. For instance, in the memory of a fragile young woman.

Nakín of the Owl Clan spent her days and most of her nights shut up in the secret room, reading the sacred texts by oil lamp. She only rarely came out, and then only for a moment. This was when her eyes and body, tired of giving warning signs, gave out completely. Whenever this happened, Nakín was oblivious to what people were doing or saying around her. Even then she was incessantly repeating to herself the texts she should never forget.

'It's our turn to be invisible now,' said Dulkancellin, who was seated next to Molitzmós.

'I can imagine what you are referring to,' said Elek.

Hatred had done its work on the fair-haired man's body. In a short space of time Elek had become so thin he looked ill. His plump body and pleasant manner had vanished. His eyes were like the ashen sea, only lighting up when he talked of killing.

'I think we can all imagine what Dulkancellin is trying to tell us,' said

Molitzmós. 'And if as I believe we are all agreed, then we must take action at once.'

The talk in the Astronomers' observatory was of ambush and surprise. They would attack the Sideresians whenever they halted. Only a few warriors in each attack: swift, silent, protected by the jungle they knew so well. They would fall on the Sideresians without giving them time to seize their weapons: cut them down, wield their axes, chop off the creeping fingers of Misáianes. Get hold of their weapons and animals. Then disappear.

Everyone there except for Molitzmós agreed it should be Dulkancellin who led the first attack.

'I would have liked to do it,' said Molitzmós. 'In order to restore my honour after what happened in the port.'

'Allow me to say,' Zabralkán burst out, 'what the best way to restore your honour will be. Molitzmós of the Sun, that will be when I see you pleased that the best person is chosen to lead each task.'

'So be it,' said the haughty lord, clenching his teeth.

The afternoon had scarcely begun, but everything was decided. Dulkancellin had chosen twenty-nine men to go with him. Elek of the Offspring was one of them.

News of their departure spread through the passageways of the House of the Stars. A crowd of people, especially women and children, gathered on the platform outside to see the warriors off.

Dulkancellin gazed at a little girl peeping out from behind her mother, and thought of Wilkilén. An old woman sitting in the traditional manner reminded him of Old Mother Kush. Kuy-Kuyen was evoked by another girl with long tresses.

The women came up to the men and one by one went along stroking their faces. This was the custom whenever a man left his village. It meant: *Remember, there is a reason for you to return.*

Dulkancellin caught sight of Nakín standing at the back apart from the others, and raised his arm in greeting. A weak smile flitted across her pale, lifeless features. What prophecies could be going through her mind at that very moment...?

But Dulkancellin was looking for somebody else. To find him, he left his column of men and pushed his way through the crowd, who fell back before him. *Why is Cucub never where he ought to be?* he wondered.

'Were you looking for me?' asked Cucub, tapping him on the shoulder.

'I was,' the warrior admitted.

Taking Cucub by the arm, he led him to one side, where they could not be overheard.

'Tell me.'

'I want to ask you something,' said Dulkancellin. 'I want you to give me your word about something.'

Cucub waited for him to explain.

'You are my brother here in this land that is foreign to me,' Dulkancellin began. 'And my brother everywhere else as well. I want to know once and for all that if I should die without being able to return to the Ends of the Earth, you will do so on my behalf. You will go back to my village, to my home. And you will leave some of my blood in the land that I love.'

Cucub found he had to choke back tears.

'You have Cucub's word. I would have to be dead not once but twice to fail you.'

The Supreme Astronomers were making their way down to the platform. Dulkancellin left Cucub and went back to his post. Zabralkán had come down from the observatory to speak to them before they departed. The old man spoke slowly, and so softly the silence had to grow around them.

'The Fertile Lands are sending you out... do not count each other and think that is the number of spears you bear. You are not thirty warriors.

235

You are the Deer and the strength of Creation is with you. We know that the Sideresians have brought unknown weapons with them. But our Magic tells you that these weapons kill some with their fire, but many more with fear. Do not let that happen! The Deer is going to fight for the Deer! Bring back the first victory!'

When Zabralkán had finished his harangue, the women shouted promises for all the warriors who returned: mallow liquor, succulent dishes, leather sandals, and love-making in the hammocks in the jungle's cool shade.

Dulkancellin sought out Cucub to make sure he would keep his promise, but the Zitzahay was no longer there. Not there, or anywhere visible. *He will not forget it*, the Husihuilke warrior told himself.

The plan was to attack the Sideresians under cover of darkness on the river sandbank, if they were still there, or wherever they made camp on the following nights. The Creatures who had spotted them and were keeping a close watch on them, would inform Dulkancellin of where they had moved to. Since the sandbanks of the Red River With Feet Apart were five suns' march away, and since the Sideresians could slip still further into the jungle, the warriors had to leave in haste.

The warriors saluted the Supreme Astronomers. The thirty of them, a chant of honour ringing in their ears, descended the great staircase.

From a window high in the House of the Stars, a scowling man watched them march away until they vanished into the distance.

Five nights later, the Fertile Lands won their first victory. The Sideresians camped by the Red River were surprised by an attack which flew through the air, leapt on them, and destroyed them. From that first battle on, Dulkancellin's companions began to talk of his bravery. They, and many more in times to come, swore they had never seen anyone fight the way he did. 'Dulkancellin goes into battle as if death did not exist,' some said. 'As though he were already dead,' said others.

Very soon, the Sideresians themselves were talking of a fierce warrior with painted face and long hair... And when they succeeded in cutting off a piece of his tunic to give to the black dogs to smell his scent, they began to call him 'the prey'.

But in the attack at Red River, the Husihuilke and his twenty-nine warriors emerged unscathed. None of the Sideresians was left alive. Those who tried to escape into the jungle were pursued by the Deer, who wielded his axe once more. Because the Deer knew that by the end of the war against Eternal Hatred, there would be the living and the dead. No prisoners, or truces, or mercy. Shortly after the combat, the all-seeing sun rose on the first of Misáianes' dead in the Fertile Lands.

As soon as they had recovered from their hunger and exhaustion, Dulkancellin sent four men back to the House of the Stars. These men left with the good news and with the animals with manes that were taken from the Sideresians. Dulkancellin had no wish to keep them, because he did not think they would be useful for this kind of combat. The only weapons they recovered were the long, sharp blades with which the Sideresians had tried to defend themselves. Elek of the Offspring asked to have one of them. When the others saw the way he handled it, they realized that such skill must come from distant ancestors who had used them in the Ancient Lands.

Dulkancellin decided they should stay in the jungle, waiting for some messenger to come to the river looking for the Sideresians. He could not then imagine there were many more battles to be fought near by.

After this Red River ambush, there were more and more reports of Sideresian forces. They were always few in number, spread out in the jungle. But however difficult the path they followed, the Creatures saw them, smelt them; they crawled, flew, and ran to tell Dulkancellin. He and his warriors were constantly on the move, seeking out the camps of the Sideresians. And whenever they came across them, they vanquished them.

More men arrived from Beleram to help cover a constantly growing area. The warriors organized themselves in small bands which in those days became known as Goads. The Deer set out to defend the uncertain possibility of staying alive with such immense courage that he flew through the air. And it was at this time that someone made up a song about Dulkancellin's bravery, which spread from mouth to mouth.

Yet as the days went by, and despite their courage, the victories became fewer and more hard-fought.

The Sideresians regrouped and began to return the blows. The Deer could no longer count on surprise in attack. The weapons that killed with fire were waiting for them, and the hungry dogs foaming at the mouth.

The Deer knew that this was only the start of the war, that the Sideresians were no more than the claws of Misáianes' outstretched hands. The master of the Sideresians wanted to take possession of every last corner of Creation. And even if the Fertile Lands defended themselves with every last bit of their strength, was there any hope against the Ferocious One?

On their side, the Fertile Lands had the magic from the south, which roamed the mountains in the shape of an old, old man. And the magic of the Open Air, which was at one with the sky. On his side, Misáianes could count on a legion of ancient wizards who had become cruel within the solitude of their walls. What each side said was very similar. And the war had only just begun.

The bands known as the Goads kept in contact with one another the whole time, and with Beleram. They knew where each other was, and they all received aid from the House of the Stars. In that way they could make up their losses and share their victories.

The first weapons and animals seized as booty were sent back to Beleram. Soon, however, the Deer understood the need to keep fixed strongholds in the jungle. He chose convenient places and sent all that was won in the battles out to them. One of these strongholds was set up on the banks of the Red River, close to where the first attack had taken place. The other was hidden beyond the rocky outcrops which a little further to the east, in the centre of the territory, became the range of mountains known as the Jaguar's Teeth. Both places served to store provisions, to supply care for the wounded, and reinforcements in men and weapons. This was where all the information was received, and the next steps decided on.

As the days went by, skirmishes with the Sideresians became less and less frequent, until they almost completely stopped. The latest news reaching the strongholds was either wrong or out of date; in the end this only exhausted the warriors in useless manoeuvres.

'They must have built their fortress somewhere in the Fertile Lands,' said Dulkancellin in a meeting with his men. 'That must be where the commanders are, those who know Misáianes' plans... and where can they protect the powder they use for their weapons? Their main force cannot be these small handfuls of men we come across. There must be a place where their power is concentrated, and it cannot be far from here.'

It was night again, and nothing was happening. In their strongholds, the warriors of the Fertile Lands slept uneasily. This calm filled with fears and suspicions was not to their liking: they preferred to fight.

Dulkancellin approached one of the sentries, seeking the company of another man who was awake. Seated on the same fallen trunk, he silently helped him keep watch in the night. *At first light, I must talk with the others,* thought the Husihuilke. *We cannot linger here if the Sideresians have already left. Who knows? Perhaps we are exactly where they want us to be.*

His thoughts were answered shortly before the night's end. The Supreme Astronomers sent out a call that Dulkancellin was the first to hear. The messenger, who had covered the distance between the House of the Stars and their camp in as short a time as possible, told him, still panting for breath:

239

'The Supreme Astronomers send word... They say that everyone is to return at once to the House of the Stars. Everyone except for those chosen to stay behind and defend the strongholds. The Astronomers say to make haste, great haste. That is all.'

This order did no more than confirm what all of them thought should be done, and it was followed enthusiastically. The men who were to stay in the jungle were chosen, as were their leaders and runners. All the others set off again.

Four long days to return. As the fifth day was dawning, Elek and Dulkan-cellin entered the observatory. They were encouraged by Zabralkán's mood: even Bor seemed less gloomy than usual. Molitzmós, who was also present, rose to greet them as they crossed the threshold.

'Greetings, brother warrior!' he said, embracing Dulkancellin. 'Many have wished to talk of your courage, but could not find the words to do it justice. We know that you alone vanquished as many enemies as ten of our best warriors could have done.'

Dulkancellin was unable to receive praise without bridling. And he blamed his unease at the way the Lord of the Sun had received him on this weakness of his.

'We fought with good results for as long as we could,' he said, hoping to silence Molitzmós with this brief answer.

'You will soon be fighting again,' said Zabralkán. 'And this time it will be a great battle.'

'What do you mean?' asked Elek.

'I mean that the Sideresians have their main fortress in the Border Hills. And that it is there that they are gathering their troops to march against us in a few days' time.'

This news from the Supreme Astronomer was no reason for him to appear so optimistic. But he had not finished.

'You explain the rest, brother Bor,' said Zabralkán.

Bor was pleased to be given the opportunity to tell them the good news.

'We have learnt with all certainty that two armies are coming to our aid. From the south, and already very close to us, are the Husihuilkes. They are led by someone we believe must be that Kupuka of whom Dulkancellin has so often spoken. There is still more. There can be no doubt our emissaries reached the land of the Lords of the Sun because from there – take heart, Molitzmós! – a powerful force is heading our way.'

Elek could see that this was the first Molitzmós had heard of this development. Not because of Bor's reference to him, but because of the stab of surprise that left the Lord of the Sun looking aghast. Dulkancellin however was already caught up in his own emotions, and so did not see the change.

'Thank you,' was all the Husihuilke was heard to say. And nobody knew who this was aimed at.

25

THE PLUMED ONE

The hoops made Molitzmós's ears seem elongated. The feathered cape sweeping the ground when he walked made him look enormous. Or at least that was how the Zitzahay children saw him: like an enormous brightly coloured bird standing by the side of the pond.

Molitzmós had his eyes half closed to stare straight at the sun. The light that evening created a space of its own around the pond: a space Molitzmós's eyes filled with people he knew, words that had already been spoken, and far-off events.

The blood that the Lord of the Sun saw pouring from the edges of the sun came from old wounds. His father and twelve of his brothers had died to win power for his House throughout the empire. He had been very young then, but still could see in his mind's eye the worst battle between the two Houses always disputing the legitimate right to the throne.

The day his grandfather was on his deathbed, he demanded to see Molitzmós. When he was near, he went over the boy's duties one last time. Molitzmós remembered how the list had begun: 'We have educated you for high command.' By then he was the only suitable heir, chosen above brothers and sisters who were too young – some of them sickly, one an idiot – and a threatening group of disloyal cousins. He had been taught the arts of alliances and betrayals. Now he had to make sure his House occupied its rightful place as ruler of the vast territory of the Lords of the Sun. His grandfather already smelt of death. Molitzmós swore him an oath he had never forgotten. Then he had to bide his time, growing up and learning that there was only one way to seize the throne: by spilling the blood of others.

The colours of the sunset stained the air a deep red round the pond. When the children hiding behind a sculpted rock saw this, they thought that nightfall would soon mean they could not spy on Molitzmós any longer. He, though, knew this was not the sunset, but the blood needed to win victory.

'I swore as much to the father of my father. And the truth is I have not yet fulfilled that oath to place our House higher than all the rest.' Molitzmós saw himself saying these words to the man from the Ancient Lands. He reflected how hard it was to know how long ago this was. Neither a long nor a short time. A gulf.

After that conversation, events had rushed onwards like the water in a river waterfall. Molitzmós, who once knew where everything began and where it was destined to end, was no longer so sure. Someone from the Ancient Lands came to speak to him of Misáianes. In his name, he offered a pact between the powerful. 'So that the House of Molitzmós shall always rule over the Lords of the Sun. And the Lords of the Sun over the Fertile Lands.' Molitzmós accepted, thinking this was the way to fulfil his promise to his grandfather. Misáianes' offer came when he had almost lost hope of being able to do so: it even offered him the chance to climb still higher. 'The Lords of the Sun can be lords of the Fertile Lands': that was even more than what his grandfather had asked. The pact had appeared so obvious that Molitzmós could not understand why a misty cloud seemed to be obscuring the centre of the light enveloping the pond.

He was keeping his side of the bargain. And if it had not been for the little Zitzahay, who always popped up where he was not wanted, the results would have been even better. He had not failed in anything, even in the secret successes. Thanks to his work blowing and blowing on the coals of arrogance, Bor was dreaming of a past of Enclosures that distanced him from Zabralkán and the rest of the Creatures.

Misáianes had wanted a crack in the Magic of the Fertile Lands... and now he had it! Molitzmós had succeeded in forcing one open, and making it bleed. The children saw the crack in the sky and thought it was the start of night.

'I have done all they asked of me.' From some part of the dying light, the Sideresian nodded in agreement. 'I deceived the reigning House with false rumours and provocations. I put many of my allies in danger with an untimely revolt. I did all this so that you could take advantage of the confusion and install yourselves in our lands. I hid the truth, confused the weak, protected the flight of your ships...' Molitzmós shouted at the light hovering over the pond. 'And in return... what has your master done? Very little. I hardly receive any messages from him any more. Should I not know what his plans are if, as he said, we are equal partners in our agreement?' The light heard Molitzmós out, then smiled from afar. This happened just as a crescent moon appeared in the sky.

Yet Molitzmós understood what he seemed not to know, and had his own answers. The Lord of the Sun never believed that Misáianes considered him his equal in power. He knew the ambitions of the Ferocious One, and because of that was glad to be his eyes and his arms in the Fertile Lands. Misáianes' most loyal subjects would be princes in the realm of vanquished Creation. And he would be one of them...

The light over the pond was fading, but Molitzmós could still see a space filled with the presence of memories.

He himself was there, expressing his disbelief at the first promise the

245

Sideresian had made him. 'Tell me, who can possibly think that the Magic of the Fertile Lands will choose me, precisely me, to go to their Great Council? Rest assured, I will not be the one who goes as the representative of our people, but someone from the reigning House. However much the Supreme Astronomers say they are impartial, I know they consider our fight for the throne to be illegitimate and cruel.' The Sideresian heard him out, and smiled. 'Molitzmós, just wait... simply wait. You'll see that one day soon a messenger will come to your door to take you to Beleram.' On that occasion, Misáianes had kept his word. As he had when he promised that Illán-che-ñe would be his servant, with no will of his own.

Many years earlier, the struggle for the throne had led the Lords of the Sun to battle. Still only a child, Molitzmós had seen his House defeated. Whenever one of his brothers did not return, his father's wives gathered to mourn the dead warrior. Molitzmós recalled their tears. When his father was stabbed in the back, everyone suspected each other. He could remember all the whispers and bewilderment. The shameful gifts that the victors offered to buy off their former enemies: Molitzmós remembered that too. But above all else, he recalled his grandfather's ire at their unworthy surrender. After this there was a period of apparent calm, when many of his House, especially those who could not disguise their hatred, had to endure all kinds of humiliation and suffering.

All this time, Molitzmós's grandfather was busy organizing revenge. Silently and deliberately, knowing he would not live to see it, he brought up the most worthy of his grandsons for future glory. In Molitzmós, their House would once again have a leader who would return it to its deserved place. His remaining span was barely enough for him to carry out the task he had set himself. That was why, on his deathbed, he called Molitzmós to him and made him swear to devote all his soul to the conquest of the throne which had been theirs in days gone by. Molitzmós loved his grandfather, and the oath he swore to him then became everything that gave his life meaning.

Despite this, the years went by without his being able to complete his mission. The reigning House was powerful. It acted astutely, and kept a watchful eye on everything.

Molitzmós's hopes rose when the Sideresian arrived: he was aware of the power of the One who had sent him. And the more he learnt about Misáianes, the more he was convinced of his inevitable victory. The Fertile Lands would cease to exist. And if Misáianes became the absolute ruler of the Fertile Lands, better by far to stay in his shadow. Molitzmós did not care what rule Misáianes intended for this world. What was the point of lamenting something that could not be avoided? It might be seen as the end of free will for the Creatures. It might be seen as the ruin of Creation, or a world subservient to the wishes of the Ferocious One. Molitzmós dreamt that this world, whatever it might be, would have a place for him and his House. The war would end one day. The Sideresians would return to the Ancient Lands, and he would be left here, with the title of Lord of Lords. What did it matter to him if he had a master on the far side of the ocean? Molitzmós would survive. And with him, his House, part of his people, their treasures and their cities. The rest was inevitable.

The light had gone from the sky. Everything was in darkness. The servants of the House of the Stars were lighting the oil in their lamps, and the trail of light they left behind showed Molitzmós they were heading towards him. There were many such servants, which meant they would soon reach him. The Lord of the Sun wanted to make use of these last moments of darkness to convince himself there was not the slightest room for doubt.

None of Misáianes' subjects could turn back. Besides, what good would that do? More than ever, Molitzmós had to make sure he carried out his orders properly, not forgetting that he was on the side of those who would finally triumph. It was not for him to get caught up in the fighting, however much he gave the House of the Stars the impression he was keen to do so. His energy must be aimed elsewhere. Misáianes' finger pointed him towards his goal: the bonds between Magic and the Creatures of the Fertile Lands. This was where his Master's greatest efforts were directed, because this brotherhood was his greatest obstacle. Molitzmós closed his eyes. When he opened them again, his resolve was renewed.

Before he left the pond, he repeated a vow. 'I swear from the shadows...' The children saw a cloud pass in front of the moon.

26

THE BLOOD OF THE DEER

✤

Dulkancellin was riding Dusky One. Cucub was on Spirit of the Wind. The two men were heading to meet the Husihuilke warriors approaching Beleram. Dulkancellin was galloping as fast as he could to cover the distance between him and his brothers. Behind him, Cucub tried as best as he could to keep up.

Dusky One suddenly pulled up on the top of a small rise. This time it was because his rider meant him to.

'There they are!' cried Dulkancellin, pointing to the road in front of them. He waited for Cucub to come alongside, then they both galloped down as fast as they could.

The place where they met was not far outside Beleram. The road the Husihuilkes were travelling on was not the narrow, hidden path that Dulkancellin and Cucub had taken the day they came to the city. The southern warriors were marching along one of the busiest roads in all Beleram. Broad cultivated fields ran along either side, separating it from the jungle. The morning was ripe with the joy of their re-encounter.

Dusky One and Spirit of the Wind plunged down the hill. Below, in the midst of abundant maize fields, Kupuka ordered the warriors to halt until he could make out what this strange mixture of men and animals coming towards them might be.

'It's my father, it's my father,' repeated Thungür next to him.

'Yes, it is your father,' said the Earth Wizard with a smile.

The Husihuilkes were filthy. They were weary. And hungry. Yet if necessary they would have been ready to face any enemy.

'We won't have to do so for now,' said Kupuka, turning to his men. 'Brothers, it is Dulkancellin who is coming. And with him is a good man.'

The Husihuilkes had lost many warriors in their skirmishes with the Pastors. Some of them were wounded, and all without exception were exhausted. In spite of this, beneath the dust and their weariness, anyone could see they were real warriors. *Perhaps now it will be possible*, thought Dulkancellin.

Thungür leapt forward to meet him. Dulkancellin dismounted and stood waiting for him. His son was no longer the boy who ran with the oriole's feather in his hand and, frightened by the forest's prediction, had asked not to be left alone. When had the change occurred? Dulkancellin did not think of the time that had elapsed, but of all that had happened, and so was not surprised to see standing in front of him a man as tall as he was, a man who grasped his arm in greeting. Yet if he blinked, it was the same person as the boy he had left. Dulkancellin greeted his son, then stepped forward a few paces to salute the warriors. The new arrivals returned his greetings in the beloved language he had not heard for so long. These were Husihuilkes. Husihuilke men in whom Dulkancellin began to recognize himself once more.

'Greetings, old man,' he said, embracing Kupuka.

The Earth Wizard looked like an apparition. He looked older than old, with his long white hair tied up and covered in dust, his nails like a mountain goat's. So animal-like, so wise, that Cucub could not help anticipating with pleasure the ridiculous expression on the Plumed One's face when he finally met him.

'Greetings, old man,' he said.

While the Zitzahay was having his fun, Dulkancellin gazed on well-known faces once more. He found neighbours and cousins; men he had fought with, and men he had fought against. There they were, from every village and clan. And there was one young man, his side covered in healing herbs. Dulkancellin did not know what to do, or even how to look at him. Who knows? Possibly it would have been enough for Kume to say some words of greeting to his father. Who knows? Perhaps his father was refusing to acknowledge him again. The fact is that the youth remained where he was, and Dulkancellin looked away.

This was a day of shocks for the father. And soon Dulkancellin experienced the greatest shock of all. Beyond the last line of warriors, Kuy-Kuyen was waiting patiently for him to discover her.

'Why did you bring Kuy-Kuyen?' Dulkancellin could not believe his eyes. 'Explain to me, old man. Why did you bring her?'

'I'll do so as soon as we set off again,' Kupuka replied. 'Reason has many facets; and these men cannot wait while you see and understand them all.'

The warriors were fascinated by Dusky One and Spirit of the Wind.

'We call them animals with manes,' said Cucub. All at once, seeing he had an audience once more, he began to raise his voice and explain the whys and wherefores of these remarkable beasts. Explanations which threatened to become endless. Fortunately, Kuy-Kuyen chose that moment to greet him.

'Greetings, Zitzahay man.'

'Greetings, Husihuilke woman.'

Cucub was doubly pleased to see her.

'I am pleased to see those eyes of yours again. And also to find someone else my own size here.'

Immediately the order was given to renew their march. Dulkancellin mounted Dusky One and asked Kupuka to climb up too.

'I'll take you with me. On the way you can show me all the facets of your reasoning,' he said. Then, turning to Cucub, he told him: 'You take Kuy-Kuyen with you.'

Hearing this, his daughter shook her head and shrank back.

'Don't be afraid,' said Cucub, holding out his hand. 'Tell him your name and you'll be friends.'

Dusky One led the way, at walking pace. Dulkancellin constantly looked round to talk to Kupuka.

'Tell me about Old Mother Kush.'

'She will even now be kneading her bread.'

'Tell me about Wilkilén.'

'She has hardly grown. But her hair is long down her back.'

'And Piukemán... Why did you not bring him?'

This time there was a long silence.

'Someone had to look after Kush and Wilkilén,' Kupuka said hesitantly. 'He'll be able to do that.'

There were many things Dulkancellin wanted to ask. And in particular one thing he did not understand at all.

'What reason could you possibly have for bringing Kuy-Kuyen to this threatened land?'

'One thing at a time,' replied Kupuka. 'There are two things you have to remember before you grow angry: first, there is as much danger at the Ends of the Earth as there is here. And secondly, Kuy-Kuyen is here now.'

What Cucub had imagined with such amusement paled in comparison to the effect Kupuka's entrance to the observatory actually created. The Earth Wizard came in still wearing the rags that had accompanied him throughout his journey. And he clung on to the wooden staff that he refused to give up, even inside the House of the Stars. Probably everyone present, including Zabralkán, was taken aback by Kupuka's wild appearance. But, as Cucub had anticipated, it was Molitzmós's reaction that was by far the most extreme. The look on his face was less one of welcome than of disgust.

Yet the reason for the meeting was not Kupuka's appearance, and this was quickly forgotten as the important matters were discussed.

These were nothing less than the spinning of a slender thread of strategy. The Deer knew his only chance in the war against Misáianes was to strengthen his hold in every possible way. Men would organize and lead the men. Magic controlled the other forces in the Fertile Lands; and in the sky they could look into the mirror where the future could be discerned. Zabralkán's concern would be for the alignment of the stars and auspicious dates. Kupuka's head was to be filled with hordes of peccaries, swarms of wasps, and poisons.

The army of men was growing stronger. The arrival of the Husihuilkes, together with the division of the Lords of the Sun advancing from the north behind the lines of the Sideresians, made them far more numerous and skilful. The Deer weighed their strength, and dreamt of victory.

The following days were ones of much hard work. And if the House of the Stars had already become crowded with people, so now too was the whole of Beleram.

The pond at the centre of the House of the Stars became the meeting place for all those seeking rest. And also for those who in the midst of the preparations for war had found a chance to become friends.

Kuy-Kuyen and Cucub were among those who met at the pond every day as dusk fell.

Kupuka and Zabralkán were another pair. The Supreme Astronomer acquired the habit of leaving the observatory to visit the area surrounding the House of the Stars. Against a time-honoured tradition, he went around without an escort. 'We need as many people as possible to carry out more important tasks...' was his answer to anyone who objected. Despite this, he never asked Bor to do without his escort. Never once. Even though he knew that if he lifted his head from the edge of the pond where he was walking on Kupuka's arm, he would be sure to see Bor's disapproving face at one of the observatory windows.

Kume and Molitzmós also met by the pond every day. Always with stern faces, and far from the others. A strange friendship indeed, and one typical of those days of turmoil.

When the moment came to march off to war, these friends went in different directions, according to the role destiny had allotted them.

Zabralkán remained in the House of the Stars. Kupuka disappeared on his own with his bag into the jungle.

Kuy-Kuyen stayed to work with the Zitzahay women. Cucub rode to the north-east, following orders from Dulkancellin.

Molitzmós left with the army, in command of a company of spear-bearers. Kume was sent with the troops heading north-west.

At dawn on the day of departure Cucub was the only one in tears. Kuy-Kuyen, accustomed to the harshness of the Husihuilke warriors, was pleased to discover that men too could water their faces with sadness.

The men Dulkancellin had sent out to reconnoitre came back with news that a party of Sideresians had advanced a long way from the Border Hills and were camped on the far side of the Red River.

'We have seen them with our own eyes. And we are pleased to say that our own forces are far greater in number.'

'Where exactly are they camped?' asked Dulkancellin.

'They are resting in the Between the Feet Valley.'

They were talking about a low extension of land at the estuary of the Red River With Feet Apart. One channel of the Red River ran through the south side of the valley; the other flowed to the north. The Deer already knew the place where the battle would be fought. He knew that on this occasion he would have more warriors than the enemy. Now he had to make sure that the Sideresians' advantages – their weapons and their animals – were reduced, and if possible turned against them.

That night the warriors of the Fertile Lands began their march. They headed towards the coast, looking for the mouth of the Red River, to the east of the site of their first battle against the Sideresians. The Deer had the virtue of being able to advance without a sound. Nobody apart from the creatures of the jungle could hear him.

The front line of the army was reserved for the Husihuilkes, something less than half of those who had come to the Remote Realm. Most of the remainder were sent with the troops heading north-west. The rest, together with a large number of Zitzahay, were guarding the House of the Stars. The warriors were armed with bows and arrows. With clubs and axes.

Next to them, in similar strength, were the spearmen. These were the most valiant of the Zitzahay, and were led by Molitzmós, second in command to Dulkancellin.

Behind them, and protecting the flanks, were the rest of the Zitzahay army. In the rearguard came the people from the villages. Some of them were too young, others too old for the main army. Most of them were coming to war after a gentle life producing their goods and taking them to market, smoking their leaves, and dancing for their dead and the newborn. Yet afterwards it was said and sung that they fought with the bravery of true warriors, and so went down in history. Cucub was one of them, his job more that of helping out where he could than of fighting.

The Deer had chosen to split its forces into two prongs, so that they could cover more of the land and discover and disrupt any attempt by the Sideresians to attack Beleram. Then on a day and at a place already decided, their two divisions would unite again.

The north-eastern division, commanded by Dulkancellin, came to a halt at the edge of the jungle. From there, hidden among the roots, high in the branches of the trees, or concealed behind trunks, they could keep watch on the Red River without anyone suspecting their presence.

The wheel of the day had turned. The storm which had been gathering on the horizon at sunset risked hiding the moon. The heavy clouds seemed to be pulled in opposite directions. One which wanted to offer the Deer the good fortune of light. The other which wanted to deny it. This struggle lasted for some time. The clouds paled when they drifted away, but swept back, black and gold-edged, to encircle the moon. Finally, deep into the night, the friendly side won its battle in the sky, and the storm abated.

On the far bank, the bonfires the Sideresians had lit showed the silhouettes of their guards, and their animals' uneasy movements. Surprise was the Deer's best chance. To preserve it, all the warriors breathed softly, and Dulkancellin told Cucub to keep the few animals they had with them as quiet as possible.

At first light, the Sideresians began to move out as the Deer had expected. They were going to cross the river: first the mounted men, behind them the foot soldiers. The warriors from the Fertile Lands also took up their final positions. The jungle breeze came to their aid, mixing light and shade so much that the enemy could not see any of their movements. Protected by all the arms of Mother Neén, the Deer waited. The Sideresian riders had almost finished wading the river. The men on foot had more difficulty because the water pushed against their thighs, and because they had to keep their weapons dry. The first riders were already reaching dry land. But the Deer was still waiting for most of the enemy to be in the water.

When that moment came, Dulkancellin straightened up on Dusky One. He drew back his bow and aimed at an enemy soldier, the one he had chosen for his first arrow. Dulkancellin had been in this position many times before in the Border Hills. Like all warriors, he knew that the man chosen to be the first victim was without a face, nothing more than a blur, because the person firing the arrow had no wish to remember him. But now Dulkancellin did want to recall the face of the man who, if he were not killed, could crush the heart of Wilkilén the very next day.

Dusky One felt his rider's fury, and added its roar to the Husihuilke chief's cry announcing the start of the battle. The cry was taken up by all the warriors as the first volley of arrows sped from the jungle. To the Sideresians it seemed as though the trees themselves were shooting at them. With poisoned or flaming tips, the southern warriors' arrows found their mark. So many men were killed, and their mounts were thrown into such panic, that the remaining cavalry tried desperately to pull back, colliding with the oncoming foot soldiers.

Taking advantage of the confusion and chaos, the spearmen rushed out of their positions in the jungle. Some threw their lances, but most wielded them directly against their foe. The Sideresians also had to face many clubs and axes, all the pain the Deer could inflict. Although many of them tried to use their weapons against the warriors from the Fertile Lands, the battle soon turned into a rout.

The outcome was to be seen by the bodies in the river. The current piled up corpses on its journey to the sea. Beasts, men and hacked-off limbs floated out to the Yentru. The Red River should have been named after this day, and not before.

The good news of the victory spread quickly through the jungle. When she heard, Kuy-Kuyen buried her little face in her hands and murmured her own words of thanks. Zabralkán called the people of Beleram to the great courtyard of the House of the Stars; Kupuka's explosion of joy echoed round the jaguar's cave where he was carrying out his own tasks. All over the Remote Realm, everyone celebrated the victory. On the battlefield, the warriors buried their dead, and recovered the animals and weapons they had won. Then they turned their faces to the sun and sang. As long as the sun was in the sky, they sang and sang. They became hoarse, and yet none of them let up in their singing.

The men in the other division heading north-west heard the news while they were advancing without encountering any Sideresians. At first, they shouted and acclaimed the good news, but soon each of them fell silent. They felt the shame of the warrior who has not fought in battle: as if they were to blame for the direction their enemy had taken. That night, as they ate roasted wild boar, they chewed on their frustration.

'Eat a little,' said Thungür, offering Kume a piece of the meat. He took it reluctantly, inspecting it slowly in front of his face.

'We will soon have to renew our march,' said Thungür, 'and who knows when we will be able to stop and eat again.'

Kume began to nibble at the sweet-tasting meat. His elder brother had never mentioned the Kukul feather. He never asked how he had let things get that far, or shown any interest in finding out how he had done it. Kume was grateful for his lack of insistence, and so perhaps in return never once rebelled against the authority his father had delegated to Thungür. This did not mean that Kume had changed his sullen manner. On the contrary, he buried himself ever deeper in it, and never opened himself to anyone.

'I don't think we have celebrated our brothers' victory properly,' Thungür went on. 'But our disappointment should help us to fight even more bravely when it is our turn to do so.'

Just like his mother, Thungür had the knack of finding flowers in the midst of a thorn bush.

'Do you know who I am thinking of?' he went on. 'Of Cucub. I'm trying to imagine him in battle.'

Kume had finished eating. He drove his knife into the ground and licked off some grease that had stuck to his forearm.

'Terrified. Hiding between someone's legs,' he replied. 'I can assure you, that's what he was like.'

Thungür had the strength and the harmonious features of his race. As well as these, Kume had his mother Shampalwe's beauty.

'Do you know exactly what became of Kupuka?' he asked.

The Husihuilkes were accustomed to thinking in a straightforward manner. Kume's thoughts were always more devious.

'How can anyone know exactly what the Wizard's movements are?' said Thungür with a smile. 'He must be somewhere in this jungle, conspiring with his friends.'

Kume pulled the knife out of the ground and handed it back to his brother. Then he walked away.

The Deer could not afford to spend long celebrating the victory, because he had to continue on northwards as quickly as possible. The advance was inexorable, but more cautious with each passing day. A strong network of communications protected his army and kept it unified. The two divisions had to stay in contact as often as they could, but there was much more to do as well. They had to keep one eye on what was going on behind them, to know what was happening in Beleram and to send word to the coast of the Yentru to hear the news from the fish-women. Someone had to try to reach Kupuka. And above all, they had to get beyond the Sideresian lines to reach the Lords of the Sun. This was the path taken by the silent jaguars, slipping back and forth with a message of feathers round their necks that only their allies could understand.

The two divisions reached the appointed meeting place with half a day's difference. From where they met, the Border Hills were clearly visible. The hills were a landmark between the Remote Realm and the land of the Lords of the Sun. They were gentle and easy to climb. Anyone who had done so remembered them as a pleasant spot. And so they were

– or had been. Because as dusk fell that night, the warriors looked at the hillsides rising to the sky like someone at the mouth of a lair, wary of the animal inside lashing out.

The plan was for them to stay there until they could establish the next and final contact with the Lords of the Sun. The last jaguar carrying its message of feathers. After that, the two armies would fight alongside each other on the battlefield, when Hoh-Quiú's men would surprise the Sideresians by attacking on another front.

Hoh-Quiú, one of the princes of the ruling House in the land of the Lords of the Sun, commanded a large army. Although the Lords of the Sun had received only fragmentary and confused information, they had understood they needed to throw as much of their power as possible into this war, and had done so.

'Molitzmós, tell us about Hoh-Quiú,' Dulkancellin said. 'He is your prince, so you must know a lot about him. This will help us understand each other on the battlefield.'

'As you say, he is a prince. Yet I have never seen him.' Molitzmós remembered perfectly well seeing Hoh-Quiú's face daubed with the blood from the heart of one of his own brothers, executed because he had not shown sufficient reverence towards the then tiny prince. 'All I can say is that he must be very young still, and because of this I am amazed he is commanding the army.'

'That must mean he is very valiant,' said Dulkancellin.

Molitzmós of the Sun did not want to give any answer, for fear that his voice would betray his hatred.

'Let's hope the jaguar does not take too long,' was all he murmured.

His wish was fulfilled. That night, escorted by the two guards who had seen him arrive, the jaguar entered the tent where a group of warriors were talking to Dulkancellin. Elek and Molitzmós were among them. Thungür and even Cucub were there too, the little Zitzahay staying close to his Husihuilke friends and stoically putting up with the Lord of the Sun's patent hostility. The jaguar's arrival had set the camp agog. The men gathered outside the tent, anxious to know what the animal's message contained. Shortly afterwards, the warriors inside appeared. Dulkancellin raised the feathered collar aloft so that they all could see it.

'Our brother jaguar has brought us the news we were waiting for,' he said. 'And it is as good as the light of the sun.'

The men responded with a shout of triumph. The groups had not been together for long, but despite this, the differences that at first had been hard to overcome had eased to such an extent that they all seemed part of one family. The Offspring with flame-coloured hair, the dark-skinned Zitzahay who looked so small next to the Husihuilkes, the warriors and the artisans. Something about their situation brought them all together.

'The army of the Lords of the Sun is close by,' said Dulkancellin. 'It should not take more than a day and a night for them to meet up with us. And that will be before the Sideresians arrive.'

Although Dulkancellin was talking to all his men, he could not take his eyes off those of Kume. His son returned his gaze, with no flicker of acknowledgement.

'It is true that the Sideresians are drawing near, and are doing so rapidly. Even so, we have time enough. We must make sure that tonight we rest. Eat and sing, because soon we will have to face a war which, whatever its outcome, will divide Time.'

Once the warriors had dispersed, Dulkancellin called Cucub over and asked him to feed the jaguar.

'Let him get some rest too. He will be heading off again at first light to take the reply that Hoh-Quiú is expecting.'

Together, Dulkancellin and Molitzmós strung the feathers onto the collar, their length and colours conveying precise information for the Lords of the Sun about where and when the battle was to be fought.

The new day dawned. The jaguar, which had seemed to wish to sleep for ever, suddenly leapt to its feet when the Husihuilke warrior approached. As always, he was on his own. And as always, he knelt in front of him and put his arms round the animal's neck to fit the code of feathers. The jaguar knew the man, and waited calmly for him to secure the collar.

'You can go now, brother,' said Dulkancellin as he tied the final knot. 'Run as fast as you can to your destination. This is our only hope that you and we will still have an earth we can inhabit together.'

The jaguar began to lope away. But it had hardly left the camp when another man halted it with a whistle he had taught it to recognize. The jaguar knew this man too. His smell was always together with the smell of the other one. This one also called him brother as he undid his feathered collar and slipped another one in its place.

'Now you can go,' he told the animal.

As if the jaguar had taken it with him on his rapid journey, the day raced past. 'The jaguar must already be with the Lords of the Sun,' some of those in the camp said. 'Not yet,' replied others. 'Hoh-Quiú and his men must have begun their march.' 'Not yet...' When two days had gone by since the jaguar left, even the least optimistic were expecting Hoh-Quiú to arrive at any moment. 'He'll send out an advance party...' 'He'll come in person...'

'I suppose you can hardly wait to see your prince.' Cucub had already noticed that those words 'your prince' had a terrible effect on Molitzmós, and so never missed an opportunity to say them.

The dislike the two men had for each other was well known, and put down to their different temperaments. Previous clashes between Cucub and Molitzmós had stayed within the bounds of a strained politeness that fooled nobody, but made their hatred more tolerable. This time, however, things were different. Molitzmós wheeled round on Cucub, grasped him by his tunic and lifted him off the ground. The Plumed One's expression

262

suggested he was the possessor of a terrible secret, which could destroy his adversary were he to let it slip.

'I could tell you…' Molitzmós hesitated. But Cucub had seen the venom flash on the tip of his tongue, and decided to continue to provoke the arrogant lord to get him to reveal the truths he was hiding.

'Dulkancellin is my leader as well as yours, and he will not be pleased by your treatment of me.'

Cucub was afraid. Looking deep into the Lord of the Sun's eyes, he could tell that Molitzmós might kill him if he baited him any further. Yet *just a little more and his arrogance will make him spill all he is hiding from his mouth*, he told himself.

At that very moment, however, cries of alarm came from the far side of the camp. Molitzmós let the Zitzahay go and ran towards the commotion. Cucub scurried after him, convinced Hoh-Quiú had at last been sighted. When the two men reached the others, they stood paralysed at what seemed like something from a nightmare.

The jaguar had returned, and was surrounded by a circle of horrified men. Round its neck was not a feathered collar, but a bundle tied in a bloodstained leather bag. Dulkancellin stepped forward and untied it from the animal's neck. As soon as the jaguar felt itself freed from the disgusting weight, it sped off into the jungle. Everyone in the circle knew the leather bag contained a human head. At first, Dulkancellin was dreading only one thing: to find that it was Kupuka's. That was the last thing he wanted. His hands struggled to undo the tight knots, but finally they yielded. Everyone could see it was the severed head of someone who had without doubt been one of the highest Lords of the Sun.

'Tell us, Molitzmós, do you know this man?' asked Dulkancellin.

'He is not young enough to be Hoh-Quiú,' Molitzmós replied. 'All I can say is that his ear-hoops show he was one of the nobles in the ruling House.'

Whoever he might have been, the message was clear. The army of the Lords of the Sun had been attacked by the Sideresians. Attacked and destroyed. It was a terrible blow for the warriors of the Fertile Lands. What would happen now? Where were their enemies?

Blow upon blow rained on the heart of the Deer: at that moment guards from the north appeared. They were pale with fear.

'They've appeared on the hillsides. The Sideresians have appeared; they will soon be upon us.'

All the men stared at Dulkancellin, waiting for his reply. For a moment, the Husihuilke felt brutally alone. In his mind's eye, he saw the forest at the Ends of the Earth. He saw Old Mother Kush and her life-restoring bread. Then, more than ever the leader of his warriors, he gave the first order.

The battle was drawing near, and it was not the one they had planned. It was going to be different, and would be fought before the auspicious day announced by the stars. And the Lords of the Sun would not be with them. From Kupuka there had come nothing but an inexplicable silence. The Deer no longer had surprise on his side. Nor did he have the jungle's protection. The battle would be fought on the open lower slopes of the Border Hills. The number and valour of their warriors seemed to be the only advantage the Fertile Lands had. The number, their valour, and the support of Magic. 'And the strength of the earth, which will not abandon us on a day such as this,' said the men.

By the time the Sideresians appeared on the horizon, the Deer had regained his courage and was ready to face them. The enemy was a black banner unfurling down the slopes. The Deer set out to fight with the colours of fire, of the sky and of the earth painted on his face and battledress.

The army of the Fertile Lands would fight in the same formation as before, this time divided on two fronts. But now they also had cavalry. Like Dulkancellin, the other Husihuilke warriors had immediately taken to the animals with manes. With Cucub's help, they had learnt to ride skilfully and artfully.

As the Sideresians advanced, so did Misáianes and the great power contained in his name. The heart of the Deer was consumed with a single thought: his enemy's true name. 'The Time we knew and loved has gone for ever. We are not here to shed tears over it, but to fight for the Time to come,' Dulkancellin told his men before the battle.

The armies were ready, each drawn up on either side of the land. The battle was about to begin, and the world fell silent. The winds withdrew to a distant sky; the sea pulled back its waves; the jungle sought refuge in its nests; mothers hushed the infants at their breasts.

'Those of us who die in this war will be remembered for ever as the mountain of bones which held up the sun. For the Sun! For the Father!' cried Dulkancellin. His last words were drowned out by the first volley of shots.

The warriors of the Fertile Lands were hit by another unknown weapon, which spat more fire and roared even louder than the ones the Sideresians had used in the port the day that Drimus had escaped from Beleram. The fire fell on them like a rock from an exploding volcano. As they saw their companions torn open by this incomprehensible force, they had to choose. And they chose anger.

But for every Sideresian who fell, many more on the side of the Deer were slain. Long before they could close on their enemy, the warriors died as the fire struck them. Many archers did not succeed in loosing off a second arrow. Even though those they had launched hit their targets, and the Sideresians also began to lose men, their fire slowed the advance of the Fertile Lands. The Deer knew that the distance between them and the Sideresians was their worst handicap, and that as soon as they managed to cross it and come face to face with the enemy, their bravery would prevail.

But it was difficult to move forward over their own dead. A volcano explosion aimed at their west flank took with it many men who had been potters, weavers and beekeepers. Their blood now stained the earth. Another explosion, then another. It was even harder trampling on their own dead when they were beekeepers, potters, and weavers. The Sideresians' surprise weapons were destroying the Deer.

In spite of everything, the army of the Fertile Lands kept going forward. The Husihuilke cavalry succeeded in reaching the Sideresians on their mounts: at last the Deer was where he wanted to be. The distance between the two armies was reduced to the length of a sword or spear, or a blow from a club or the edge of a stone. Or to nothing, which meant another death. Fighting with a fury that made them seem ten times more than they actually were, the warriors of the south scattered death among the Sideresians. So much so that for a moment the Sideresians were overcome by panic. Dulkancellin killed with every blow of his axe, until he and Dusky One were covered with blood. Three of his warriors remained close by him, to protect his flanks and his back, because death was seeking out the Husihuilke chief from all sides.

Elek of the Offspring was fighting in memory of his massacred people with the weapon he had won at the Red River. From his position, Thungür saw the Sideresian arrive who was to bring death to his pumpkin-haired brother. But Thungür was unable to go to his aid: all he could do was shout his name. Elek was one of those who died that day, desperately defending themselves. Unable to avoid it, Kume rode over his prone body.

The Deer's best warriors had been decimated. Although the great explosions were no use to the Sideresians any more, it seemed as if they had landed the fatal blow. Dulkancellin was bleeding from a wound just below the heart. He knew everything would soon be over for him, and clung to Dusky One's mane for one last effort. He raised his face to the sun to say goodbye.

Cucub was also saying his farewells: he could see the Deer was losing the battle. The Zitzahay was still at the post Dulkancellin had allotted him, behind the rearguard with a few others. Hidden in the undergrowth, it was their task to receive the wounded and help the warriors who came back in search of replacements for weapons or shields they had lost on the battlefield. When he was told of his role, Cucub had felt split in two. Cucub the little village musician was relieved. Cucub the man in love with Kuy-Kuyen felt ashamed.

It was this second Cucub who was keen to join the fray. He was amazed to find himself thinking this way, but his mind was almost made up. There were several others who could do what he was doing. Besides, no wounded were arriving now. At first, many warriors had come to them, but most had bound up their wounds and returned to the combat. The others had died. Molitzmós, who was among the first to be wounded, was in neither position. The Lord of the Sun had a deep wound in his side, and looked like someone whose life was about to end.

Cucub stared at him, unable to rid himself of the unpleasant feeling that if he stayed where he was, he was behaving like the wounded lord. Finding this idea unbearable, he finally resolved to join the battle. There was a pile of spears and arrows all round him. But, true to his nature, Cucub chose something different.

'I'll take your knife,' he said to Molitzmós. 'It's a noble weapon that deserves its opportunity.'

The Lord of the Sun either could not or did not know how to reply.

'That's odd,' said Cucub, raising the blade to his nostrils, 'the blood on this smells like your own.'

Kuy-Kuyen's beloved took the knife and ran out to join the fighting. This would be the first time he killed a man, or the last time he died. He could never clearly recall what thoughts were going through his mind as he ran forward. What he did remember was that he suddenly came across the enemy for whom the stars had destined him. It was Illán-che-ñe.

267

As soon as he recognized the Pastor, Cucub felt an ancient, absolute duty that made him invincible. The Pastor stepped forward, brushing his weapon against his thigh and pressing Cucub back. When he was close, he launched himself at the Zitzahay, but the little man was no longer there. Time and again, Illán-che-ñe's dagger plunged into nothing but air. This trickery had its effect: Illán-che-ñe was so caught up in it that he forgot his enemy. The Pastor only realized his mistake when a stone knife ripped open his stomach. Cucub pulled it out and stared at him. The Zitzahay was neither trembling nor triumphant. He lifted his gaze to find his next adversary, but saw that something had changed in the battle.

The Sideresians were retreating, wheeling round as if to face a new threat. Cucub did not immediately realize why a shout of victory went up from the Deer, rose to the top of the hillsides, and returned a hundred-fold. He could not see that from the west the Lords of the Sun had arrived, giving the Sideresians no time to turn their big, heavy weapons on them. The division of the Lords of the Sun was greatly reduced: they had lost more than half their men in an ambush. Despite this, the winds of war were changing.

After the initial surprise, the Sideresians managed to regroup. Firing from the backs of their animals, they succeeded in restoring the balance. By now it was growing dark. Soon night and exhaustion would end the battle for that day. Possibly both armies wished the same, because neither had the strength to go on. But in a last effort, the Sideresians let loose their black dogs...

As if vomited straight from Misáianes' mouth, the pack of hounds surged through the ranks. A hundred slavering jaws. Sniffing at the air, they launched themselves at the warriors of the Fertile Lands. They hurtled along, looking for one man in particular. Their sense of smell led them to their most sought-after prey... Dulkancellin saw them milling around him, snapping at Dusky One's feet. The animal resisted as best it could. Wounded and exhausted, the Husihuilke defended his mount as best he could. But in the end, they were both toppled. Before Dulkancellin could get to his feet, they were upon him. He fought for his life, the hot, foul-smelling dogs swarming all over him.

This would have been his last day on earth, his moment of departure… It would have been, had it not been for Thungür, Cucub and the other warriors who rushed to defend him. They managed to rescue him from the dogs' fangs, mauled but still alive. Dulkancellin had been given a few more steps to take in this world.

Night fell. Both armies needed rest: neither was able to continue, or to pursue their enemy. They were like two wounded animals withdrawing to their lairs to lick their wounds. When they returned to the fight, one of them had to die.

That night, the healing hands of Magic could be felt in the medicines that repaired wounds and relieved pain that otherwise no man could have borne.

'Go and get some rest, Thungür, I'll look after him,' said Cucub.

It might have been Dulkancellin's face under the purple swellings, but when Cucub removed the leaves that had soothed his fevers, he found it hard to recognize him.

'Brother,' he told him, 'the sun often talks to musicians. Today it spoke to me and said…'

The Husihuilke opened his eyes and tried to speak.

'Sleep,' said Cucub, cooling his brow. 'Sleep in peace. I have not forgotten my promise.'

These must have been the words that Dulkancellin was hoping to hear, because at once he fell into a deep sleep. He dreamt of his wedding dance with Shampalwe.

The night went by too quickly for all those who would have needed ten calm nights of sound sleep. First light brought the men to the bonfires where they could find food. While they ate, they named the dead and identified the living. Many, probably most of them, were wounded. Despite this, very few refused to haul themselves to their feet to face a second day's fighting.

Less affected because they had come late to the battle, the Lords of the Sun's troops had camped apart from the others, and spent the night in silence. They lit no fires and prepared no food. There was nothing to indicate that a small army was resting there, until the first light of dawn, when they joined the main force. Hoh-Quiú came up to Dulkancellin, greeting him respectfully.

'We know of each other thanks to the jaguars... And, if I had not seen you fight, I might still have thought that the betrayal was your work.'

Dulkancellin struggled to understand what the young prince was trying to say to him. The words slipped away from him, and he had to search deep in his fevered mind to find them again.

'Betrayal?'

'The last jaguar led us into an ambush. And if we were not all caught in it, that was thanks to an old man who suddenly appeared to warn us of the danger before the trap finally closed on us. The old man was sweaty and covered in mud. After telling us exactly where the battle was to be fought, he disappeared again.'

'The old man is called Kupuka,' murmured Dulkancellin.

'He did not say his name. All I can tell you is that it is thanks to him that we are here.'

The Husihuilke felt some strength returning, and was gradually able to see things more clearly.

'Apparently there is much to try to understand,' he said.

'If we are fortunate, we can do that tomorrow. Today we have to end a battle that will not be easy.'

The prince spoke as if he were an old man too.

'One of your people by the name of Molitzmós should as befits his rank be here with us. But he cannot do so: as I understand it, he is gravely wounded.'

'And aren't you?' asked Hoh-Quiú, as tenderly as of a son.

The prince of the Lords of the Sun had said the battle would be no easy matter. For a second day they would have to cross a battlefield facing the enemy fire. The Sideresians would by now have turned all their weapons to face them. And the warriors of the Fertile Lands were wounded and weary.

Dulkancellin allowed the prince to speak the final words to the warriors.

'We are here to face whatever happens. Because when there is no more hope, there is honour.'

The sadness of the Sun, who would see its children die. The pain of the Earth, who would receive them before their time. The Father and the Mother saw themselves in them.

It happened as expected; the same as on the previous day. The first cannon roar… the first volcano explosion against the advancing warriors of the Fertile Lands, struggling to reach the Sideresian lines. The second roar… The second volcano explosion, and torn bodies littered the hillside. The third volley took longer, giving them time to close on their enemy. The fourth explosion never occurred.

A furious charge engulfed the Sideresian line. The flocks of the jungle, led by a gigantic old man, flung themselves on the Sideresians and their fire. Hundreds of animals that made the earth quake and transformed the air into wind, and the wind into dust: clouds of horseflies and wasps, enormous birds, wild pigs, pumas and jaguars… all of whom Kupuka drove on with his incantations.

Caught unawares by this jungle horde, the Sideresians abandoned their front line and ran to seek protection.

Misáianes' greatest fear had come true. The Ferocious One, who was also well aware of his weak points, had made it his first order: '*Keep Magic away from the Creatures. Make them forget each other, so that they cannot recognize one another.*'

The Earth Wizard's army possessed the only force that Misáianes feared. Rising from the deepest part of Creation, it swept away the arrogance of the Sideresians' cannon to give the Deer the chance to cross the battlefield. That was enough. The rest was a matter of courage.

Still the combat continued, and still the dead piled up. But by the end of that morning, after a battle worthy of being sung about, the warriors of the Fertile Lands could contemplate victory. Or what was left of them. The few still alive, next to the mountain of dead. That which could not bring laughter, or love, or merry drinking, was a victory. Merely the first in a war whose beginning was lost in the mists of time. As was its end!

The Sideresians withdrew from the battlefield, abandoning most of their weapons. Among those who succeeded in escaping was the one who without a doubt was their commander. Dulkancellin had seen him wrapped in a black cloak. The Sideresian general watched the battle from the top of a hill, mounted on an animal harnessed with gold. He looked down on it all, motionless and distant, as if the result of that morning's combat were of no interest to him. Or as if convinced that this defeat would be short-lived. When Dulkancellin tried to find him, he and his golden animal had vanished. Nor had anyone he spoke to seen Drimus enter the battle.

'He must have been sent with some other purpose,' said Dulkancellin.

'He probably stayed in the fortress where the remains of his army have taken him the bad news.'

'The fortress,' said Dulkancellin. 'Where exactly can it be?'

'I know where it is,' said Kupuka. 'Less than a day's march towards the coast.'

But even though Kupuka knew where the fortress lay and could lead them there, it was unthinkable for them to set out at once. The men needed to rest. Some of them could not go, even after resting.

The wounds they had endured so bravely while fighting now returned once they had completed their task. Many who would never have surrendered to the Sideresians now fell to gangrene. Kupuka's medicine was their best hope. The Earth Wizard made Cucub his assistant, and tried his best to save those who could be saved, or to make death easier for those destined to die.

Dulkancellin himself tried to show a strength he no longer had. The dog bites were raw swollen lumps. His mouth was cracked, his saliva thick. His fever-racked body was weakening all the time.

Molitzmós was weakening too. Kupuka could not understand it.

'Look at this man, Cucub. His life signs are threatened. He is growing pale and can hardly speak, and yet his wound does not seem so bad.'

Molitzmós lay senseless, his skin icy. A feeble breathing was all that made him different from a dead man.

'He will recover,' said Cucub. 'You'll see, I'm not wrong.'

Kupuka thought the same.

Dulkancellin and Hoh-Quiú were giving fresh orders when Thungür came up to his father.

'I need to talk to you about Kume,' he whispered in his ear.

'Speak out loud. This lord here has the right to know.'

'Very well,' said Thungür, ashamed. 'Kume is not here. Neither among the living nor the dead.'

As ever where Kume was concerned, Dulkancellin's pain was greater than he expected. Death in battle brought honour and gave those left behind a sense of pride. But what did this disappearance mean? Kume's behaviour had been at fault ever since Cucub had arrived. Now he had disappeared, and Dulkancellin could not forget that a betrayal had been foretold. Kupuka understood what the father was thinking.

'Don't be too hasty,' he murmured.

Some time later, Dulkancellin was sitting drowsily in the shade. Hard at work, Cucub nevertheless paid close attention to his breathing.

'Come here.' Dulkancellin called him over without opening his eyes.

With one bound, Cucub was beside his friend.

'What do you need?'

'I need to tell you I know how you fought.'

Cucub's smile was so radiant Dulkancellin could see it with his eyes closed. But Cucub was never one to leave things as they were. Loose-tongued, extravagant in manner, with little sense of judgement, he took a deep breath and said in a rush:

'Brother, it is true I am a minstrel and not a warrior; Zitzahay and not Husihuilke; small even among the smallest. And yet despite all this, I wish to wed Kuy-Kuyen.'

27

THE SON

He was whining with a shrill whimper that stopped when he took a breath, then immediately started up again. Tears were dripping from the tip of his nose, and his hump-back was shaking with his sobs. Drimus the Doctrinator was weeping for the dogs that had died in battle, stroking with his constantly moist hands the animals who had survived and were now sprawled out on the sand floor.

'My little ones! He has not abandoned us. He has not failed. He sent us here knowing full well the one great risk. We were the ones who made mistakes, and are now paying for them with our tears. But I promise you, this grief will soon be a distant memory.'

A black cap covered his skull, framing his face as Drimus rubbed it against his dogs' bellies. Picking one of them up, he cradled it in his arms.

'They succeeded in doing what our Misáianes was afraid of. They must now be thinking they have halted the expansion of his Mandate.' The Doctrinator's words came from his mouth with the tone and rhythm of a mother crooning to a little baby. 'But you and I, my little ones, you and I know that is not the case. The Master is intact; his plans have merely been delayed. The scraps from these lands remain, and we can eat our fill of them.'

Leogrós had come up to the Doctrinator without his noticing it. He listened to him muttering for a while, then cleared his throat to show he was there. The two men blamed each other for what had happened, and so stared defiantly at one another. Leogrós was rock-like, refusing to reveal what was going on inside him. However great the anger or scorn he felt, or however harsh the words he was about to utter, neither his attitude nor his voice betrayed any of it.

'We were expecting more of them,' he said, pointing to the dogs.

'Oh, Leogrós, Leogrós!' Drimus said with a sigh.

The position in which Leogrós had surprised him was hardly worthy of his lofty role, so the Doctrinator left the dog on the floor, and made to stand up. Even though he saw a gloved hand held out to help, he preferred to ignore it and scramble up on his own.

'Oh, Leogrós, Leogrós!' he kept repeating as he went over to a water barrel.

He served himself some, and drank it in noisy gulps that were visible down the front of his gullet. Leogrós was always disgusted at the sight of the white, pastry-like skin there. By the time he had finished drinking, Drimus had managed to contain his agitation and was as calm as his companion.

'Oh, Leogrós...! We were all expecting more from everyone.' He ran his tongue over his lips, feigning resignation. 'He expected much more of us. He honoured us with the mission of being his hands. And look how we rewarded him, Leogrós! Will we be able to return to him without the victory with which he entrusted us? Tell me: what will become of us if his will is not behind us?'

As usual, Drimus felt so much self-pity as he spoke that the tears started to flow once more.

'I just heard you telling your pups: all that is left in this land is scraps. If you know that, why so many tears? This battle has used up all their reserves. I'm surprised at you, Drimus. I thought you were capable of enjoying it when hares believed they were wild beasts, when you are in fact that wild animal licking its paws.'

Drimus passed from tears to laughter, without any great change to his features. How not to trust in the Master and the power of the Enclosed Brotherhood? If that wandering magician and his herd of pigs, that band of disloyal wizards who had chosen to distance themselves from Wisdom – if they were the best the Fertile Lands had to set against them, then there was nothing to fear. Let Leogrós put his faith in his arsenal of powder and weapons! Let him believe, for now, that his war was the one that would bring victory. The poor wretch would see soon enough that nothing would have been possible without the efforts of the Enclosed Wizards. When everything was in its proper place, then he would become aware of his true destiny. For the moment, better to let him finish off the already dead.

Misáianes worked on his chosen ones in such a way that they all believed they were his favourites, and that the role they played was crucial to the fulfilment of the Great Plan. They were suspicious of and mistrusted each other because they never knew exactly what the others' orders were. Still less which of them the Master would finally anoint when the time came.

'Have faith in our weapons!' Leogrós insisted. 'They are more than enough to exterminate every last one of those on this continent which, before you even realize it, will be our palace.'

Peeling off a glove, Leogrós rubbed his cheeks in a familiar gesture. He liked the touch of his hand on the thick beard, just as he liked to look at his own features in the glass he brought with him wherever he was. He knew the hunchback could not appreciate the glory of war. But the fact that the Doctrinator was unaware of it did not mean that Misáianes felt the same. The Master, who saw everything from beginning to end, compared warfare to the wind. *'It will blow through this world, sweep away the heights of the revolt, reduce everything to the same level.'* When Leogrós heard Misáianes talk, he felt for the first time that someone understood his own dreams. Not only did he understand them, but he gave them a perfect shape, and had the power to make them come true. 'War, our war, is first of all slaughter. Then it is eternity,' he had whispered to him. 'And it is in war that Time will find its only chance to continue to pass.' Let the hunchback continue to fantasize over the supremacy of his doctrines! One day he would see that the laws of distant skies had to bend before the rules of war.

'I accept your view,' said Drimus, although this was far from his true way of thinking. 'In return, explain to me what your plans are.'

Outside the fortress, on his stomach in a small hollow on the hillside, Kume was waiting for nightfall. He had followed the Sideresians' retreat until he came within sight of a wall of wooden posts forming a semicircle around a group of hastily constructed buildings. From his hiding place, Kume could make out the ones higher up the slope, placed there to take advantage of a flat stretch of ground on the hillside. All these buildings were made of wooden posts like the wall, and roughly covered in straw. Only one was bigger and taller than the rest. *That's where their leaders must be*, thought the Husihuilke.

The place where the Sideresians had chosen to build their fortress was close to the Yentru coast. At that height, the ground was sandy and the vegetation had thinned out.

All that afternoon, Kume watched the Sideresians coming and going. Between the fortress and a nearby stream, two lines of men were rhythmically passing from hand to hand empty buckets and full ones. Others dragged their heavy weapons to gaps opened in the semicircular wall. After that, the only men he could see were the guards keeping watch from their towers, who were relieved at nightfall.

Kume had not planned what he was doing; he had not even stopped to think about it. He did it because that was what his spirit urged him to do. The same urgency that had driven him to carry out the most important acts of his life, although he never knew where it came from. Only one thing was certain: when he felt its call, Kume became utterly determined to see it through, whatever the cost. Once again he had acted in the grip of this force. He knew what he had to do in the midst of the battle. And if he glimpsed how it all would end, that did not weaken his resolve.

His wait would have made anyone but Kume reflect. In his place, another person would have baulked at how little chance he had of achieving what he proposed. Someone else perhaps would have realized that such determination might be turned against those he pretended to favour. A third person might stop to wonder if all this was not excessive pride, which could ruin everything. Kume had none of these thoughts. All he concentrated on were the practical details of what he was going to do. He was like a child about to start a game.

At last night fell. Luckily for him, it was moonless, and filled with the sounds of nocturnal insects. There was only one thing Kume wanted before he headed towards the fortress: water. He wanted water to drink… he watched it spilling out of the buckets the Sideresians were passing to each other, and remembered he had not had a drink since the battle. He crawled slowly towards the stream. The light from the torches around the fort did not reach this far, so that Kume was in no real danger. He heard the sound of the water before he reached the bank, and saw a cloud of fireflies hovering above it. The Husihuilke greedily drank his last fresh water. Then he looked around him: everything was still and silent. No reason to wait any longer.

The information he already knew, and what he had seen that afternoon, was whirling around his head: he must forget nothing if he were to carry out his mission. While they had been staying in the House of the Stars, the warriors had been taught about the Sideresians' weapons. Everything the Supreme Astronomers had learnt was explained to them in great detail. They were shown the arms captured in the first skirmishes.

They saw and smelt the grey powder feeding them. More than anyone else, Kume had shown a great interest. His admiration was so great his brother warriors were disturbed; Molitzmós was the only other one who shared this feeling, and who devoted himself to studying them without resentment. This was what had brought the two of them together for their discussions by the pond, of which Kume now recalled many important details. Of course at that time none of them knew of the heavy weapons that the Sideresians used in the battle of the Border Hills. But from what Kume understood, from the way that they blew things apart they must need the same powder.

As he fought alongside the other warriors, Kume had understood the Sideresians would return far too soon. They must have more of these huge weapons in their fortress, and more of the powder that fed them. If this was the case, the victory of the Fertile Lands was little more than a dream. But if he could find and destroy the arsenal of grey powder, the Sideresians would be unable to use these weapons. Then the Deer would have time to regain his strength in many ways before the Sideresians could return. Kume might have shared his plan with Molitzmós, but he had seen the Lord of the Sun fall in battle. And he knew that if he tried to explain to anyone else, that would rob him of his only advantage: the time their enemies needed to reorganize.

Beyond the light from the fortress torches, Kume went over in his mind what he had to do next. He wanted to be sure he had enough time between the signals the guards exchanged in their towers. These wooden towers were built at each end of the fortress's front wall. By waving a torch, one sentry could tell that the other one was in position, and that everything was as it should be.

Kume edged as close as he dared to the sentry at the western end of the fortress. Now everything depended on his aim. If he did not hit his target, if he left the Sideresian with enough life for him to be able to cry out, then all was lost. The arrow and its poison had to strike him deep in the heart, so that there was no distance between life and death. The Husihuilke was ready. The sentry responded to his companion's signal, then hung the torch in a bracket and stood peering out over the dark countryside. The arrow whizzed through the air and plunged into the Sideresian's chest so precisely it seemed almost to be taking pity on him. This end of the fortress was left unguarded. Kume ran to the wall. He climbed up it, then up the crossed supports of the tower. When he reached the top, he waited. The next signal came at the appointed time. Kume took the torch from the bracket and signalled that everything was in place.

Far from being behind him, the most difficult part still lay ahead. This time it did not depend on the Husihuilke's good aim, but whether destiny wanted the same as him. He had to climb down from the tower, discover where the Sideresians kept their grey powder, and then set it alight. He had only a short space of time to do all this. When the sentry in the tower did not respond to his companion, the alarm would be raised.

Kume climbed down. Reaching the foot of the tower, he gazed around the inside of the torch-lit fortress. That night, destiny and Kume were at one. On the same side as the one he had chosen – chosen because he had seen the men's huts by the far wall – he saw a long, low stone building. Too low for men, made of stone to offer protection, on its own for safety, and, above all, kept under guard. Kume had no doubts, and no time for any. If this was where the Sideresians kept their powder, he would do his bit. If not, he would try to escape with his life.

He moved cautiously towards the stone building. It would not be long before the sentry in the eastern tower signalled with his torch and, not receiving any reply, would realize something serious was going on. Kume used projecting stones to help him climb onto the roof. From there he leapt down onto the man guarding the entrance, who was dead before he knew what was happening.

At that very moment, Kume saw the torch waving high in the tower. He peered inside the building. In the darkness all he could see was a pile of objects he had no time to properly identify. Running to the nearest torch, he seized it. As he was returning, he heard the voice of alarm being raised all round the fort. How comforted Kume would have been, had he known what he was about to destroy! Almost all the reserves the Sideresians had in powder, weapons, and shot.

Kume had no time to inspect anything. He took a few steps inside the arsenal. Thanks to the torch he was carrying he could see some barrels: he threw the torch at them, then ran out as quickly as he could. He had no way of knowing all that the Sideresians were about to lose. But they could do nothing in the face of an explosion that destroyed everything.

When this happened, from his hiding place in the dark Kume saw the stones erupt and a fire break out that would last longer than he did. He tried to remain hidden among all the confusion of men, shouted orders and cries, still hoping he could escape. But he soon saw the pack of black dogs coming closer, sniffing at the ground. Kume tried not to give off a smell of fear, of Husihuilke, but it was impossible. Drimus's dogs were the first to find him. And it was only the Doctrinator's voice that could drag them off him.

Kume fought like ten pumas. Like a hundred, a thousand pumas surrounded by men who had been ordered to capture him alive. The only fighting code that Kume knew was that of the Husihuilkes. For that reason he could not comprehend a death different from the one they would give their enemy. If he had been able to, he would have taken his own life rather than let himself be made prisoner.

Stretched out on the ground and savagely beaten, he heard Drimus approach and squat beside him.

'You miserable vermin! My pups deserve to have your rotten meat for their dinner,' he said, quietly and calmly. 'But that cannot be. Your death will leave you intact on the outside, but drilled with holes inside. That way your sad army will see you, and recognize their own fate in you.'

Drimus took Kume by the hand and forced him to feel his hump. Kume clenched his fist and tried to resist, but no longer had the strength.

'Feel it, you cur,' the Doctrinator insisted. 'Feel that bump of wisdom: that is what distinguishes me from the rest. I want you to die knowing that the delay you have caused will not change destiny. We shall be the masters of these lands, and every Husihuilke will pay for what you have just done.'

We have to be as close to one another as two grains of sand, Kume remembered.

From that moment on, he never said another word. Not one when they stripped him, not one when they forced him to his knees, not one when the hunchback promised him the worst kind of torture imaginable, spraying his face with saliva.

Kume watched them preparing his death without being able to comprehend it. His enemies drove a sharpened post into the ground. He thought of all those he loved. As death penetrated his body, Kume's scream collided with the sky.

Thirteen times thirteen warriors, plus seven more. That was the number Cucub had counted of those able to march on towards the Sideresians' fortress. The others were too badly wounded. They would be taken back to the House of the Stars, accompanied by men who could attend and aid them.

Molitzmós had come out of his stupor that afternoon. He came round all of a sudden, and leapt up in a way impossible to imagine in someone who only moments before had been on the verge of death. In the short space of time when he was lucid, he kept repeating that he was going to ride alongside Dulkancellin. It all happened in a flash: he woke up, threw off the blankets covering him, stood up, asked for all the details of the battle, and swore that this time he would do all that his wound had prevented him from doing until now. The warriors around him could make no sense of his excited gestures until he began shouting for the weapon he could not find.

'Here it is,' said Cucub. 'You can rest easy: it has played its part.'

Molitzmós gazed at Cucub with feverish eyes. He was still very pale, and perspiration ran down his face. The Lord of the Sun did not even manage to take his weapon back. He stood rooted to the spot, blinking furiously. The image of Cucub, arm outstretched to hand him back his knife, suddenly became clouded. He tried to focus, but could not; he tried to walk, but lost his balance. Two men rushed to catch him, and laid him out on the ground. By the time Dulkancellin and Hoh-Quiú came to see him, he had slipped back into his stupor. Kupuka thought his moment of recovery must have been the spirit of Molitzmós saying farewell. For once, the Earth Wizard was mistaken. Molitzmós went no further than into a deep sleep.

'You ought to return to Beleram with the wounded,' said Dulkancellin.

'You are the one who ought to do that,' Kupuka replied.

It seemed vital for the Earth Wizard to be in both places at once.

'I can guide you quickly to the fortress,' he said. 'And as for the wounded... those who arrive at the House of the Stars will be in Zabralkán's good care; the others will not survive anyway.'

It was still not first light on the day after the battle when the army of the Fertile Lands divided. The caravan heading south travelled slowly, weighed down by the cost of victory. The warriors setting out for the Sideresian fortress left well armed and mounted on the backs of the animals with manes, although many of them had to learn to ride along the way.

'Spirit of the Wind is not Dusky One,' Cucub warned Dulkancellin. 'Try to understand him. For my part, I'll make use of the journey to find a name for this one I have chosen.'

Kupuka, Hoh-Quiú and Dulkancellin rode out in front. Thungür and Cucub made sure they stayed close to them, as if they thought that by keeping their eyes fixed on Dulkancellin they helped him stay upright. The warrior's condition was worsening. In spite of all Kupuka's care, the infection of the wounds was spreading, and the fever hardly ever left him. But Dulkancellin rode at the head of the warriors, and there was no force on earth or in heaven that could have persuaded him otherwise. Dulkancellin was someone born worth ten men. They all knew as much, and made no attempt to dissuade him. No one except Kupuka, who had to be content with riding alongside him and easing his pain. To make matters worse, the Husihuilke had not slept all night. The lack of sleep made the night seem endless, and it was filled with Kume's absence. Where could he be? Why had he disappeared? The father could never have imagined that while he lay awake, Kume was performing such a noble deed. Afterwards, he had no wish to know whether his son had acted out of pride, bravery, or sadness.

The time Kupuka had estimated that it would take to reach the fortress was much shorter now they were riding. There were still hours of daylight left when Dulkancellin ordered his men to halt. From that distance, they could see the signs that the fortress had been abandoned. It was no more than a desolate, burning shell. Seeing this, the warriors rode on. As the silence had indicated, no one tried to stop them.

The wooden wall was breached in several places, and one side was still in flames. Dulkancellin and Hoh-Quiú went in first: the ground was strewn with rocks, fires, all kinds of objects left behind in a recent flight. In the midst of all this desolation, they saw Kume's body thrust through with a stake.

After Kume, after the pride, bravery and sadness of Kume, everything had changed for the Sideresians.

The certainty of victory, the joy at savouring their revenge, the pleasure at being able to offer Misáianes a handful of his new lands, had gone up in flames. Without the protection of their powder, Leogrós's plans came to nothing, and his army was shown for what it really was: a miserable, fearful rabble whose only wish was to flee. It was true that Kume's torture had for a moment concealed their true natures. Thanks to its ferocity, they had once more seemed terrifying. But that appearance did not last long. They soon returned to making their pleas to leave – pleas which would become demands if their leaders would not listen. Leogrós knew there was nothing to do but comply. It was impossible to win this war with the few weapons they had been able to save; nor could they attempt to resist until the arrival of a new fleet. No promise of riches or power was enough to buy off the dread the Sideresian army felt.

'But I cannot go back after a defeat like this,' murmured Leogrós.

Drimus listened to him with drooping mouth and eyes wide open.

'What shall we do then?' asked the Doctrinator. 'What shall we do?'

'To begin with, we must leave here,' Leogrós replied. 'But not as far as they expect. Not so far, and not for so long.'

Leogrós gave the order to prepare to abandon the fortress towards the end of the morning after the battle. The Sideresians hastened to carry out all the necessary tasks: to recover and take to the beach anything that might be useful, destroy what they could not take with them, and supply the ships with enough drinking water. Drimus personally kissed the forehead of the wounded, whispering to each of them that there was no other way, that they should die praising the Master. By the time everything was ready, it was mid-afternoon.

So the Sideresians headed down to their ships. The Creatures who saw them leave spoke of how they constantly looked back behind them.

Kume's dark body was contorted in agony. His naked form still showed traces of its former beauty. The men from the Fertile Lands could not bear to look at the way he had died; still less the warriors from the Ends of the

Earth. When a warrior killed another warrior, it honoured them both. What Kume had suffered was not death. It brought with it shame that no one wanted to take with him to eternity.

Kupuka went to investigate the area where the fire had started. He found traces that helped him work out something close to the truth of what had happened. When he returned, he spoke briefly to Dulkancellin. The Husihuilke listened to him, then spoke to all the men.

'This warrior died in battle, and no one will say otherwise. This man called Kume, son of Dulkancellin, died fighting. And nobody will ever say anything different.'

Turning towards the coast, Dulkancellin urged Spirit of the Wind on. The animal galloped off, leapt over the remains of the wall, and headed for the Yentru.

The others quickly followed. Although many of them got close to him, Dulkancellin was the first to reach the shore. Here too he saw fires, as if these were Kume's last signal guiding his father to the exact spot where the Sideresians were putting to sea.

They had set fire to the ships they could not use, and it was this that led Dulkancellin to the point on the coast where they were embarking. Spirit of the Wind rushed across the sands like the shadow of a bird to catch them before they could escape. Dulkancellin no longer felt any fever or wounds: no longer a man but fury in person. By the time he reached the sea, the black ships were too far away for any archer. Dulkancellin shouted incomprehensible curses as he rode into the water, desperate for there to be no distance between them and his revenge.

One man responded to his challenge. Leogrós started back towards the shore in a small boat. His face wore the same expression as it had throughout the battle.

Everything that happened next was closely observed by Drimus. The hunchback thrust his head and eyes forward. The rest – his panting laugh, his hunched body and his skip of joy – were hidden behind one of the ship's masts.

The Husihuilke warrior waited, Spirit of the Wind's front legs pawing at the waves. The leader of the Sideresian army was drawing closer. The man who must have given the order for Kume's torture was right there, with the wind blowing his cloak around his body. When he reached a certain distance from the shore, Leogrós opened the cloak. He was carrying a weapon in his hands. Dulkancellin drew back his bow. The arrow and the fire crossed. The fire took the warrior's life with it; the arrow dropped into the sea. Dulkancellin felt an intense pain in the chest, and knew then he was already in the land of death. The figure of Leogrós wavered and went dark before his eyes. Was that Shampalwe husking corn? Yes, it was Shampalwe dancing with her hair gathered up under a crown of shells, the day their love began. Still, before death closed the door, the greatest warrior of the Ends of the Earth had time to stare at the sea and imagine it was the Lalafke. Time to stare at the sky and confuse it with his forest in winter. And at the last moment of his life, he imitated his brother Cucub, and began to dream.

Those who in later years sang of these events said that his arrow had crossed the Yentru Sea and buried itself in Misáianes' laugh. But the men who saw it said the arrow had simply fallen into the sea. They also spoke of how little Cucub sobbed, still clinging to a brother who was no longer there. Of Thungür's silence, and Kupuka's prayer.

28

THE BROTHERHOOD OF THE OPEN AIR

Cucub stuck his fingers in the pot, then put them, sticky with honey, into his mouth.

'Well…?' asked Kuy-Kuyen. 'Is it back?'

The Zitzahay frowned. No, the old taste of cane-sugar honey was not there. Of course, the honey in the pot had tasted good. It was good, but different.

'We have to accept it,' said Cucub. 'Nothing will ever be the same as before. I can remember Dulkancellin's words: "The Time we knew and loved has gone for ever."'

Hearing her father's name made Kuy-Kuyen sad, but although Cucub saw this, he continued on the same theme.

'This market is a good example. It might look the same. But those of us who grew up among these stalls know it has changed.'

Little by little, Beleram was returning to normal. People gathered in groups and began to make their way back to the villages, talking once again of crops and harvests. And the market, even if it had different produce, opened as usual.

The House of the Stars was also emptying of people. The first order Bor gave to the servants was to restore to the empty chambers the splendour that had been neglected in the time of war. He busied himself not only with the rooms but the courtyards and the observatories. *As if he were trying to get rid of all traces*, thought Kupuka as he saw him scurrying around tapestries and statues.

The Earth Wizard had other priorities, which seemed to him far more important. The war had greatly diminished the number of young men, and to him this was something that needed restoring. Kupuka did not let any family leave without pressing them with recommendations.

'Go back to your village. Plant your corn, get used to the animals with manes. And above all, remember that we need births.'

We need births! Wherever he could, and at every moment, Kupuka stressed the message. Not content with that, he would introduce young warriors to recent widows:

'Look how beautiful she is! Ask what her name is. Take her with you into the jungle! And remember, the shade of the copal tree is good for conceiving boy children.'

The Lords of the Sun did not take women from other races. Hoh-Quiú reiterated the prohibition, and was implacable in punishing any transgression. Bor seemed to agree with the prince in this matter.

'What will those children be?' he lamented. 'Zitzahay or Husihuilkes?'

'They will be men,' retorted Zabralkán.

The Zitzahay people gradually left the House of the Stars. The others stayed on for the space of several moons.

The cacao festivities were approaching. Before this, it was the last day of a Council that had started out by asking: Who are these strangers arriving on our shores? and was finishing with the question: How are we to prepare for their return?

'I will tell them what they should do,' said Kupuka, taking Kuy-Kuyen by a tress of her hair, and Cucub by the hand. 'And whilst we are busy with times to come, you concern yourselves with your wedding day. Now that

Thungür has agreed, you, little one, must put on all your best arm-bands and your sandals. And you, Cucub, make sure there is enough to eat and drink, because no one else will do it for you.'

Then, understanding what they were thinking, he added:

'Don't think that by getting married you will be betraying the dead or abandoning the living.' Kupuka took Kuy-Kuyen's face in his hands. 'This smile of yours comes from the sun. Keep smiling, Kuy-Kuyen. Smile against the darkness that is still all around us.'

That day, shortly after the three friends had left the great courtyard, Molitzmós appeared. During his recovery, he often continued to suddenly wake up and then equally suddenly fall back into a stupor. He walked slowly around the pond. He still occasionally shook from head to foot, and felt a great desire to sleep. Sometimes, in his lucid moments, he had feared that the plant he had taken was stronger than he had thought, and that it would carry him off into a sleep from which there was no return. Fortunately, the mixture of flowers and roots was exact. He had swallowed the concoction shortly before the start of the battle, to produce the lethargy that had so puzzled Kupuka. And if it had sedated him more than expected, it made the pain of stabbing himself with his own knife more bearable.

The drink and the wound. Molitzmós had done both things in order to avoid having to fight the Sideresians. And now, had it been possible, he would have done the same, to postpone the moment when he had to meet and salute Hoh-Quiú. Yet he knew that this humiliating duty could not be delayed. To find the strength to bear it, he reflected that possibly everything that had happened could be turned in his favour. Now that the Sideresians had left, he was in a good position. Molitzmós of the Sun had become Misáianes' vanguard. He was sure he would soon hear from the Master of the Ancient Lands. While he waited, Molitzmós would continue with what was most important: deepening an irreparable wound. That was where he should persist.

And the best place for him to do that was in the person of Bor. The Supreme Astronomer's spirit was fertile ground for sowing the evil that Misáianes had called for. The daily visits Bor had paid Molitzmós during his recovery, looking for someone who would support his claims, showed Molitzmós he was not mistaken. The Supreme Astronomers were at odds with each other, and there could be no better beginning.

Separating Magic from the Creatures was the start of the new mandate in which Molitzmós and his House would be great again.

Zabralkán and Bor stared at each other. Bor had called for this urgent meeting. 'Just the two of us,' he had insisted.

The last day of the Council was to be held a few days later. Zabralkán knew that what Bor was going to tell him was closely related to that, and was bound to be important. Bor had been noble in his support of the Fertile Lands, but always with a final reservation, like a person trying to help resolve someone else's problem.

'Very well, the Creatures have done everything they could. And we must recognize their bravery and celebrate their victory.' Bor had thought out carefully what he was going to say, and made it sound convincing. Later, as the Astronomer got close to the heart of his argument, he gradually lost his composure. 'But we know that victory will be short-lived. The Creatures will not withstand another attack by Misáianes, which will be reinforced in many ways.'

Zabralkán nodded, and Bor was encouraged to go on.

'We are the Magic... the Magic of this side of the sea. The Enclosed Brotherhood and the Brotherhood of the Open Air were born of the same light back in the Ancient Lands. When we both succeed in rising above the Creatures we will meet in the skies, and be in harmony once more.'

Zabralkán no longer agreed with what he was hearing.

'Between us, we encompass the whole of Wisdom,' Bor continued. 'We can and must find agreement in our territory of stars. We are not medlars or iguanas; we are not even men. We should not ally ourselves with them, but with our peers. The alliance of the two Brotherhoods is the only force before which all the others, Misáianes included, will bow down.'

Zabralkán sat with eyes closed.

'Do we really love the Creatures?' Bor almost shrieked, to make him listen. 'If we do, I see only two possibilities: to return to the place we should never have left and enlighten and protect them from there. Or to vanish with them from the face of the earth.'

Zabralkán slowly opened his eyes. Rose even more slowly from his seat. Hesitated for a long while over whether or not to say something. And in the end, walked out without a word.

The horn was blown at regular intervals to herald the start of the Council. Neither the chamber nor those who had to take the decisions were the same. Four of the representatives were no longer there. Dulkancellin, Elek, and the Pastor had died in battle. Still enveloped in her memory, Nakín by now was little more than a slender piece of bark inscribed with signs from the past. But others had arrived to replace them.

They sat in concentric rings around the White Stone. Zabralkán, Bor, Kupuka and Hoh-Quiú formed the innermost circle. The others were filled by representatives from all the peoples of the Fertile Lands. Zabralkán raised his hand and the murmuring ceased.

'Let us begin,' said the Supreme Astronomer.

The old man paused, but no one spoke. Nobody could think of doing so before he had addressed them all.

'Which of us is unaware that our victory, however glorious, is not a definitive one? If it had been, we could have celebrated and then each one of us departed for his own land. Yet here we still are, almost as troubled as we were. A not unwise voice has said that Misáianes will return, re-inforced in many ways, and that the Creatures will not be able to resist another attack.'

Bor began to think things were going well for him. It was possible that Zabralkán's silence a few days earlier meant he had taken a decision which the stars had then confirmed. It was possible that Zabralkán had at last understood.

'How long will it take Misáianes to return?' asked Zabralkán, this time expecting an answer.

'Not long,' said Kupuka.

'We will be waiting for him with a large army,' said Hoh-Quiú.

'It will not be enough,' the Earth Wizard said.

All of them only had to remember the evils Misáianes had sent in advance of his ships, many of which were still afflicting them, to under-stand how true this was.

'You have spoken well, brother Kupuka,' said Zabralkán. 'An army will not be enough. Is everyone agreed?'

Everyone there could see plainly how much the victory had cost them. That was enough for them. That and the memory of the heroism of some and the feats others had performed. None of them hesitated.

'Agreed,' said Hoh-Quiú, the first of all.

'Agreed,' said the voices of the Offspring.

'Agreed,' said the Husihuilkes.

'Agreed,' said the Zitzahay.

'Agreed,' said the lesser Astronomers.

'How are we to strengthen ourselves while we wait for the day of their arrival?'

Zabralkán asked each in turn what they thought needed to be done, big or small; each of them replied with sensible suggestions according to their customs and natures.

'All we have heard from our brothers is good and necessary,' Zabralkán thanked them. 'And if we imagine each of these actions brought together, they can build a great stone wall around us which will undoubtedly protect us. To raise it will be the hard work to which we must now dedicate ourselves. Yet before we assume our duties and separate, let us be sure we remember the most vital thing. Because every time we remember it, we will be surer of it.'

Zabralkán raised both arms in the direction of Bor, who so far had remained silent. Everyone was wondering what this gesture meant, when the aged Astronomer asked his brother to tell them all where he considered that their true strength against Misáianes lay.

Bor turned pale. Surely Zabralkán did not think the representatives would understand the reasons for the re-encounter with the Enclosed Brotherhood? Molitzmós might, endowed as he was with powers that went beyond his condition as a simple creature. But how could the warriors of the south and their wizard do so? How were the Zitzahay craftsmen, or the young fishermen of the Offspring to understand?

'It would be better to hear it from the mouth of Zabralkán,' said Bor.

What was taking place, unnoticed by most of them, was a trial of strength between the Supreme Astronomers. A battle between the two in which Zabralkán was asking Bor to assume his position and defend it; to state out loud for all to hear the place he claimed for Magic: close to the stars, and far from the Creatures. Faced with this silent demand, Bor appeared to yield and instead to choose a place next to them.

'I say that what Zabralkán has to tell us is what I believe, but in clearer words,' Bor continued, as if he had changed his mind.

Zabralkán realized this was not the time to challenge Bor. Perhaps there was still a way back for his brother.

'You do me honour,' said the old Astronomer. 'But I say that Kupuka is the best one here present to tell us what is most vital for us. You, brother

Bor, said "It would be better to hear it from the mouth of Zabralkán." I say it would be better to hear it from the mouth of Kupuka.'

Until now, the Earth Wizard had been as silent as Bor. But Zabralkán's ploy had less to do with this than with showing Bor how far he had to go to rejoin the rest of them.

Barefoot and smelling of the jungle, Kupuka began by laughing. Sitting alongside the splendour of two Astronomers and a prince, the Wizard seemed more than ever like a muddy animal.

'Zabralkán, who is ancient compared with everyone, is not old compared to me. Yet he has been cleverer. He has robbed me of my calm and put me to the test. "Tell us what is most vital for us..." Kupuka's tone of voice robbed the complaint of any sting. 'But Zabralkán is a true brother, and has made it easy for me. Now all I have to do is to repeat what he himself said as clearly as possible. Zabralkán said: "It would be better to hear it from Kupuka." There is the most vital point.'

Those who understood the direction the Wizard was taking began to smile.

'"We will do better to hear it from the mouth of Kupuka." This is telling us that an Astronomer from the Remote Realm is no more than a Wizard from the Ends of the Earth. And I will add: a Wizard from the Ends of the Earth is no more than a walnut tree; a human birth is no more or less than a blossoming flower, an Astronomer studying the stars is no more and no less than a fish spawning. The hunter is no more or less than the prey he hunts in order to live; a man no less and no more than the corn he needs to feed him. That is what Zabralkán was telling us; and that is what is most vital. Creation is a perfect weave. Everything in it has its proper size and place. Everything is linked together in an immense tapestry that not even my beloved weavers of the south could reproduce. Shame on us if we forget we are a loom. And that wherever that endless thread snaps is where Misáianes can start to pull until the whole work is undone.'

With this, Kupuka took a root out of his pack and began to chew on it. Cucub's face spoke of life as he stared at the old man from one of the outer circles. Molitzmós's face spoke of death, as his mind was on destruction.

'Now it is the turn of the considerably astute to repeat what those who are considerably old have said.' Zabralkán spoke in the same light tone as Kupuka.

Smiles appeared again. Realizing he had struck the wrong note, the Supreme Astronomer resumed his usual solemn appearance.

Sitting opposite each other with a circle between them, Bor and Molitzmós could study how the others reacted. Each new misjudgement that Zabralkán made strengthened their shared conviction.

'Because... can we put Magic above Creatures, or the reverse?' Zabralkán went on. 'Can we put day higher than night? Do they not need each other to exist? Kupuka has reminded us that Creation is a tapestry in which every thread is vital. It is Magic's task to see how they all fit together. This and only this is its Wisdom, made up of the things of this earth. Perhaps Magic can see how the earthworm and the mountain fit or oppose one another. But to do so, it first must ask the mountain and the earthworm. If we ever forget that, Wisdom will become arrogance; and what now is medicine for us will turn to poison.'

A long time later, when every last detail of the work that needed to be done had been settled, the circles disbanded. Zabralkán sought out Bor, and led him apart from the others.

'It is possible that the man in front of me is Bor, my brother. But until I am sure, I will be on the alert.'

For a fleeting moment, Bor sensed that Zabralkán's stern warning might bring him back, and almost accepted it. But from a corner in the same chamber, Molitzmós and his whispers drew him away again.

29

CACAO

The cacao festivities lasted seven entire days. The processions crossed Beleram to the platform in front of the House of the Stars. Musicians and flower girls, dancers and jugglers. Men carrying poles as wide as the avenue where turtle-doves, doves, parakeets, owls, and kestrels perched, often flying off to land on the shoulder or head of their bearers. When the processions reached the House of the Stars, the Supreme Astronomers came out to celebrate in their golden vestments.

But now all that was over, and the people of Beleram were gathered in the market for the best part of the celebrations. The cacao beer was poured from large pitchers into small ones. The men drank their fill; the sweet fermented water ran from their mouths. Some stalls sold honey-coated plums, others were piled high with breads and tortillas. Hot burners offered dishes of fowl cooked with thistles and leeks, and fish stews.

Everyone ate until they had more than enough. And drank until first they laughed, then staggered, then slept the sleep of the intoxicated. That year, the celebrations were more intense than ever. The first light of day found hundreds sleeping where they had no longer been able to stand.

The braziers went out. In the bottom of the cooking dishes, the dried-out stews grew cold.

Soon afterwards, though, the stallholders awoke. It was time to clean up round their fires and prepare food for the coming day. An enthusiastic drinker of cacao beer, Kupuka had ended up sleeping in the open air along with many other snoring bodies. The sounds of cleaning and the smell of fresh cooking woke the Earth Wizard. He had just decided to stay where he was, lying face up in the sun, until the effects of the drink had worn off, when he remembered Kuy-Kuyen's wedding. He got to his feet and hastened off.

In far greater haste, with no drink and no wedding, Hoh-Quiú was leaving Beleram.

'I have been away from my country for too long,' said the prince. 'And I am sure that my usual enemies are making a lot of noise. How insignificant they seem compared to the enemy we all face! Yet I must return to confront their petty intrigues.'

Molitzmós had learnt to turn Hoh-Quiú's frequent arrogant comments to his own advantage, using them to convince himself he was right to hate him. The prince seemed never to fail to express them when Molitzmós was present, unaware that he was fuelling his enemy's determination.

What strange creatures men are, thought Zabralkán as he listened to Hoh-Quiú. *Even if a great flood threatens to engulf them, they seem rather disappointed when life returns to its normal course.*

Molitzmós waited for the prince to finish. Then he went up to him and asked his leave to stay on a few more days in Beleram. As an excuse, he mentioned the wedding of his brother Cucub, and the fact that he still had not recovered sufficiently to make the journey.

'You may stay,' the prince said. 'But choose a speedy animal and catch up with us before we reach the Border Hills.'

Loaded down with gifts and abundant provisions, and taking with them several of the finest animals with manes so that they could multiply in their lands, the Lords of the Sun were the first to leave Beleram.

The wedding to Kuy-Kuyen offered a good opportunity to sing. So Cucub spent the morning phrasing and rephrasing his song. 'I crossed to the other fear...' No, that opening did not suit the occasion. 'I asked the river for permission...' That was better, because it reminded him of the ceremony where he would have to ask Thungür's permission to wed Kuy-Kuyen.

Earlier, she had wanted to know when she would have her own song.

'You will soon be Zitzahay enough to find one,' Cucub had replied. 'And it's possible that by then I will be so much a Husihuilke I will have forgotten mine.'

'I crossed to the other far...' Cucub went on singing while waiting for the appointed time. He sang and considered how he looked. In addition to bathing in the river, today he had for a long while stayed close to a dish of burning aromatic copal sticks. His body had absorbed its perfume, and so had his clothes before he put them on. Cucub rejected some of them as too worn-out. But he added new ones, so that the result was the usual motley of textures and colours. On top of this wedding attire, he was loaded down with his customary extraordinary jumble: belts, darts, his flute and blowpipe, stone axe-heads, feathers and seeds.

'Love is singing,' Molitzmós said behind his back.

Cucub was enraged just by hearing him, and had no wish to hide it.

'And the lack of love hides to listen.'

The Lord of the Sun burst out laughing.

'I have stayed to be at your wedding, and look how you thank me!' he said. 'I came to find you to give you the knife that performed so well in the battle of the Border Hills.'

Cucub did not stretch out his hand.

301

'Take it,' said Molitzmós. 'You cannot refuse a wedding gift without some important reason. Do you have one?'

Cucub did not reply, but accepted the knife with a nod of the head.

'I have heard you are to leave with the Husihuilkes,' said Molitzmós.

'That is so. I am going with Kuy-Kuyen. And I will take care of her family, just as I promised Dulkancellin.'

'That is good!' Molitzmós smiled both on the inside and the outside. 'So Thungür will no longer rule in the house?'

'Thungür and some other Husihuilkes are to stay here in Beleram. They are needed to help transform the Zitzahay into able warriors.'

The two had nothing more to say to each other.

'I salute you,' said Molitzmós, turning to leave. But he turned back and added: 'One more thing. One day I will reach the Ends of the Earth and come knocking on your door.'

Cucub recognized the threat only partially concealed behind the polite words.

'It's possible that by the time you arrive, Cucub will have many sons who will come out to welcome you.'

The wedding had its delicious foods, its music, and its bowls overflowing with cacao beer. In the centre of a ring, Cucub danced. And talked and talked, although his tongue often seemed to disobey him.

'My Kuy-Kuyen is as beautiful as the summer moon like no one has ever seen and look at all the garlands of flowers she herself wove so that you will eat and drink to Cucub who is going to take this woman with him to the Ends of the Earth... And tell me if anyone here has seen a woman as beautiful as her and tell me what sweetens a man's night more, Kuy-Kuyen or sweet cacao. Drink with me because I am Cucub and happy and I am emptying this bowl in honour of my brother warrior whom I know is here. I'm dancing... he is dancing. Dance and tell me if my Kuy-Kuyen is not as beautiful as the moon, and serve me more cacao. Kupuka is dancing and drinking with me because we know he is among us watching this wedding since death gave his permission. Look at your daughter, Dulkancellin, and drink to her… Come and I'll serve you some cacao beer. What do you say, Kupuka? If one can cry one can also drink, and as you have come to our wedding, Dulkancellin, I swear once more on all your blood… Tell me, brother, is there any woman as beautiful as your Kuy-Kuyen? And let's drink and drink… while we are drinking you will have a good excuse to stay with us.'

Cucub ended his dance on the floor, and fell fast asleep until the next dawn. Some of his guests must have carried him from the courtyard in the House of the Stars to his hammock in the jungle, because that was where he woke up. Only his bride was with him, eating plums. Kuy-Kuyen saw him wake up, and offered him a handful. When Cucub bit into one, the skin crunched, and the sweet juice ran between his fingers.

The Offspring of the Stalkers of the Sea had become a people without adults. Despite this, it was decided they too should return to their villages and renew their ways of the sea. They had to continue the traditions of the Northmen in building boats and learning the skills of sailing them. The Offspring were given charge of the Yentru coasts and its tides. But they were very young, and wanted to do even more than was asked of them. 'To wrest the sea from Misáianes we will need to learn more than sailing along the coasts,' they said. Their ancestors had been content to build small craft that travelled close to the shore, trading between Beleram and the villages of the Remote Realm. Now they dreamt of reaching the far south, where the Yentru and the Lalafke met. 'We will sail to the Ends of the Earth.' 'We will reach Cucub's house by boat.'

Nakín of the Owl Clan had completed her journey back to the Magic Time. Zabralkán gave her medicines and soothing words to help her through the painful stages of allowing herself to fade away. The day after the wedding, several people felt her spirit float along the passageways as if a wind were blowing through the House of the Stars. That was the last they knew of her... Nakín must already be on the far side of time, with the colour coming back to her cheeks. Caught up for ever in her memory.

Molitzmós on the other hand left suddenly. His only farewell was to Zabralkán. As for Bor... He would soon see him again. They had managed to speak together on their own only once. Enough for them to understand they needed each other, and that for their own good and that of everyone else, they should stay in contact. Molitzmós turned back to look at the torches lit once more in the House of the Stars. Then he galloped through the night to reach the Lords of the Sun close to the Border Hills.

The Husihuilkes were also leaving Beleram. Ahead of them lay great distances and a desert where, in addition to its natural rigours, they faced the threat from the Pastors. It seemed unlikely that the Pastors of the Desert would try to attack them, but as so few of them were returning, the warriors of the south made careful preparations for the journey.

Many of those not returning had been killed in the war and buried in the Remote Realm. But those who had been chosen to train a Zitzahay army also stayed behind. They gathered together to say goodbye to their brothers and send gifts and their wishes: 'Tell my wife to plant these seeds.' 'These feathers are for my mother.' 'Tell my children what a beautiful city Beleram is...'

The Husihuilkes took with them animals with manes that soon became hundreds. The people of the Ends of the Earth quickly adopted them, gave them sonorous names and kept them close to their houses. Eventually they became part of the warriors' bodies, and they never fought without them.

Kuy-Kuyen climbed up on Spirit of the Wind behind Cucub, grasping his clothes tightly. Thungür had already said goodbye to the Wizard of the Earth, and came over to them.

'If at the next ceremony of the sun any woman should ask after me, give her these seeds and tell her to plant them,' he said, handing his sister a small leather pouch. 'And these feathers are for Old Mother Kush. You two will have to tell Wilkilén and Piukemán all that has happened here.'

Just as Dulkancellin or any other Husihuilke warrior would have done, Thungür wasted no words on saying what everyone already knew.

'May the sun accompany you on your way, and also remain here with us, because he is able to do so. Farewell.'

So it came to pass. Hoh-Quiú returned to his throne, Kupuka to his cave. The Beleram market recovered its variety, and Nakín her colours. The Offspring were busy with their boats, while others plotted. Zabralkán felt an age-old sadness. The Husihuilke were heading back to the south. Another age was beginning...

30

IN HUMAN TONGUES

The last I will say about these events is that those Husihuilkes safely reached their lands. As they travelled through the desert, not even the silhouette of the Pastors of the Desert was seen on the horizon. They met with no greater hardships than those to be expected on such a long journey. And perhaps, thanks to the animals with manes, a few less.

Soon after they had crossed the Marshy River, the column from Beleram began to diminish, as some of the warriors left to head back to their own villages. The first group took a short cut to the west to reach Sweet Herbs. Then the inhabitants of the high villages left the main group. A little further south, and those who had to cross the Forgotten Pass took their leave: people from the far side of the Maduinas Mountains, from rival clans.

That was why when the Ministering Falcon passed overhead, Piukemán saw fewer than half of those who had set out, on the journey back.

'Old Kush, come here! Hurry!' he called out to her, as if she too could see them coming.

'What's the matter?' asked the old, old woman, her face covered with new wrinkles, but her eyes as bright as ever.

Piukemán was twisting and turning his body, trying to make the Falcon fly back again.

'Come back! Come back!' The Ministering Falcon was flying round in circles. 'Fly lower so I can see who it is!'

'What are you talking about, Piukemán?' asked Kush.

'What can he see with the bird's eyes, Grandmother?' Wilkilén did not want to hear her brother crying out again in a way that terrified her. But this time Piukemán was smiling.

'They're back,' he said.

Kupuka spied the Falcon in the sky above them. 'Come down!' he begged him. 'Fly down so that the boy can see us.'

The Ministering Falcon was smiling.

'Very well, if you won't come closer, I'll have to follow you,' complained the Earth Wizard. 'I have a debt to repay Piukemán.'

So Kupuka set off after the Falcon.

'You go ahead. I will catch up with you.'

It was a day of sun at the Ends of the Earth.

'Run, Wilkilén,' said Old Mother Kush. 'Tell the neighbours our warriors are back, and tell them to spread the news. While you are doing that, I will make fresh bread. I hope they will be here soon to eat it.'

It was a night of stars at the Ends of the Earth. And Kush's house smelt of corn bread.

'Someone is drawing close to the Falcon's nest,' Piukemán whispered slowly, so as not to disturb the bird.

Old Mother Kush and Wilkilén went over to him, fearful of finding out who was there and who was not. Together, Piukemán and the Ministering Falcon peered at the face of the old man.

'It's Kupuka,' they whispered.

It was dawn at the Ends of the Earth, and the bread was made. Kush, Piukemán and Wilkilén were waiting beside the walnut tree halfway between the house and the forest. Piukemán could sense the old woman's soul tremble.

'Grandmother, tell me who is coming.'

'I cannot see your father or your brothers.'

'It's Kuy-Kuyen and the little man,' said Wilkilén. 'And the Wizard. And they are bringing animals whose hair looks like mine when Kush undoes my tresses.'

Old Mother Kush took Piukemán by the hand and walked down the path where Wilkilén was already running.

'Welcome, Shampalwe,' she said.

Kuy-Kuyen looked to the Earth Wizard for help. The grief the old woman felt at not seeing all those she loved must have driven her mad.

'Because that is what I hope she will be called,' Old Mother Kush continued, placing her hands on her granddaughter's waist.

There were so many questions to ask and answer.

'I am leaving,' said Kupuka, refusing to enter the house. 'If I went into that nest, I would eat bread until I almost burst, and then lie down to sleep for the length of seven suns...'

'And what is wrong with that?' asked Kush.

The Earth Wizard gave one of his goat laughs.

'I will be back one day. And I hope that by then there will be many children here, as well as this Shampalwe whom Kuy-Kuyen has brought with her. I also hope that all of them will have a proper fear of me.' Kupuka took Piukemán by the shoulders: 'The day I return, you will no longer be afraid of flying.'

The Earth Wizard left them. Anyone following him would have seen him reach his cave on all fours.

Afterwards, Old Mother Kush shared out the bread.